Praise for the novels of Anna Snoekstra

"In Anna Snoekstra's dark and edgy debut, a young woman slips easily into the life of a girl missing eleven years, only to discover the grisly truth behind the disappearance. Will she be the next victim? Truly distinctive and tautly told, *Only Daughter* welcomes a thrilling new voice in crime fiction."
—Mary Kubica, *New York Times* bestselling author of *The Good Girl*

"*Only Daughter* by Anna Snoekstra is a dark meditation on the secrets we keep about our families and about ourselves. Twisty, slippery, and full of surprises, this web of lies will ensnare you and keep you riveted until you've turned the final page."
—Lisa Unger, *New York Times* bestselling author of *Ink and Bone*

"A wickedly twisted and fast-paced plot that leaves numerous questions unanswered…readers who enjoy a creepy thriller that will keep them guessing will be unable to put this down."
—*Booklist* (starred review)

"Escalating tension and menace will keep readers glued to the pages, leading to a highly satisfying resolution that is both surprising and believable. Snoekstra's excellent debut stands out in the crowded psychological suspense field with smart, subtle red herrings and plenty of dark and violent secrets."
—*Library Journal* (starred review)

ONLY
DAUGHTER

ANNA
SNOEKSTRA

MIRA

ISBN-13: 978-0-7783-1944-3

Only Daughter

Recycling programs
for this product may
not exist in your area.

First printing: October 2016
10 9 8 7 6 5 4 3 2 1

For my mother.

I've always been good at playing a part: the mysterious seductress for the sleazebag, the doe-eyed innocent for the protector. I had tried both on the security guard and neither seemed to be working.

I'd been so close. The supermarket doors had already slid open for me when his wide hand clamped on my shoulder. The main road was only fifteen paces away. A quiet street lined with yellow-and-orange-leaved trees.

His grip tightened.

He brought me into the back office. A small cement box with no windows, barely big enough to fit the old filing cabinet, desk and printer. He took the bread roll, cheese and apple out of my bag and laid them on the table between us. Seeing them spread out like that gave me a jolt of shame, but I tried my best to hold his eye. He said I wasn't going anywhere until I gave him some identification. Luckily, I had no wallet. Who needs a wallet when you don't have any money?

I attempted all my routines on him, letting tears flow

when my insinuations fell flat. It wasn't my best performance; I couldn't stop looking at the bread. My stomach was beginning to cramp. I've never felt hunger like this before.

I can hear him now, talking to the police on the other side of the locked door. I stare up at the notice board above the desk. This week's staff roster is there, alongside a memo about credit card procedures with a smiley face drawn on the bottom and a few photographs from a work night out.

I have never wanted to work in a supermarket. I've never wanted to work anywhere, but all of a sudden, I'm painfully jealous.

"Sorry to bother you with this. Little skank won't give me any ID."

I wonder if he knows I can hear him.

"It's all right—we'll take it from here." Another voice.

The door opens and two cops look in at me. It's a female and a male, both probably about my age. She has her dark hair pulled back in a neat ponytail. The guy is pasty and thin. I can tell straightaway that he's going to be an asshole. They sit down on the other side of the table.

"My name is Constable Thompson and this is Constable Seirs. We understand that you were caught shoplifting from this store," the male cop says, not even bothering to hide the boredom in his tone.

"No, actually, I wasn't," I say, imitating my stepmom's perfect breeding. "I was on my way to the register when he grabbed me. That man has a problem with women."

They look at me doubtfully, their eyes sliding over my unwashed clothes and greasy hair. I wonder if I smell. My bruised and swollen face isn't doing me any favours. It was probably why I got caught in the first place.

"He was calling me foul names when he brought me back here—" I lower my voice "—like *skank* and *whore*. Disgusting. My father is a lawyer and I expect he'll want to sue for misconduct when I tell him what went on here today."

They look at each other and I can immediately tell they don't buy it. I should have cried.

"Listen, honey, it's going to be fine. Just give us your name and address. You'll be back home by the end of the day," the girl cop says.

She is my age and she's calling me pet names like I'm just a kid.

"The other option is that we book you now and take you back to the station. You'll have to wait in a cell while we sort out who you are. It will be a lot easier if you just give us your name now."

They're trying to scare me and it's working, but not for the reason they think. Once they have my fingerprints it won't take them long to identify me. They'll find out what I did.

"I was so hungry," I say, and the tremor in my tone isn't fake.

It's the look in their eyes that does it. A mix of pity and disgust. Like I'm worth nothing, just another stray for them to clean up. A memory slowly opens and I realize I know exactly how to get myself out of this.

The power of what I'm about to say is huge. It courses through my body like a shot of vodka, removing the tightness in my throat and sending tingles to the tips of my fingers. I don't feel helpless anymore; I know I can pull this off. Staring at her, then him, I let myself savor the moment.

Watching them carefully to enjoy the exact instant their faces change.

"My name is Rebecca Winter. Eleven years ago, I was abducted."

1

2014

I sit in an interview room with my face down, holding my coat tightly around myself. It's cold in here. I've been waiting for almost an hour, but I'm not worried. I imagine what a stir I've caused on the other side of that mirror. They're probably calling in the missing persons unit, looking up photographs of Rebecca and painstakingly comparing them to me. That should be enough to convince them; the likeness is uncanny.

I saw it months ago. I was wrapped up with Peter, a little bundle of warmth. Usually I got teary when I was hungover and just spent the day hiding in my room listening to sad music. It was different with him. We woke up at noon and sat on the couch all day eating pizza and smoking cigarettes until we started feeling better. That was back when I thought my parents' money didn't matter and all I needed was love.

We were watching some stupid show called *Wanted*. They were talking about a string of grisly murders at a place called Holden Valley Aged Care in Melbourne and I started looking for the remote. Butchered grannies were definitely a mood killer. Just as I went to change the channel, the next story began and a photograph came up on the screen. She had my nose, my eyes, my copper-coloured hair. Even my freckles.

"Rebecca Winter finished her late shift at McDonald's, in the inner south Canberra suburb of Manuka, on the seventeenth of January 2003," a man said in a dramatic voice over the photograph, "but somewhere between her bus stop and home she disappeared, never to be seen again."

"Holy shit, is that you?" Peter said.

The girl's parents appeared, saying their daughter had been missing for over a decade but they still had hope. The mother looked like she was about to cry. Another photograph: Rebecca Winter wearing a bright green dress, her arm slung around another teenage girl, this one with blonde hair. For a foolish moment, I tried to remember if I had ever owned a dress like that.

A family portrait: the parents looking thirty years younger, two grinning brothers and Rebecca in the middle. Idyllic. They may as well have had a white picket fence in the background.

"Fuck, do you think that's your long-lost twin or what?"

"Yeah, you wish!"

We'd started joking about Peter's gross twin fantasies and he forgot about it pretty soon. Nothing stuck around long in Peter's mind.

I try to remember every detail I can from the show. She was from Canberra, a teenager, maybe fifteen or sixteen at the time she went missing. In some ways, I was lucky the side of my face was bruised and swollen. It masked the sub-

tle differences that distinguished us. I'll be well and truly
gone by the time the bruising fades. I only need to buy myself enough time to get me out of the station, to the airport
maybe. For a moment my mind wanders to what I would
do after that. Call Dad? I hadn't spoken to him since I left. I
had picked up a pay phone a few times, even punched in his
mobile number. But then the sickening sound of soft weight
crashing against metal would fill my head and I'd hang up
with shaking hands. He wouldn't want to talk to me.

The door opens and the female cop peeks in and smiles
at me.

"This won't take too much longer. Can I get you something to eat?"

"Yes, please."

The slight embarrassment in her voice, the way she looks
at me and then quickly averts her eyes.

I had them.

She brings me a box of piping-hot noodles from the take-
away next door. They're oily and a bit slimy, but I've never
enjoyed a meal so much. Eventually, a detective comes into
the room. He puts a file on the table and pulls out a chair.
He looks brutish, with a thick neck and small eyes. I can
tell by the way he sits down that my best chance with him
is ego. He seems to be trying to take up as much space as
possible, his arm resting on the chair next to him, his legs
wide open. He smiles across the table.

"I'm sorry this is taking so long."

"That's okay," I say, wide eyes, small voice. I turn my face
slightly, to make sure he's looking at the bruised side.

"We're going to bring you to the hospital soon, okay?"

"I'm not hurt. I just want to go home."

"It's procedure. We've been calling your parents, but so far there's been no answer."

I imagine the phone ringing in Rebecca Winter's empty house. That was probably for the best; her parents would just complicate things. The detective takes my silence as disappointment.

"Don't worry, I'm sure we'll get a hold of them soon. They'll need to come here to make the identification. Then you can go home together."

That's the last thing I need, to be called out as a fraud in front of a room full of cops. My confidence starts to slip. I need to turn this around.

I speak into my lap. "I want to go home more than anything."

"I know. It won't be too much longer." His voice is like a pat on the head. "Did you enjoy those?" He looks at the empty noodle box.

"They were really nice. Everyone has been so amazing," I say, keeping with the timid-victim act.

He opens the manila folder. It's Rebecca Winter's file. Interview time. My eyes scan the first page.

"Can you tell me your name?"

"Rebecca." I keep my eyes down.

"And where have you been all this time, Rebecca?" he says, leaning in to hear me.

"I don't know," I whisper. "I was so scared."

"Was there anyone else there? Anyone else held with you?"

"No. Only me."

He leans in closer, until his face is only inches from mine.

"You saved me," I say, looking him right in the eyes. "Thank you."

I can see his chest swell. Canberra is only three hours from here. I just need to push a little harder. Now that he's feeling like the big man, he won't be able to say no. It's my only chance to get out of here.

"Please, will you let me go home?"

"We really need to interview you and take you to the hospital to be examined. It's important."

"Can we do that in Canberra?"

I let the tears start falling then. Men hate seeing girls cry. It makes them uncomfortable for some reason.

"You'll be transported back to Canberra soon, but there is a procedure we need to follow first, okay?"

"But you're the boss here, aren't you? If you say I can go they have to do what you say. I just want to see my mom."

"Okay," he says, jumping out of his seat. "Don't cry. Let me see what I can do."

He comes back to say he's worked it all out for me. I will be driven to Canberra by the cops who picked me up, and then the missing persons detective who worked on Rebecca Winter's case will take it from there. I nod and smile at him, looking up at him like he's my new hero.

I'll never reach Canberra. An airport would be easier, but I'm sure I can still get away from them somehow. Now that they see me as a victim, it won't be too hard.

As we walk out of the interview room, everyone turns to look at me. One woman has a receiver pressed to her ear.

"She's here now. Just let me ask." She puts the receiver against her chest and looks up at the detective. "It's Mrs.

Winter—we finally got a hold of her. She wants to talk to Rebecca. Is that okay?"

"Of course," the detective says, smiling at me.

The woman holds out the receiver. I look around. Everyone has their heads bent but I can tell they are listening. I take the phone and hold it to my ear.

"Hello?"

"Becky, is that you?"

I open my mouth, needing to say something, but I don't know what. She keeps going.

"Oh, honey, thank God. I can't believe it. Are you okay? They keep saying you aren't hurt, but I can't believe it. I love you so much. Are you all right?"

"I'm okay."

"Stay where you are. Your father and I are coming to get you."

Damn.

"We're just about to leave," I say, in almost a whisper. I don't want her noticing my voice is all wrong.

"No, please, don't go anywhere. Stay where you're safe."

"It'll be quicker this way. It's all sorted out."

I can hear her swallowing, heavy and thick.

"We can be there really soon." Her voice sounds strangled.

"I've got to go," I say. Then, looking around at all those pricked-up ears, I add, "'Bye, Mom."

I hear her sobbing as I hand the phone back.

The last glow of sunlight has disappeared and the sky is a pale grey. We've been driving for about an hour and the conversation has dried up. I can tell the cops are itching to ask me where I've been all this time, but they restrain themselves.

This is lucky really, because they would most likely have a better idea than I do where Rebecca Winter has spent the past decade.

Paul Kelly croons softly on the radio. Raindrops patter on the roof of the car and slide down the windows. I could fall asleep.

"Do you need me to turn the heater up?" Thompson asks, eyeing my coat.

"I'm okay," I say.

The truth is I couldn't take my coat off, no matter that I was starting to feel a bit hot. I have a birthmark just below the crook of my elbow. A coffee-coloured stain about the size of a twenty-cent piece. I'd hated it as a kid. My mother always told me it was the mark left by an angel's kiss. It was one of the few memories I have of her. As I grew up I sort of started to like it, maybe because it made me think of her, or maybe just because it was so much a part of me. But it wasn't a part of Bec. I doubted that either of these idiots had looked closely enough at the missing persons file to see the word *nil* under *birthmarks*, but it wasn't worth the risk.

I try to force myself to plan my escape. Instead all I can think about was Rebecca's mom. The way she had said "I love you" to me. It wasn't like when my dad used to say it, when someone was watching or when he was trying to get me to be good. The way she had said it was so raw, so guttural, like it was coming from her core. This woman that we are zooming toward really does love me. Or she loves who she thinks I am. I wonder what she is doing right now.

Calling her friends to tell them, washing sheets for me, dashing to the supermarket for extra food, worrying that she wouldn't sleep because she was so excited? I imagine what will happen when they call her to tell her that they lost me on the way. These two cops would probably get into a lot of trouble. I wouldn't mind that, but what about her? What about the cleanly made-up bed waiting for me? The food in the fridge. All that love. It will just go to waste.

"I need to go to the bathroom," I say, seeing a sign for a rest stop.

"Okay, honey. Are you sure you don't want to wait for a servo?"

"No." I'm sick of being polite to them.

The car veers onto the dirt road and stops outside the brick toilet block. Next to it is an old barbecue and two picnic tables and behind that is solid bushland. If I get a decent head start, they won't be able to find me in there.

The female cop unclicks her seat belt.

"I'm not a kid. I can take a piss by myself, thank you."

I get out of the car, slamming the door behind me, not giving her a chance to argue. Raindrops fall onto my face, ice against my sweaty skin. It feels nice to be out of that sweltering car. I glance back before I walk into the toilet block. The headlights beam through the rain, and behind the windscreen wipers I can see the cops talking and shifting in their seats.

The toilets are disgusting. The concrete floor is flooded, and scrunched-up wads of tissue float around like miniature icebergs. The place stinks of beer and vomit. A bottle of Carlton Draught rests next to the toilet and the rain beats against the tin roof. I imagine what my night tonight will be like, hiding in the rain. I'll have to wander until I reach a town, but then what? I'll be hungry again soon and I still don't have any money. The last week has been the most horrible of my life. I'd had to pick up men in bars just to have somewhere to sleep, and one night, the worst one, I had no other option but to hide in a public toilet in a park. Jumping out of my skin at every noise. Imagining the worst. That night felt like it would never end, like the light would never come. The toilet block looked a bit like this one.

For a moment my resilience slips and I imagine the other alternative: the warm bed, the full stomach and the kisses on the forehead. It's enough.

The bottle breaks against the toilet seat easily. I pick a large shard. Squatting down in the cubicle, I hold my arm between my knees. I realize I've started to whimper, but there's no time now to be weak. One more minute and that cop will be checking on me. Pushing down on the brown blotch, the pain is shocking. There's more blood than I expected, but I don't stop. My flesh peels up, like the skin of a potato.

The lining of my jacket slips against the open wound as I pull it back on. I throw the gory evidence in the sanitary bin and wash the blood off my hands. My vision is beginning to blur and the oily noodles swirl in my stomach. I grip the sink and breathe steadily. I can do this.

The slam of a car door is followed by footsteps.

"Are you all right?" the female cop asks.

"I get a bit carsick," I say, checking the sink for blood.

"Oh, honey, we're almost there. Just tell us to pull over if you want to be sick."

★ ★ ★

The rain is heavier now and the sky is a rich black. But the icy-cold air helps to fight the nausea. I clamber into the back of the car and pull the door shut with my good arm. We veer back out onto the highway. I rest my throbbing arm up next to the headrests, afraid of the blood beginning to drip down to my wrist, and lean my head back against the window. I don't feel the sickness anymore, just a floating feeling. The even patter of the rain, the soft tones of the radio and the heat of the car lull me into a near sleep.

I'm not sure how long we've been driving in silence when they start talking.

"I think she's asleep." The man's voice.

I hear the squeak of leather as the woman turns to look at me. I don't move.

"Looks like it. Must be tiring work being such a little bitch."

"Where do you think she's been this whole time?"

"My guess? Ran off with some man, married probably. He must have gotten sick of her and given her the boot. I reckon he was rich, too, by the way she's been looking down her nose at everyone."

"She said she was abducted."

"I know. She's not acting like it, though, is she?"

"Not really."

"And she looks in pretty good nick, considering. If she was kidnapped, he must have been pretty fond of her. That's all I'm saying. What do you think?"

"I don't give a shit honestly," he says. "But I reckon there might be a commendation in it for us."

"I don't know. Shouldn't she be in a hospital or something? I don't know if ass hat was really meant to just let her leave when she clicked her fingers."

"What is the protocol, then? I know what we're meant to do when these kids go missing, but what about when they come back?"

"Fucked if I know. Must have been hungover that day."

They laugh, and then the car is quiet again.

"You know, I've been wondering all day who it is she reminds me of," the female cop says suddenly. "It just hit me. It was this girl back in high school who told everyone she had a brain tumor and took a week off school for the operation. A bunch of us started a drive to raise money for her. I think we all thought she was going to die. She came back right as rain on Monday, though, and for a few hours she was the most popular girl in school. Then someone noticed that none of her hair was shaved, not even an inch. The whole thing was a crock of shit from start to finish.

"That girl, she looked at you just like our little princess back there looked at us when we met her. The way she takes you in, surveys you with that cold glint in her eyes like her head is going a million miles a minute trying to figure out the best way to fuck with you."

After a while I stop listening to them talk. I remember I have to speak to the detective when I get to Canberra, but I feel too dizzy to try to plan my answers. The car pulls off the main road.

I wake to the jolt of the brakes and the light going on as the female cop opens her door.

"Wake up, little lady," she says.

I try to sit, but my muscles feel like they're made of jelly. I hear a new voice.

"You must be Constables Seirs and Thompson. I'm Senior Inspector Andopolis. Thanks for pulling the overtime to bring her down."

"No worries, sir."

"We better get started. I know her mother is over the moon, but I have a lot of questions for her first."

I hear him pull the door next to me open.

"Rebecca, you can't imagine how pleased I am to see you," he says. Then he kneels down beside me. "Are you all right?"

I try to look at him but his face is swirling.

"Yes, I'm okay," I mutter.

"Why is she so pale?" he calls sharply. "What's happened to her?"

"She's fine. She just gets carsick," the female cop says.

"Call an ambulance!" Andopolis snaps at her as he reaches over and undoes my seat belt.

"Rebecca? Can you hear me? What's happened?"

"I hurt my arm when I was escaping," I hear myself say. "It's okay, just hurts a bit."

He pulls my jacket to the side. There's dried blood all the way up to my collarbone. Seeing that makes my vision fade even more.

"You morons! You absolute fucking idiots!" His voice sounds far away now. I can't see the reaction from the cops; I can't see their faces paling. But I can imagine.

I smile as the last of my consciousness fades.

2

Bec, 10 January 2003

Bec had decided months ago to live her life as if she was being watched. Just in case there was a film crew hiding behind a corner or her mirror was two-way. It meant no more yawning without covering her mouth or picking her nose on the toilet. She wanted to always look exactly like a happy, pretty sixteen-year-old girl should.

This felt different, though, this prickling on the back of her neck. This felt like there really was someone watching her. She had been feeling it for a few days now, but every time she whipped her head around there was no one there. Maybe she was going mad.

It would be scary for your worst fears to be coming real all around you and everyone to just dismiss you as crazy. Their next-door neighbour, Max, used to yell all night. Her mom told her he must just be arguing with someone on the phone, but she'd peered through her curtains when he'd woken her at 4:00 a.m. one morning, and there he was, screaming at no one in the dark. He threw a rock through their kitchen window a few weeks later. Her dad made a call that night, and Max was taken away. When he came back, he didn't yell anymore. He just sat on his stoop and stared into the middle distance, slowly getting fatter and fatter.

Would it be better to feel afraid all the time or to feel nothing at all? She hadn't decided yet.

The sun glared down at her through a milk skin of clouds. She would probably be burnt if she stayed out here much longer. But she liked this image of herself. Lying on her back in Lizzie's swimming pool. Green bikini, freckled arms outstretched, belly button filling up with water as she breathed. She wondered if she was being watched right now. The bedrooms of Lizzie's brother and father looked down onto the pool. She'd caught both of them staring at her a few times over the past year. It should gross her out, but it didn't.

The sound of feet slapping against the concrete, a moment of stretched silence and then the surface of the water exploded as Lizzie cannon-bombed. She came up for air giggling madly, her wet hair plastered over her face.

"I almost got you!"

"You're such an idiot." Bec laughed, trying to dunk her back under the water. Lizzie grabbed her waist and they screeched and cackled as they attempted to wrestle, slippery limbs like eels tangling together. Bec dunked Lizzie hard and she came up spluttering.

"Truce?"

Lizzie held out her pinkie finger, still coughing. They gripped pinkies and Bec swam quickly out of the way before Lizzie changed her mind. Bec leaned over the tiled edge of the pool, getting her breath back. She wished this was her house and Lizzie was her sister, although they looked nothing alike. While Bec was lean and relatively flat-chested, Lizzie's body was all soft and curvy in the right places. Sometimes when Lizzie put on red lipstick Bec thought that her best friend looked just like Marilyn Monroe, but she never told her.

"Oh, now my head is spinning again." Droplets of water clung from Lizzie's eyelashes as she stared intently at Bec.

"It's your own fault." Bec rested her head on her arm. Her hangover was slipping away. The dizziness was gone and her stomach was beginning to calm.

"Last night was awesome, wasn't it?" A dangerous little smile crept over Bec's face as she said it. Lizzie didn't even know the best bits.

"We're so lucky." Lizzie sighed and pushed herself off the edge. "You'd better go, dude. You're going to get in the shit with Ellen."

"Crap! What time is it?" Bec pulled herself out of the pool, the baked concrete searing her bare feet as she hopped toward the lounge room. She grabbed her phone off the kitchen bench. It was two thirty; she would only just make it if she hurried. She had an SMS. It was from him. Just woke up. Always have the most amazing nights with you.

Bec was glad Lizzie wasn't there to see the goofy smile that plastered her face as she ran up the stairs to grab her work clothes. The message ran over and over in her head. It must mean he liked her. She was sure now. She slammed into Lizzie's brother, Jack, on the landing. His door was open and the grinding sounds of his metal music pumped from his bedroom. He had put a hand out instinctively; it felt hot on her lower back. For a quarter of a second they were so close it was like they were embracing; she could feel his breath, smell his smell. He jerked his hand away.

"Sorry!"

He looked awkwardly at the floor, his face colouring. She realized suddenly she was basically naked and gave a little shriek of laughter as she ran into Lizzie's room. Pulling off her bikini, she left it a wet green lump on the carpet and put her work uniform on. It stank of deep-fryer oil and stuck to her wet skin. She wished she'd given herself time to have a shower and wash her hair. Bec would usually never go anywhere without straightening it. Grabbing her makeup bag, she smudged on her concealer, smeared on the thick foundation, blush on top, then mascara. She liked to wear liquid eyeliner these days, too, but it was too easy to muck up if she was in a hurry. She'd gone to school looking like a panda once and never wanted to repeat the experience. Pulling on her ballet flats as she walked, she grabbed her bag and took the stairs down two at a time.

"See ya, bitch!" she called to Lizzie, who stuck her middle finger up from the swimming pool.

The gate banged shut behind her as she rushed down the street. It was now 2:43 p.m. She should make it. Her pace slowed. It was too hot to run. The air felt heavy, pushing her down into the road. This was a stinker of a summer. Day after day of over forty degrees. She ran her fingers through her hair; it was almost dry already. Hopefully it wouldn't frizz.

Sunday was his day off. She wished he was going to be there anyway. They could compare hangovers, rehash the events of last night and laugh. Her thumbs flashed across the keypad: On my way to work now. Boo, wish you were there :). Reading over it again and again, she wasn't sure. She didn't want to be too obvious, although she'd read in a magazine once that obvious was good. You have to give them the confidence to make a move. The smiley face had to go, she decided; it was too childish. Her finger hesitated over the send button, her heart racing. Closing her eyes, she forced herself to push it. The private little smile crept over her face again and Bec wondered if Lizzie had any idea. She liked having this secret. It felt dangerous, like playing with fire.

For a moment the other secret leapt into her mind. The memory of it was like red-hot metal, searing and violent. She tried to push it back down; she shouldn't be thinking about that.

Gum leaves crunched under her feet as she turned the corner onto the main road. The smell of baking eucalypt was pungent. It made her eyes water. The leaves were crisp and black around the edges, like the heat in the air had burnt them. For a second she wondered if she might vomit, if last night's beer was going to make a reappearance after all. She stopped walking and held on to a branch to steady herself, squeezing her eyes shut.

Last night had been fun; it was worth feeling a bit sick today. The best nights out always happened by surprise. She'd been closing up. Mopping the floors and washing out the deep fryer with two fingers pinching her nose. Matty was doing the grill. His thick fingers were black from the grease. She didn't understand why he never wore gloves. She used to be a bit scared of Matty, with his hulking frame and tattooed arms, but then she realized he was one of the sweetest men she'd ever met. More like a teddy bear than a biker.

"I'm meeting Ellen and Luke at the pub after this. Do you want to come?"

"Do you reckon we can sneak Lizzie in, too?" He'd said yes, but she would have gone even if he hadn't.

The five of them played pool, Matty and Luke taking it in turns and buying her pots of beer. She hated beer, but didn't want to ask for cider; she loved feeling like one of the boys. The pub was dark and smelt musky. When she'd opened the doors to the toilets, she saw her own dilated pupils in the mirror, before they responded to the bright fluorescents. She'd smeared on a bit more makeup, wishing she'd brought something to change into. But she hadn't let that spoil the night.

Bec had tried not to stare at Luke. But she was willing him to come over, to get closer. Eventually she sat a game out and so did he.

"How are you going, mate?" She loved it when he called her that, as if they were complete equals. She hated nothing more than being treated like a little girl.

When he sat next to her, she could feel the radiating heat of his body. They made smutty jokes as they watched the others play; she lit up when she managed to make him laugh. He told her secrets. She listened. She wished he would kiss her. He didn't. But he took her hand once and squeezed it, his eyes staring at her intensely. He didn't have to say anything; she could guess what he was thinking. She was too young. When they were working late one night he'd told her that a friend of his had a rule. You could date someone half your age, plus seven years. Any younger than that was wrong.

"So, when do you turn seventeen?" he'd said, like it was a joke. It had been three months away then. Only one now. She would just have to be patient.

Bec's foundation was starting to melt off. She pushed herself to walk a little faster. McDonald's had air conditioning. Not that it helped much in the drive-through. Fingers crossed she was just at the main counter today. Then she felt it again, that prickling feeling. She turned. There was no one behind her. The street was strangely empty. Everyone was locked away in air conditioning. She quickened her pace, the back of her neck still prickling.

When she got off the bus after work the sky was black. The air was still heavy and hot. Her suburb was always silent when she came home late. When she walked around Lizzie's street at night, it felt like it breathed—lights on, windows open, people laughing, music playing. There was the welcome smell of hot dinners wafting out of the screen doors.

In Bec's suburb, everyone shut their curtains tight, so you could just see the blue glow of televisions around the edges.

She couldn't wait to get home, to open her front door to a cool house. Her family sitting in front of the television, laughing along to some dumb sitcom. To feel the relief of being comfortable, included and safe. Of being home.

At least, she wished that's what it would be like. But that was someone else's family. Not hers.

Her limbs were starting to ache as she walked up the hill to her street. It had been a long shift. Ellen was angry with her; she'd been ten minutes late after all. When she'd seen her reflection in the stainless steel, she saw her running makeup and frizzy hair. There was nothing she could do about it either. Sitting in the drive-through window, she could feel her forearms starting to burn; she hadn't even put sunscreen on.

That doomsday feeling started to creep up on her. That

feeling when she was so tired that everything started to feel wrong. She tried not to think about Luke. If she did, she would start to pick it apart; to worry. To realize he didn't like her at all, that she was being an idiot and everyone was laughing at her.

She approached her house slowly. It was dark. Every window pitch-black.

3

A tube of white light surfaces in the thick black. I close my eyes again. It's too bright. My throat is dry and my head throbs. Groaning, I rub my eyes. Something catches on my cheek. Blinking the blurriness away, I look at my wrist. Around it loops a plastic hospital band, with the words *Winter, Rebecca* in bold type. Looking around groggily, I see the officer from last night asleep in a chair at the foot of the bed.

Oh, God. This is going to be so much more difficult than I'd thought.

Standing in that dark toilet block, the cold and fear and exhaustion had seemed like the bigger of two evils. But now, waking up in this hospital bed with a sleeping detective blocking the door, I realize that maybe I'd made a mistake. I'd been so stupid to think that I could just start a brand-new life, that it would be that easy.

The room is quiet. There is only the sound of the cop's sleeping breath and the muffled chatter from a few rooms away. There's a window to my right. Maybe I could make it.

As quietly as I can, I push myself up to sitting. My arm is bandaged and stinks of antiseptic, but it barely hurts. Must be because of whatever is in the drip attached to my hand. Looking down, I see that I'm wearing nothing but a thin hospital gown and underwear. Someone undressed me. For a moment I could laugh—how many times have I woken up in a strange bed out of my clothes?

The detective snorts a loud snore, waking himself up.

"Bec," he says, rubbing his eyes and smiling.

I stare at him. No way I'm getting out that door now.

"Do you remember me from last night? Vincent Andopolis." He looks at me carefully. This is happening too fast. I have no idea how to answer him.

"Everything's a bit fuzzy." My voice is still thick with sleep and painkillers. Best to keep it simple while I try to figure out what the hell I'm going to do.

I do remember him. He's the missing persons detective who'd called my two chauffeur cops "morons." I hadn't been able to make out much of him last night; he looks different in the cold, sterile hospital lights. His grey eyes and wide shoulders hint at the attractive man he must have once been, but his gut pushes tightly against his shirt and his hair is more salt than pepper.

"Have you been here all night?" I ask.

"Couldn't have you disappearing again. Your mom is ready to sue us as it is," he says with a lopsided grin. "How is it feeling?" He motions to my arm.

"It's fine," I say, although it's throbbing painfully, then notice a small pile of things on the chair next to his. He follows my gaze.

"Your parents are talking to my partner." He clears his

throat. "There are a few things we still need to do before you can be reunited."

There is a pair of pyjama pants, a T-shirt and some underwear all neatly folded on the chair, with a hairbrush on top.

"They've already been in here?" Surely not.

"They couldn't really believe it until they saw you."

My mind reels. They've been in here. They watched me sleep. Yet they still believe I'm their daughter. I guess the bruise on my face worked on them, too. The biggest hurdle was already over and I wasn't even conscious for it. I can't help but smile. Andopolis beams back at me.

"I have to be honest, Bec. I couldn't be happier to see you. It's like a miracle."

A miracle. What a dope. How could this guy be a missing persons detective? The panic I felt a few seconds ago flushes out of me. Perhaps it won't be so hard to go through with this.

"It is a miracle," I say, flashing him my best shit-eating grin.

He says nothing, just gazes at me. I guess he thinks we're sharing a moment.

"When can I get out of here?" I ask.

"Probably by the end of the day. We've just got a few things to get through and then you'll be all set."

"Like what?"

"Well, I've got a few more urgent questions for you. Then there are some tests to run, just to make sure you're well."

I try not to blink. I'm screwed.

He pulls a notebook out of his pocket. "The New South Wales police informed me you stated that you were abducted."

I nod. The less I say the better until I figure out what the hell I'm going to do.

"Do you know the person or people who took you? Before you were taken, I mean." I can see the eagerness in his eyes.

I shake my head.

"Do you remember where you were held? Any details would be helpful."

"It's all blurry. I can't really remember," I say slowly. He watches me calmly, as though he expects me to say more. The silence swells between us.

At last he looks away, flicking his notebook shut and returning it to his pocket. "I'll give you some time, and we can resume this after your tests are done."

"Then I can go home?"

His eyes fix on mine, as though he's waiting for something.

"Is going home what you want?" he asks finally.

"Yes, of course."

I try to smile reassuringly, and after a few moments, his lopsided grin returns.

"The nurse will be in soon."

The door clicks shut behind him and I jump out of the bed. My head swims but I ignore it. Letting the drip trail behind me, I go to the window first. It's just a panel of glass, sealed on all sides, no way of opening it. I guess they're afraid of people jumping; three floors could still do some damage. Outside, people stream around the entrance. Doctors and paramedics enter; sick people hobble out. There are cars and taxis and ambulances. Even if I were to put on the clothes

Rebecca's parents left, it would be a stretch to be able to just walk out of here.

I go over to the chair and hold out the pink T-shirt and cat-print pyjama pants that the parents left in front of me. Looks like I am about her height and weight. They'd just about fit. Lucky. I pick up the brush. Glinting copper hairs are caught between the bristles.

When the nurse comes in to take me for tests, I'm back in bed, innocent as a baby lamb. If I can get through this, I'll have earned a new identity. The rewards of this game are just too great to give up on.

I keep my fists clenched as the doctor prods me. He's worked his way down my body, looking for any kind of injury. Now he talks loudly to me from between my legs.

"This will be a little cold."

"It might sting a bit."

"Almost done now."

I wear a humiliated expression, but really I've gotten used to having men poke around blindly down there.

"Thank you, Rebecca. You've been a good sport," he says. "You can get up now."

He pulls the curtain closed behind him, as though I have any modesty left to preserve. I pull on my underwear, listening as he talks to the nurse.

"Can you prepare the swab for a mitochondria? We'll need three vials for the syringe, as well."

I don't think so. There's no way I'm giving them my DNA or my blood, and not just because they'll know I'm not Rebecca Winter. But because then they might find out who I really am. The curtain opens.

"Ready, then, Rebecca?" the doctor asks.

The nurse meets my eye as she scampers back in, then quickly looks away.

"I need to go home now."

Putting my head down, I let my hair cover my face. I'm preparing.

"I know it's all a little intrusive, but we're almost done. We just need a swab of the inside of your cheek and some blood."

"No more pain, please. I can't." My voice is pitch-perfect, all panicky and high.

Woven between my fingers is a clump of copper strands from her brush. I tug at my own hair, nowhere near hard enough for anything to come out.

"Will this do? I can't deal with any more." I raise my hand, the clump of her hair dangling downwards. I don't look up but I hear the tiniest intake of breath from the nurse.

Then I start crying. Really bawling, like a little kid. Letting the sobs roll out on top of each other. My whole body shakes with it. It's not hard once I start; I've had a lot to cry about these last few weeks. The nurse steps forward, carefully taking the hair out of my hand with her plastic gloves. Easy.

The car climbs the steep hill of Rebecca Winter's street, and finally, I can see them: a middle-aged couple who look totally ordinary. My new mother and father. Their backs are braced, their heads down. They are standing in rigid silence in front of their big white house. An old gum tree next to the garage throws dappled light onto the facade. Idealized middle-class suburbia just waiting for me.

The mother's head snaps up as she hears the car. My heart hammers harder. The hospital could have been a fluke. Unconscious, with a bruised face, maybe they'd seen what they wanted to see. Now that my eyes are open, now that I'm moving and walking and talking, there is no way I'll fool her. I can sense Andopolis's eyes flicking up at the rear-vision mirror to look at me. She'll realize my deception the moment she lays eyes on me. It doesn't matter how much time has passed. Surely a mother would know her only daughter.

"Usually we would have a support agent here for something like this," he says. "Your parents didn't want it, though."

I nod. I'm too nervous to be appreciative, although this almost definitely will make it easier. Convincing the parents was going to be enough of a feat. It wouldn't do me any good to have some bleeding-heart liberal with a smile slapped across their smug face trying to "help." They'd know how victims really did act in this kind of situation.

"You will need to talk to a counselor soon, okay, Bec? But we'll take it all one step at a time."

I smile weakly at him. No way I'm talking to a counselor.

We pull into the driveway. For a moment I wish I could stay there; I wish I could hide in the back seat for just a little longer. Andopolis gets out and walks around to my door, opening it for me. Now that I see them, I'm not sure if I can do it. Rebecca—Bec—was a person, not a character, and I'd never even met her. Never even heard her voice.

I can't look at the mother as I step out of the car. I keep my face turned downwards, my eyes focusing on the white geraniums flowering by the path.

"Becky?" she says, moving closer. She touches my arm tentatively as though I might not be real.

I look up; I have to look up. Her eyes stare into mine. They're filled with such fierce love, it's like the rest of the world has disappeared. It's just her and me; nothing else matters. She wraps her arms around me and I can feel her heart against my ribs, her warmth mixing with mine. She smells of vanilla.

"Thank you, Vince," I hear the dad say over her shoulder.

"You're more than welcome," says Andopolis. "Bring her in around three."

"See you then, mate."

I hear the door open as Andopolis gets in his car. Then the engine starts and he drives away. The mom releases me and the father looks me up and down. He's the ultimate white-collar worker, with his suit and open shirt, his dark eyes and clean-shaven face. He must have dressed for work even though he knew he wasn't going, still in shock that he was taking the day off because his long-lost daughter was coming home.

"I don't know what to say, Becky."

He pulls me in for a hug. It's different from the mother, a little awkward. I can smell his aftershave and, behind that, a strange rotting smell.

The mother turns and pulls open the door. I think I see her wipe her face.

"Come inside, Bec."

Her voice cracks and I realize I've passed the test. I'm in. This is my house, my life.

From now on, I am Rebecca Winter.

I'd forgotten how amazing a hot shower is. Being able to wash my hair and shave my legs feels fantastic, even though I have to do it with my injured arm sticking out of the stream. I wrap a towel around myself and happily breathe in the steam. If I'd made the other choice, I'd be cold and alone somewhere right now, wearing my dirty clothes that would probably be still damp from the rain. The thought makes me shudder.

Walking out of the bathroom, I realize I don't know which one was Rebecca's room. I open the door next to the bathroom. It's a cupboard full of folded linen. I slowly open the door opposite, hoping they can't hear me from the kitchen. This one is a bedroom, nothing on the walls and no furniture except for two single beds. Was this meant to be my room? There's one more door, so I decide to try that one, walking softly on the carpet so they won't hear my footsteps from below.

Posters of Destiny's Child and Gwen Stefani glare at me. The bed is made with pink sheets. A Cabbage Patch doll perches on the bedside table. Year Ten textbooks are stacked on the desk, the first four in the Harry Potter series are aligned neatly on the shelf above, and everywhere, there are photographs. There she is, smiling and posing, her arms around various friends, mostly another girl with long blonde hair. It's like life stood still in this room, waiting for the same sixteen-year-old to return.

I peer at the pictures of her, gripping the towel around my naked body, my wet hair dripping on the carpet. Even in photographs you can see the life and vitality of this girl. She looks confident and at ease. Looking at her face from all angles, I realize she looks a little less like me than I originally thought. Her nose is smaller, her eyes are bigger—even the shape of her face is slightly different. A decade can change a face a lot, though. I can blame any differences on time.

Time is the other problem. Adding it up in my head now, I

realize Bec would be around twenty-seven. I'm only twenty-four. For once I find myself hoping I look older.

I slide the slatted closet door open. Her clothes are hung up neatly, but I can smell the stale air inside. This door hasn't been opened in a long time. Seeing Bec's school uniform hanging in front of me makes me feel strange, a little sick inside, so I quickly grab some jeans and a T-shirt and close the door again. Anything is better than these kitten pyjama pants that make me want to gag with their cuteness. They fit me well enough, but still, they're childish. It feels wrong to be almost twenty-five and wearing a sixteen-year-old's low-slung jeans and Guess top. Having the fabric so close to my skin, I can smell an unfamiliar musky human smell. It must be the scent of her body, still clinging to the cotton of the T-shirt. A shiver snakes down my spine.

The mother and father sit on the two-seater sofa in the lounge room, an untouched sandwich in front of each of them and another in front of one of the empty chairs across. I sit down, noticing the other armchair has a cat curled up in it. I've always wanted a pet.

"Thought we'd have lunch in here today, keep you as comfortable as possible," says the mom.

"Great, thanks!" I say, not really knowing what she means. I wish I knew more about Rebecca, had a clearer view of what kind of person she was. Since I don't, I decide I'm best off playing the role every parent wants: the dutiful daughter. I'll be wholesome, appreciative and innocent. I take a bite into the sandwich, realizing again how ravenous I am.

"This is so yummy. Thanks for making it, Mom."

"Of course, sweetheart." She smiles broadly. It's working.

"I talked to Paul and Andrew last night," the dad says.

"Really?" Turning things into a question is an easy way to keep a conversation going when you have no idea what the person is talking about.

"Yes. They'll be flying in later this evening."

I look around the room. There are framed photographs on the walls: two identical little freckled boys grinning, with Bec standing proudly between them. Growing until they reached her shoulders and then, abruptly, just the two of them, smiles not as wide, continuing to grow into teenagers' clothes and stubble and then jawlines and suits. They must be her brothers.

"I can't wait to see them," I say.

"Good." He smiles and takes a bite of his sandwich.

"Bet you'll want to call Lizzie," says the mom.

I nod, shoveling the rest of the sandwich into my mouth. I don't know who Lizzie is.

"Just don't be calling anyone who you think might get in touch with the media. That's the last thing we need," the father says.

"Do you really think someone would do that?" I ask, playing innocent.

"You never know, sweetheart."

Of course they would, but it doesn't matter. I'll be avoiding Rebecca's old friends as much as possible. I already have enough lies to keep track of. I pick the crumbs off the plate with my finger. I want another sandwich, but don't really want to ask. Looking up, I realize they are both staring at me. I remember what the lady cop said in the car, that I wasn't acting like I'd been abducted.

"I'm so happy to be home, to be safe again," I say.

The mother starts crying at that, her chest heaving with

painful, guttural sobs, her hands held over her face like a shield. It is a long time before she stops.

When we get to the police station, I ask the parents if they'll come in with me. I grip the mom's hand tightly; I need her there with me to answer some of the questions. These people are trained at spotting a lie; no matter how good I am, it's their job to see through me.

"If you want us to I'm sure we can ask," says the mom, taking a step forward. The dad holds her arm, stopping her.

"I think Vince will want to talk to you alone, Bec. But we'll wait right out here." The mother takes a step back and looks down, her eyes still red and puffy.

The uniformed policeman at the desk ushers me through. Rebecca's T-shirt is starting to feel a little snug.

A man wearing a brand-new suit walks toward me, his hand outstretched.

"Rebecca Winter?" he asks. I nod and he gives my hand a brisk shake.

"I'm Detective Vali Malik, Vince's partner."

"Bec!" Andopolis says, coming over to us, a file under his arm. "You look much better."

He never mentioned having a partner. "Thanks," I say.

"Come with me," Malik says, turning on the heel of his perfectly polished shoe.

Trailing behind the two of them, I peer into a room to my left. Inside is a large board covered in notes that I can't quite read from here. Stuck to it is a map, a large photograph of Rebecca smiling into the camera and a close-up of a cracked mobile phone in grass. There are a few men sitting at a large table and one of them looks up at me as I pass. Andopolis's wide hand presses against my lower back, gently pushing me forward. He smiles reassuringly.

"Right in here," he says as he holds a door on the right open for me.

I'm expecting another cold concrete box like the one in Sydney. Instead they bring me into a sunny room with couches, a miniature table and a plastic tub of toys in the corner. Like Sydney, there's a large mirror across one of the walls. I wonder if the cops I just walked past are going to come and watch. Malik motions toward one of the couches. It squeaks as I sit down.

"Would you like anything, Rebecca? Tea, coffee?"

"I'm okay," I say. "Thank you."

"How does it feel to be home?" Andopolis asks, sitting on the couch across from me.

"It's amazing."

Malik sits on the chair to my left, opening a folder.

"That's great to hear," he says and smiles.

"Your tests have come back looking good," Malik says, flicking through some papers in the folder.

Victory. Even I can't believe I actually pulled that off. But I can't get cocky now. I need to concentrate on this new stage of the game.

I take them in for a moment. Malik must be at least fifteen years younger than Andopolis. He is all sharp lines and impeccable grooming. Next to him Andopolis looks old and rumpled.

"You weren't there this morning when I woke up," I say to Malik.

"No. I was talking to your parents." He smiles his quick, efficient smile again and continues. "I'm happy that you're back with your family, Rebecca, but we really have to focus on the investigation. The longer we leave it, the less likely we are to get answers."

He was right. I didn't want them getting any answers; I had to hold them off as long as possible. Their notebooks come back out. Ding, ding. Round two. I'd knocked it out of the park at the last round at the hospital, so hopefully I could do as well now. After this, things would only get easier.

"Can you describe the location of where you were held?" Malik, diving straight in there.

"I didn't really..." I pause for effect. "I didn't really see the outside. It could have been anywhere. Sorry."

"That's okay, Bec. Don't pressure yourself. How much time do you think passed between your escape and when the police picked you up? You were picked up in Sydney, so presumably you were held near there," Andopolis asks.

I think about that last night in the cheap hostel at Kings Cross. It was only a week ago, but it feels like much longer. I'd counted my money out on the mattress, knowing I wouldn't have enough, that I'd have to check out in the morning. I remember trying to sleep. From the window I could hear women screaming outside, bottles smashing, men swearing. I knew that the next day I'd be out there with them.

"No. Not really, sorry."

It smells weird in here, like a hospital. I guess the toys have to be cleaned every time a kid picked them up. I look at the miniature chair and table, wondering if Andopolis ever sat down there with a child, asking them to use a dolly to play out whatever abuse they'd encountered.

"I know this is hard, but we need you to tell us everything you can remember," Malik says.

I take a breath, getting ready to tell them what they're gagging to hear. I'd planned it all out: torture chambers, men in masks, everything. They'd lap it up and I'd lead them on a wild-goose chase around Australia. But then, just as I'm about to begin, the photograph from the investigation room comes into my mind. Rebecca Winter, young and happy. Did I really want to make her fate so ghastly? I look between their waiting faces. I was being silly. Whatever I said had no bearing on whatever really happened to her. It was stupid to even think about that. It was my life now, not hers. I had to be smart about this. Of course, as soon as I tell them a story, they'll start digging through it and finding holes. Less is more. The cleverest thing to do is to tell no story at all.

"That's the problem," I say, quietly. "I don't remember anything."

"Nothing?" Malik tries to cover his frustration, but I can hear it there in his voice.

"What about more recently? Do you remember who hit you? Who caused that bruise?" asks Andopolis, eyeing the side of my face. I look down, as though I'm ashamed of it. Really, the story is sort of embarrassing. I was running from a fruit vendor. I'd stolen two apples before I tripped and fell on the curb. No one hit me.

"No."

"What about your arm?" Andopolis asks, softly. If he's annoyed he doesn't show it.

I shake my head.

"When I first came to see you," Andopolis says gently, "you said that you hurt it when you escaped. Do you remember that?"

"Yes." No. I'd forgotten.

"So you do remember escaping?" Malik asks.

I take a breath. I'm going to have to give them something.

"I remember breaking the window glass," I say, remembering the bottle smashing in the bathroom. My body shudders at the memory, they notice.

"My arm got caught, but I kept going. I just remember knowing I didn't have much time."

"Why didn't you have much time?" Malik asks, quick as a whip.

Because I knew the cop outside was going to come in and check up on me. I wonder if there was some way of asking if she lost her job without seeming vindictive. Probably best not to.

I wish I could press Pause on this situation. Go outside for a cigarette and have a real think on the best way to handle it. I was prepared for just one detective, and having the two of them on each side is intimidating. One question rolls out over the next before I've had a chance to think.

"How long did you look for me?" I ask. I feel safer when I am asking the questions.

Malik looks at Andopolis. He probably wasn't even a detective back then, just a rookie in uniform.

"The investigation went on for a long time. We searched everywhere," Andopolis says slowly.

The intensity in his eyes was starting to make more sense. He must have a lot of burning questions for me.

"Did you have a suspect?" I ask.

"We had a few people of interest."

"Who?"

"Why don't we start from the beginning?" interrupts Malik. "What was the last thing you do remember? Before the abduction."

He was putting the focus back onto me. My mind flicked back to the television show.

"I was at work, at McDonald's. It's all blurry after that."

Andopolis smiles at me, that proud, lopsided grin. I got that one right. He puts the file down on the table between us and opens it. Inside is a spread of what looks like staff photographs, head and shoulders of five different people, all smiling in their McDonald's uniforms.

"Do you remember these people?" he asks.

"Yes," I say. "Of course. But...you know. It's been a long time." My heart is pounding and the T-shirt squeezes under my arms, making me sweat. This feels like a test.

"Do you remember her?" He points a finger at a young girl. She's very pretty, even in the ugly uniform. Her blonde hair is pulled up into a ponytail and her eyes sparkle. I realize I do recognize her; she was in most of the pictures on Rebecca's wall.

"She was my best friend," I say, and then I remember the father's words from earlier. "Lizzie."

"And the others?" Malik asks. That must mean I got it right.

"I remember Lizzie. The rest... I know that I know them..." I try to look upset. "I hate being confused like this."

"It's okay, Bec. We'll take it slow." Andopolis's voice is soothing. "These are the last people who saw you before you disappeared. This is Ellen Park. She was your manager."

She looks like she's in her midtwenties maybe, with a look of premature worry in her eyes.

"This is Lucas Masconey." He points to a good-looking guy in his early twenties.

"And Matthew Lang. He was the cook." This guy is big

and beefy with a bunch of silver rings through his ear. "Do you remember him?"

"Kind of," I say.

"Anything specific?" Malik presses. This Matthew guy must have been a suspect. Trust the cops to go for the most obvious person.

"No," I say, a little too harshly.

I look down at my hands and force myself to breathe. I had to do something; I was already breaking character. I couldn't be anything other than a victim, not even for a moment.

"So, how long until you gave up looking?" I ask.

Andopolis looks up at me, something dark passing across his face.

"It's not that we gave up. The investigation just went cold." He averts his eyes as he continues and I realize what he's feeling: guilt. "Every lead was followed. Do you understand?"

"Yes."

I see the guilt there again, even though he tries to hide it.

"Let's try to concentrate on that day," says Malik. "We were talking about your last shift at McDonald's."

I had to get rid of Malik. I could see he was a good detective, yet he didn't seem to have much of an ego. He just saw this case as his job and I was an important part of it. But that's all.

"Actually, I wouldn't mind a cup of tea. If that's okay," I say quietly, looking at Malik.

"Okay," he says. "Won't be a minute."

As soon as the door clicks shut I lean forward.

"I don't like him!" I say in a panicked whisper.

"Why?" Andopolis asks, surprised.

"He scares me. I don't feel right when he's here. Can't it just be you?"

I can see Andopolis's chest swell ever so slightly. Idiot. He didn't like him either; he probably didn't want to share his case with some new hotshot.

"I trust you," I add. "Please?"

"Let me see what I can do."

He pushes himself off the couch and walks out of the room. I wonder what conversation they're having behind the mirror right now. I force myself not to look.

After a few minutes Andopolis comes back with a cup of tea and the tiniest trace of a triumphant smile on the corners of his mouth.

"Okay, Bec, it'll just be me from now on."

"Thank you!" I say.

"It's fine." He puts the tea down on the little table next to me. "If you ever feel upset or uncomfortable I want you to tell me. I'll do everything I can to try and fix it. Deal?"

"Deal," I say, giving him my best innocent eyes. He thinks we are on the same side.

"Great. Now, when you're ready, we really do need to talk about that night. The night you were taken. Anything you remember would be so helpful in finding who did this."

He was treating me like a fragile child, which was exactly what I wanted.

"I do remember something," I say.

"What?" he asks.

I stare into the middle distance for a while, counting to ten in my head, letting the heavy silence fill the room.

"I was cold and scared," I say when I reach ten. "Everything was black."

I talk slowly, letting the suspense build. "I remember hearing sirens. They were getting closer and closer. I thought

I was saved. But then they kept going. They got quieter. I knew they weren't for me."

I look up at him and his face is twisted with guilt and shame. I have him.

"I'm tired now. And I'd like to see my parents."

As the father drives us home, I want to fall asleep in the back seat. I really am tired.

"Do you mind if I have a little nap before they get in?" I ask. I've already forgotten the brothers' names.

"Of course. You must be exhausted."

Lying down between Rebecca's sheets, I wonder for a moment whether they were changed. Or whether these are the same sheets that she had lain in, eleven years ago, on the morning that she would leave her house and never return. They must have been changed, surely.

Soon, I hear the front door opening and then two male voices. Her brothers must be here. They'll expect me to go down and greet them, but the idea of getting up again seems impossible. My arm is throbbing. The bandage feels too tight. I'll go in a minute, I decide. Let the mother be the one to fill them in on the details, on the memory loss and my arm.

Turning over, I realize I don't care if they changed Rebecca's sheets or not. They feel warm and silky soft. Having my own bed in the hospital had been good, but this was amazing. Feeling so safe and comfortable made the week that had just passed feel unbelievable, like some sort of nightmare.

When I wake it's starting to get dark. I don't even remember falling asleep. I pull myself out of bed, a foul taste in my mouth, brush my fingers through my hair and open my bedroom door. I have to face them sooner or later and the longer I put it off the harder it will be. Walking down the stairs, I notice the house is strangely quiet, but all the lights are on. For a moment I think maybe they've gone out, but surely they wouldn't have left me here alone so soon.

I hear very faint movement on my right. I turn toward it and the kitchen opens up in front of me. There they are. The mother, the father and the two brothers sitting around a circular kitchen table. Dirty plates are in front of each of them. They must have just had dinner. No one is speaking or even looking at one another.

I hesitate for a second in the doorway, waiting for them to move, to notice my presence, but they don't. They sit together in silence with straight backs but empty eyes and lowered heads. I guess it's been a tough day for them, too. Still, something feels strange, slightly off, about this sparkling image of family. But I have bigger problems right now, so I ignore it and walk in to join them.

4

Bec, 11 January 2003

It was almost one in the morning when Bec finally closed her bedroom door, slipped between her bedsheets and switched off the light. She'd been too tired to move quickly. Standing in the shower for almost twenty minutes, she scrubbed the grease off her arms and tried to get the smell of burnt meat out of her nostrils. She groaned with relief at finally being horizontal. The cotton sheets felt clean and soft against her skin. She considered telling Ellen she didn't want to do closes anymore. One hour of extra pay wasn't worth this aching, overtired feeling.

Her mind was moving too slowly to think about it now. Tomorrow was her day off anyway; she'd decide then. A whole day to do whatever she wanted. It would be great. Lying down in her own quiet room felt too exquisite to ruin it by worrying, The hot weight of the cat, Hector, pressed against her leg as he stretched, his bell jingling softly.

Something shifted. That's what woke her. The creaking sound of shifting weight. There was someone in her room.

Bec was too afraid to open her eyes. She didn't want to see what was there. It was enough just to feel its presence, that heaviness of the air that meant another person was breathing it. Underneath the warmth of her sheets, her skin prickled cold. It couldn't be happening again.

She listened. Seconds flicked by. Not a sound. Maybe it was a nightmare.

Bec knew she should open her eyes. Just to check. Just to be sure. A sound rose from beneath the silence, so soft it was barely audible. The gravelly hum of the cat's purr. Very slowly, she opened her eyes.

The first thing she noticed was that Hector wasn't on her bed anymore. She could see the small pear shape of his furry back. He was sitting in the corner, looking at something, purring. Bec knew she should laugh at herself; it was just the cat. But her limbs were still frozen. Something wasn't right.

As her eyes adjusted she had to hold in a gasp. There was a shadow in the corner that shouldn't be there. She could only just see it, onyx against charcoal, a splodge that didn't belong. Her heart slammed against her ribs as it began to move.

Very slowly, it twisted. Limbs stretching. Growing bigger in a way that wasn't human. She clamped her eyes shut, a scream trapped in her throat. Bec didn't want to see what it looked like when it stepped out of the corner. She didn't want to see its face.

Ice-cold fear soaked through her as she waited for the shadow to touch her. To feel that cold hand on her cheek again. She held her breath, just waiting.

The door squeaked.

Had it gone? Bec wanted to let out her breath, but she felt

like fear had paralyzed her. Then something heavy slammed against her knees. She scrambled out away from it, the sheet wrapping around her ankle so that she fell onto the carpet with a thud. Pain spread down from her shoulder but she tried to ignore it, reaching up to turn on her bedside light.

For a moment the light blinded her. And then she saw him. The cat, Hector. Sitting in the middle of her mattress, blinking at her. She picked him up, swearing, and he howled at her. The noise seemed piercing in the silence. She held him against her, the feeling of his tiny heartbeat against her chest calming her enough that she could get up and close her bedroom door again. She wedged her chair under the handle.

Something had been in here; it wasn't just the cat. She was sure of it. Her hands were still sweating and shaking and adrenaline raced through her veins.

Bec picked up her phone; she needed to talk to someone. To tell someone what had just happened so she didn't feel like she was mad. The last time was probably just a nightmare, but this time was real. It was past three in the morning, though. Lizzie would be pissed off if she woke her up.

She looked at herself from the outside for a moment. Lizzie would probably laugh at her, like she was a little kid afraid of ghosts. How lame. She wrote a text instead: There was something in my room. I think my house is haunted. She put the phone back on her bedside table.

Just before she turned the light off she noticed the little silver bell was gone from Hector's collar. A ghost couldn't do that.

Perhaps he hadn't been wearing it before, she told herself, and wrapped herself in a ball under the blanket.

★ ★ ★

It had taken her a long time to get back to sleep. When she had, her dreams were feverish and violent. She woke up with a start, slick with sweat. Checking her phone, she saw it was quarter past eleven. There were three missed calls from Lizzie and two messages. The first: Ha-ha scary. Then after the missed calls: You okay? Bec texted back: Yep. Still on for the city? I'll tell you all about it.

Her room looked different in the morning light. Peaceful and entirely her own. Johnny Depp's and Gwen Stefani's faces, photographs of her and her friends, Destiny's Child posing together perfectly. The slats of her closet doors, the shelf of books above her bed; everything was so warmly familiar. Last night's nightmare seemed exactly that: a nightmare. Not something that could have really happened in her own bedroom. But when she closed her eyes, Bec could see the dark shape again, bending in that unnatural way in the corner. That was a real memory, as clear as mopping the floors at work and walking home from the bus stop.

Her phone buzzed, Lizzie: One hour, Silver Cushion. She pushed herself out of bed and had a look at her shoulder in the mirror. There was a pale grey bruise from where she'd fallen out of bed last night. That bloody cat.

She'd thought the house might look different, somehow. As though some kind of trace would be left behind by the extra presence that had been there last night. But no, everything felt exactly the same as she opened her bedroom door. The cream carpet had the same velvety feel between her toes as she padded down the hallway.

Peering into Paul and Andy's room, she wanted to laugh. That was definitely the same: clothes and Legos strewn all over the floor, sheets on the two single beds twisted into heaps. She remembered how much of a scene they'd made when her mom suggested it was time one of them move into the spare room. She pulled their door shut. The sweaty old socks were starting to reek. You could smell puberty approaching.

The white wooden banister felt as smooth and warm under her palm as it always did. Her bare feet made squeaking sounds as she walked across the polished floorboards of the bottom level. The sound of giggling came from the kitchen; the boys must be home. She checked her parents' room; their precisely made double bed alone in the middle of the spotlessly empty space. The spare room next door was filled with plastic tubs of winter clothes. Her mother's writing desk propped in the corner, still unused. She looked into the laundry. Behind the washing baskets was a door that continued on to their garage. It was slightly open. The garage was the creepiest part of Bec's house and none of them went in there if they could avoid it. Dark and dank smelling, crammed with piled-up cardboard boxes and a dirty concrete floor. They didn't even park their car in there anymore. She was sure the place was infested with spiders. The blackness of the room seemed to spill out from the crack in the doorway, the dark of nighttime trying to recapture her and pull her back into the nightmare. She pulled the door shut.

Nothing had changed in the lounge room either. Couches remained an awkward distance apart and the wooden doors closed over the television so her parents could pretend they didn't have one. Satisfied, she went into the kitchen. Whatever it had been, it was definitely gone now.

Paul and Andrew sat next to each other on the round kitchen table, a box of Coco Pops between them and their bowls filled with brown milk. They were laughing like mad, still in their shorty pyjamas with their dark red hair sticking up at weird angles. Bec felt a sudden stab of love for them. She longed to ruffle up their hair, but she knew they would find it patronizing.

"Ready?" Paul asked.

"Yep," said Andrew.

They picked up the bowls of chocolate milk.

"One...two...three!"

They both began chugging down the milk from their bowls; throats working, brown drops falling onto the table.

"Done!" screamed Andrew, dropping his bowl down and wiping his mouth with the back of his hand.

"Oh, shit!" Paul yelled, the word sounding forced from his mouth. They looked at Bec for a moment to see if she'd get him in trouble for using it, then couldn't hold in their laughter.

"You guys are disgusting!" she said, but she was smiling, too. The horror of last night was starting to wear off.

"You look like Hitler!" she said to Paul, who still had a brown milk moustache on his top lip.

"Goot a morgan!" he said, making Andrew burst into giggles again. She shook her head and poured out her own sugar-free Muesli.

"What are you doing today, Becky?" asked Andrew.

"I'm going to go meet Lizzie in the city."

"Can we come?" asked Paul straightaway. Two sets of identical pale blue eyes fixed on her. She knew they must be really bored. They'd been on summer holidays for two months now and they weren't allowed to go any farther than the local shops by themselves. Her mom was so overprotective, she thought, as though their suburb was the only safe place in the world. It was Canberra, for God's sake. She didn't know why they just didn't go out anyway. She wouldn't tell on them, that was for sure, but she didn't want to suggest it. Somehow that felt wrong.

"Please?" Paul said.

She felt bad, but she really needed to talk to Lizzie about what had happened last night, and she couldn't do that with her little brothers running around everywhere. Plus, there was another thing she had to do with Lizzie that would be impossible with them around.

"Sorry, guys," she said. "Next time."

"Tomorrow?"

"Well, I'm at work tomorrow but how about Sunday?"

"Okay," said Andrew. But she could tell they were both upset; the smiles were gone. Bec hated upsetting her brothers. It did something to her heart that nothing else could.

"We can go to the pool if you want?"

"And you won't tell us off if we bomb?"

"Nope. Cross my heart," she said, miming a cross over her chest. They looked at each other and then turned to her, beaming.

"Awesome," said Paul. She patted them both on the head, which made them groan but she couldn't help it, and went upstairs to get dressed.

Lizzie was waiting for her on a bench in Garema Place, a few feet away from the Silver Cushion. Canberra was filled with weird sculptures, but this one was Bec's favourite for some reason. It looked like a giant half-full wine bag propped on some black steps. In summer the sun reflected off its metallic silver surface so it hurt to look at it and definitely hurt to touch it. Bec plopped down on the bench next to Liz.

"Why are you all the way over here?" she asked.

"Emos," she said, and Bec looked over. Four teenagers with striped black-and-red socks, bad eyeliner and floppy hair sat around the Silver Cushion.

"I worry it's contagious," Lizzie said, shuddering. Bec could tell she meant it, too; there was nothing Lizzie hated more than bad clothes. That's why they worked so well as best friends; they were like each other's perfect accessory. Today they both had on summer dresses and brown sandals; they didn't need to call each other. They were just effortlessly coordinated. Not just in clothes, but everything. It was as if they were made of the same stuff, as if they had the same heart.

If she hadn't already sent the message, she wouldn't have told Lizzie about last night. The image of them sitting there was perfect: two carefree, pretty teenagers ready for anything the endless summer threw at them. The shadow in her room didn't fit with that.

"So what happened?" asked Lizzie, and the perfect image flickered and died.

"Talk and walk?"

"Could it have been your brothers just trying to freak you out?" asked Lizzie, after Bec had briefly explained what had happened.

"No, no way. They would have been wetting themselves

laughing if they managed to scare me that much. Plus, it didn't feel, you know, human."

"So you think it's, what, like a poltergeist?"

"I think, like a specter. Not a ghost or spirit, but something evil and solid that's not meant to be there."

"Wow," said Lizzie, not quite looking at her, "how horrible."

She was worried Lizzie might laugh and call her crazy, but she seemed just as genuinely shocked as Bec.

"It *was* horrible."

"Do you think it will happen again? Maybe you should stay at mine tonight, dude?"

"Maybe. Ugh, I don't even want to think about it anymore."

"I know something that would take your mind off it." Bec recognized the glint in Lizzie's eye.

"I thought you'd never ask!"

They were mucking around as they ran up the last few steps of the escalator. The white facade of the department store shone in front of them. They stopped laughing abruptly as they walked into the store.

The most important thing when shoplifting is to be as quietly confident as possible. Bec had learned that in the early days. The moment you start looking shifty or laughing too loudly, a security guard is shadowing you and that's your chance blown for the day.

The second most important thing is to pick something with a lining. Bec had a look through the racks in the teenager section. Trying to find a label her mother would know was worth a lot of money. Scanlan & Theodore, perfect. She was getting so good at this it was almost unconscious. She looped the straps from the dress behind onto the hanger in front. It now looked as though there was one dress on the hanger, where in fact there were two. The maximum for a change room was six. So she quickly picked five other bulky dresses. The thin silky fabric was barely visible amongst the thick knits and ruffles of the other dresses. The harassed-looking girl at the changing rooms counted her hangers without really looking, gave her a red piece of plastic with the number six on it and ushered her through.

Bec pulled the silky fabric over her head and looked at herself in the mirror. She would have taken it either way, but it was nice when it actually suited her. This one was a teal colour, which looked pretty against her pale skin, and the soft folds hung nicely from her figure. She'd have to find some excuse to wear it in front of Luke. She slipped it off again and took the little pair of scissors out of her hand-bag, cutting the lining neatly around the plastic anti-theft tag attached. When it came off cleanly, she slipped it into the pocket of one of the other skirts and rolled up the dress and put it in her handbag. She'd come in with six hangers and she came out with the same.

"Sorry, they just didn't look right," she said to the shop assistant, who obviously couldn't care less.

"Did you find anything?" she asked Lizzie, who was waiting for her.

"Nah. Let's go."

The air outside felt even hotter after the air conditioning inside the department store. It was windy, too, rubbish and dead leaves slapping against their bare ankles as they walked. The adrenaline abruptly left Bec's body and exhaustion took its place.

"What did you get?" she asked Lizzie.

"Two Marc's dresses. I'll show you later. I was just going to get one, but I knew that girl wouldn't even notice if I came out with nothing but hangers. What about you?"

"Scanlan & Theodore. Just one, but it was meant to be like three hundred."

"Nice!"

Bec was beginning to sweat. She could taste the salt collecting on her top lip. She rubbed her hand over the back of her neck; it was slick with oily perspiration, disgusting.

"Should we go to Gus's?" asked Lizzie.

Gus's was always cool and dark inside, with an all-day breakfast menu.

"Sounds good."

Even if she had to spend a bit of money on food, it was worth it not to have to go home.

She stopped walking. The money. How could she not have thought of it before? She'd been sure that whatever it was that had been in her room wasn't human. But what if it had been? What if it was the most obvious explanation: a burglar?

"I think I might just go home, actually. I feel really tired suddenly."

Lizzie stopped and looked at her with genuine worry.

"Are you sure you're okay?" she asked.

"Yeah," Bec said, although she didn't really feel it.

Lizzie pulled her into a quick, tight hug. It was too hot for anything longer.

"Call me if you change your mind about stayin' at mine, okay?"

"All right, thanks," she said.

Bec sat on the bus, her panic growing. It was taking forever, stopping every few blocks to let someone on. They might as well not have bothered with air conditioning; every time the doors swung open the hot wind blew in. Riding the wind was the faint but sharp smell of something burning; the bushfires. Bec wrinkled her nose. She'd been worried when she first saw an article about it in *The Canberra Times*. A black-and-white photograph of a raging fire on page four. She usually didn't read the paper, but she'd read this article. No one seemed to think it was a big deal, or maybe they were just distracted by everything else that was going on. Right next to the article was a full-page advertisement: "If You See Something, Say Something," run in large bold letters. She knew all about that. If she'd called the number underneath she'd have a one-in-ten chance of talking to her mom. It was the new anti-terrorist campaign that seemed to be everywhere right now. Not just in the paper but on billboards and on television. To make it worse, her mom would come home from work with endless dumb long-winded stories of people spying on their neighbours. Bec had no idea about politics and stuff like that. Still, it seemed strange to her that people were more worried about their neighbour's new car than a fire so close you could actually smell it.

Bec didn't even thank the driver as she got off the bus. She charged up the street to her house. When she was halfway she started to run, not caring about ruining her hair and sweating through her makeup. The scorching-hot air blew hard against her face, stinging her eyes, but she didn't care. Nothing was more important than knowing if the money was still there. She kept running until she was on her doorstep, pulling out her keys, slamming the door behind her.

"It was just a joke!" she heard Andrew whine from the kitchen.

"It's not funny." She hesitated on the foot of the stairs. Her dad sounded really angry.

"Don't be too hard on them." Her mother's voice was quiet. "They're just kids. They don't understand."

"You're so weak," he said quietly.

She didn't want to hear this; she ran up the stairs two at a time.

"Bec?" she heard her mom call from downstairs. She ignored her, flinging open the door to her room and grabbing her talking Cabbage Patch doll from on top of the chest of drawers. Hiking up the dress, she pulled open the Velcro patch at the back, where the battery pack was meant to fit inside. Instead there was the yellow and orange of twenty- and fifty-dollar notes. Thank God. It was her pay for the whole of last year. Almost six thousand dollars pressed tightly inside the belly of her toy. She heard the slow, steady steps of her mom on the stairs. She carefully put the doll back into place and pulled the dress out of her handbag, holding it up in front of herself and looking in the mirror.

"Are you all right? Why are you running around for?" her mom asked, eyeing the dress.

"I wanted to try it on again," she said, smiling. "What's going on, anyway?"

Her mother looked at her hands.

"Paul and Andrew have been sneaking into the neighbours' house, apparently. Max said that he caught them under his bed whispering."

"Whispering?"

"They were pretending to be the voices in his head." Her mother sighed. "They're just too young to understand. They think it's a joke. They say it's okay because he's crazy."

"Well, Max is crazy, isn't he?" Bec asked, still looking at the reflected dress. She wanted to point out that if her mom let the boys out a bit more, then they probably wouldn't have done it.

"No, he's sick. He's schizophrenic."

Bec was pretty sure that schizophrenic meant crazy but she didn't want to talk about it anymore. Her mom's eyes focused on the dress.

"Oh, Bec, that looks really expensive."

"It's Scanlan & Theodore and you don't want to know how much it cost," Bec said, raising her eyebrows.

Her mother folded her arms.

"You work so much and then blow your paychecks as soon as they come in. You could save up for something really nice."

"This is really nice!" Bec said, feigning offense, but inside she felt smug. This was getting too easy.

"Well, I guess it's your money. But don't go running around the place. You'll get heatstroke," her mom said, walking out of the room and closing the door behind her with a soft click.

Bec felt guilty for a second as she looked at herself in the mirror, the stolen dress hanging down in front of her, her hair frizzy and her face shiny. But then she caught sight of the reflection of the Cabbage Patch doll and all she could feel was triumph.

5

2014

For a moment I think I'm back home. I cross my fingers under the blanket and hope my stepmom is at her early prenatal Pilates class, so I can have breakfast with Dad without having to listen to her yap and whine like a pampered poodle. I open my eyes and the room seems to physically tilt around me. The outdated teenage posters, the photographs on the wall, the Cabbage Patch doll looming from the bedside table. The last week comes flooding back, running from Perth, Sydney, the hospital yesterday. I try to swallow a lump of anxiety. Becoming a whole different person is going to be hard.

I take a mental tally. I had the parents fooled completely but I'd have to tread very carefully with Andopolis. He didn't seem to be as much of a dope as I originally thought, but I could still have him wrapped around my little finger if he felt as guilty as it seemed about failing Rebecca. It was the twins who had me worried. They were warm, wrapping me in a bear hug when I'd interrupted their dinner, but I sensed some hesitation in both of them. I've never played the part of big sister before, and I don't really know how it goes. They were both attractive and successful: one is a lawyer and the other in med school. I also had real trouble telling them apart. If I was a twin I'd do whatever I could to look as different as I could. That doesn't seem to be the case with Paul and Andrew. They're both clean-shaven, with closely cropped ginger hair and perfectly fitting T-shirts. It would be best if they left soon.

I push myself out of bed and open Rebecca's closet. The musky smell isn't so strong anymore, or perhaps I'm just getting used to it. I flick through her clothes slowly, sizing up each item. Surprisingly she actually has a few good brands in here. Parting the clothes, I notice a pink quilt and a few stuffed toys stuffed in the back. I almost laugh. She hadn't wanted to seem like a kid anymore, but she hadn't wanted to throw them out either. For an instant, I can imagine her as a real person rather than a picture on a missing persons sign.

I decide against the designer brands and pull out a light cotton dress. Something about the drop waist and pale fabric screams innocence. I'm seeing Andopolis today and I want to reinforce the image he has of me as much as possible. The bruise on my face was fading to a gross yellow colour. I couldn't rely on it for much longer; I needed to dress the part, too.

Slipping the dress over my head, I feel something hard in the pocket. It's a folded-up piece of paper, *Exorcism Spell* at the top in bold letters. *Magic for the Modern Witch* is written in the banner in Gothic lettering. I can't imagine Bec had been into pagan stuff. Her room looked so preppy. Then again, teenagers like to keep secrets. I fold it back up and toss it into the closet with other things she was hiding. If she'd managed to conceal it all this time I wasn't going to expose her.

When I was sixteen, I hid joints in the seams of my curtains. I'd been in my hippie stage then. I'd met a group of older kids, with dreadlocks and tie-dyed T-shirts, busking near the railway station. For a full month I had them convinced I lived in a commune near Fremantle where no one was allowed to wear clothes. That was before I realized the art of subtle lies. Somehow one of them found out who my dad was. They called him an "oil tycoon" and didn't appreciate it when I laughed. Hippies always talk about love and kindness, but I don't know if I've ever met a group of people so snarky. I squeeze the seams of Bec's blinds. Nothing.

As I walk out of the room, I can hear the mumble of the brothers' voices. I stand there for a moment, hoping to catch something, but the talking stops abruptly. They must have heard my footsteps. For a moment I consider knocking, but I don't know what I would say to them.

Downstairs, the dad sits in the lounge room, watching television. Although I'm not sure if he's watching it so much as just staring at it. His eyes look glossed over. It's creepy. He doesn't look up when I come in, so I keep walking into the kitchen. The mom stands at the sink washing dishes.

"Morning," I say, making her jump.

"Sorry, Bec. I was in my own world. Do you want some breakfast?"

"Sure, if that's okay."

"Of course," she says, pulling the plug out and taking off her rubber gloves. The water shrieks as the sink empties.

"Thanks! Do you need a hand?" I say, remembering to play the dutiful daughter.

"Oh, no, you just sit and relax. When is Vince coming by?"

"I'm not sure. He just said morning."

I watch as she whisks eggs with milk and then pours them into a frying pan. My mouth begins to water at the smell of them. Now that I've known real hunger, I don't know if I'll ever see food in quite the same way again.

"I got you a phone," she says, nodding to the brand-new iPhone on the counter.

"Wow!" I say. "Thank you so much!"

As I turn it on I get that glowing feeling in my chest that I get from things that are shiny and new. I try to swallow it away—the pursuit of that feeling has gotten me into a lot of trouble.

"It has your old number on it," she says.

"That's great. How did you wrangle that?"

"It was easier to just keep paying the plan."

I put the phone down on the table. Rebecca was most likely dead, but the parents had paid her phone plan every month for over ten years. It feels weird now to be excited by this new toy. It was kind of sad.

"Here you go, sweetheart," the mom says, putting the steaming eggs in front of me. "Don't worry, I haven't forgotten your coffee."

I smile up at her. This is what a mother's love must feel like. I wonder if my mom had been like this for me, waiting on me like I was something precious. I doubt it. I think I would remember her better if she had been like that. When I think of her, the framed photograph my father keeps on our mantel is the only thing that comes to mind. If it wasn't for that I might not even know her face. I begin shoveling the eggs into my mouth. They are perfectly creamy, with just a hint of saltiness.

"Thanks, Mom," I say, swallowing.

I don't notice the mug slip out of the mom's hand, only the sound of it smashing as it hits the ground.

"Fuck, are you okay?" I say, instantly regretting the swearword, though the mother doesn't seem to notice. She's on her hands and knees on the tiles, frantically wiping up steaming black coffee. Shards of the mug are around her. I get up to help her.

"I'm sorry!" she says in a whisper, looking up at me.

"It's okay. I'll help you."

"Oh, no, don't do that. It's my own fault. I'm so stupid."

I grab a plastic bag and kneel down next to her to pick up the pieces of porcelain.

"I'm so sorry, Bec," she says, still talking in a hushed voice.

"It's fine. What's the big deal?"

"You won't tell them, will you?" she says.

She stares up at me like a scared child. The rag she is using has red spots on it as well as the dark brown of the coffee.

"Did you hurt yourself?" I say, grabbing her hand. The skin between her thumb and forefinger is cut open.

"It's fine. It's my punishment for being clumsy."

"I'll do this. You wash your hand and put a Band-Aid or something on it."

"Oh, Becky. You were always such a lovely girl. I wish I had paid more attention to you before. I'm so sorry."

For the first time, I feel deep pity for her. She blames herself for what happened to Bec.

"It's okay, Mom. Just fix up your hand." The blood streaming from her cut is starting to make me feel a bit sick. She gets up and washes her hand. I finish wiping up the coffee and put the bits of porcelain in the bin.

"See, good as new!" I try to sound reassuring, although I'm not used to playing the nurturer.

"I should have shown you how precious you were," she says. Her eyes are distant. I think about Dad, how he would never say something like that to me. He didn't think of me as precious. I just got in the way.

"It's okay," I say, trying to comfort her. "I'm back now and I'll be a good daughter."

"I don't need you to be anything other than yourself," she says.

She squeezes my hands tightly. She means it. I don't need to play a role to make her love me; she already does.

"I need you here. You won't leave me again, will you?" she says quietly, staring down into the sink. She looks so tired and defeated.

"No," I say.

She looks up at me and seems to really see me, her eyes full of hope and love and fear. It's overwhelming.

"Do you promise?" she says.

"I do," I say, and I mean it. I'm not sure when exactly I made the decision, but I know for sure I'm not going back. I've worked so hard for this new life. I've paid for it with my own flesh. Without a doubt, this time I'm playing for keeps.

As I walk toward Andopolis's blue Holden Commodore, I notice him tuck something under the collar of his shirt. He smiles at me as I open the door and buckle myself in next to him.

"Morning!" I say, my voice all brightness and warmth.

"Good morning. How are you feeling today?"

"Really good. It was so great to be back in my own bed."

"I'm glad."

His car stinks of hot food. He must have eaten breakfast as he drove here.

"So where are we going?" I ask.

"I thought we'd take the long way to the station." He starts the ignition and puts the car in Reverse. "See if anything stands out to you."

He turns to look out the back window and his shirt tightens across his chest. I can see the outline of a crucifix on a chain around his neck. I look out the window to hide my smile. A Catholic. That explains the guilt complex. This was going to be too easy.

"I know it's painful but I want you to try to remember the night you were taken." He winds down his window and mine with the controls on his door. "See if any sounds or smells stand out."

We drive in silence for a while. Canberra flashes by. It looks so different to Perth. We weave around the suburbs; there are pockets of bush everywhere, contrasting with the stark architecture.

The houses are manicured and new, with freshly painted fences and cleanly cut grass. There are no old terrace houses or cottages like I'm used to; everything looks like it was built in the last fifty years. As we get closer to the city, the roads become wide and grand. There are endless fountains and large important buildings all around. Everything is perfectly clean and symmetrical. There is none of the big-city griminess; instead it all feels sanitized.

We pull up around into the back parking lot of the police station.

"Will it just be us today?" I ask. Having a spurned Malik sniffing around is the last thing I need. A slip here would be disastrous.

"Our counselor really wants to speak with you."

I don't think so.

"I only want to talk to you," I say.

"Don't worry, we'll take today slowly. I think she could really help you, when you're ready."

Maybe this guy really is an idiot.

With his hand on my back again, he leads me into the same room we were in yesterday. The couches and the kids toys are still there but today there's a television with an old VCR set up, as well. He doesn't mention them as he sits down across from me on the couch.

"How did it go last night?" he asks.

"It's like a dream." I let my voice go all syrupy with sentiment.

"I can't even imagine."

The way he looks at me is a little strange. When his smile drops, what's left is so intense. I know he feels guilty, but this seems like more than that. His eyes are haunted. I wonder for a moment if he has pictures of Rebecca stuck up in his house. It wouldn't surprise me.

"What's that for?" I ask, motioning to the television. Really, I just want him to stop staring at me. It's giving me the creeps.

"It's a way to jog your memory," he says, then puts a hand up defensively. "Not of your abduction, not yet, but of the time before."

Before? Why would he need to know what happened before Rebecca went missing? I don't understand how it's relevant, but if it's going to waste some time I'm all for it.

Andopolis picks up the remote from the couch's arm. He holds it in his hands for a second.

"I know this might be somewhat upsetting for you, but I think it's important. Okay?"

"Okay." Hopefully it's some home movies. Maybe I can learn some more about her. *Me.*

He presses Play. Black lines flicker across the screen before a grey room snaps into focus. A teenage girl sits at a table in front of the camera, her face in her hands.

"Elizabeth Grant, session five, thirtieth of January 2003, 9:47 p.m.," a voice says from behind the camera. A man sits down across from the girl. I can see only the back of his head, but I realize with a start that this is Andopolis.

"I've told you everything already." The girl's voice is choked. "I don't know why we have to keep talking about it."

It's an interview room, not unlike the one I was held in back in Sydney.

"We need all the details, everything, even if it doesn't seem relevant."

The girl looks up. Her face is a mess. Black smudges of makeup are under her eyes, her face is blotchy and red, and her nose is running. Through it all, I recognize her. It's Rebecca's best friend, Lizzie.

"Okay," she says.

I feel bad for her. She is way too young to look that exhausted, that beaten down.

"You've told me about the last few weeks, but I'm wondering if there is anything else you've remembered that stood out. Anything she said that didn't seem right, about school or her home life."

"No," she says, "nothing."

She's hiding something, I can see that, but I wonder if Andopolis can. He takes her in for a moment, letting her squirm in the silence.

"Your friend is missing," he says eventually, his voice different now, cold. "Who knows what violence is being inflicted on her right now while we play these games."

"I'm not playing games!" Liz wails.

I turn to look at Andopolis. That was really harsh. It didn't seem at all like him to be so cruel. He keeps watching the screen, unfazed.

"Then think harder," he continues on the screen, "think of any time where Rebecca seemed different. Where something seemed out of the ordinary."

Lizzie takes a few deep breaths. I lean forward, watching her.

"There is something. I don't think it'll help, but if you want to know…" She looks up at him, clearly terrified, then continues when he doesn't reply. "It was ages ago. Last summer. I was away visiting my aunt. When I came back, Bec seemed different."

"Different how?"

"I don't know. It's hard to explain." Lizzie's words start tumbling on top of each other. "She just… It was pretty subtle. It was probably nothing. I don't think anyone else even noticed. No one said anything, anyway. But we're best friends. We're like sisters."

Lizzie swallows, her chin wobbling.

"No more waterworks, please," Andopolis says.

What an asshole. I inch away from him on the sofa. On the screen, Lizzie puts her shaking hands on the table, trying to calm herself.

"I'm sorry," she whispers, swallowing again.

"What kind of things changed about her? I need specifics," Andopolis says.

"It's hard to explain. She was jumpy. She got spooked really easily. She would freak out over really small things. And, like, the way she held herself changed. She'd always stood straight, trying to look as tall as she possibly could. When I got home she looked different. Clothes hung on her in a weird way and it took me ages to figure out why. Then I noticed that she kind of hunched. Like she was shielding herself or something like that."

"Growing pains?" Andopolis asks.

"You asked!" Lizzie says, her bite surprising me. Maybe Liz was more than just a scared little girl. "It was more than that, too. She didn't confide in me as much as she used to. And also, Jack told me she came to my house while I was away. Why would she come over when she knew I wasn't there? It was weird."

"Did you ask her about it?"

"No."

Leaning in closer, I watch Liz. Trying to see if there is something else there, something more she is not telling Andopolis. But the closer I get, the more her face dissolves into tiny coloured blocks.

Andopolis turns off the screen.

"So, what happened?" he says, staring at me square. "What

happened the summer before you went missing, the summer of 2002?"

This, I hadn't prepared for.

"I don't know. Nothing," I say. "She just imagined it, I think. It was just me growing up."

"She imagined it, or you were growing up? Which one is it?"

I feel like I'm being grilled. It's like he's forgetting that I'm a grown woman, not a scared teenager like Lizzie.

"Both, I think. It was a long time ago." I needed to change the subject, fast. He might know more about this than he was letting on.

"Lizzie looked so sad," I say. "Poor thing. I wish I could reach through the screen and give her a hug."

"You can't turn back time, Bec," he says, deep pain in his voice, that haunted look still in his eyes.

This isn't going well. I can't get a read off him. The sweet man with the lopsided grin seems like a different person. Maybe I should have picked Malik.

"Now's the time. I need to know, right now." He's still staring.

"Huh? Know what?"

"If you're protecting someone," he says.

That completely throws me, and I hope he can see it.

"I'm not. Of course I'm not! Why would I protect the person who did this to me?" My voice is high and quavering. I look at him like he's betrayed me.

He falls for it.

"I'm sorry, Bec. I didn't mean to upset you." He reaches out an arm to console me, but thinks better of it. He's apologized, but it's not enough. I feel like the power has shifted. He's taking the control back, way too quickly. I can't have that.

Later, as he drives me home, I let the silence stretch between us. People hate uncertainty. I find that if I'm really nice to someone and then suddenly cold for no reason it drives them crazy.

"Are you all right?" he says, finally.

I don't answer. He pulls over.

"What's wrong, Bec?" he says. "Are you still upset about what I said at the station?"

I shake my head.

"Then what?"

I count to ten in my head, stare at my knees.

"How long is this going to go for?"

"Are you feeling sick?" He thinks I mean the drive.

"No. I'm just sick of trying to remember things I don't want to remember."

"You don't want to catch who did this?" He looks genuinely shocked.

"I just want to go home and be happy with my family." That was probably a little too aggressive. I bite the inside of my cheek until the tears come.

"Why won't you let me just be happy?" I say, staring up at him like he's some kind of monster.

"I'm doing this for you, Bec! I want to find the person who took you away and punish them for it."

"Doesn't it matter what I want?"

"Of course it does," he says quietly, although we both know it doesn't.

I say nothing and after a few seconds he turns the ignition back on. Damn it. I'm sick of playing this game with him. I just want to be able to relax, to be comfortable in my new life. There has to be some way to make him back off a bit. It's too hard to think when I'm constantly acting. I need a moment alone.

I look at my phone, pressing icons like I don't know how to work it.

"Yes!" I say quietly after a few minutes of driving in silence.

"What is it?"

"I've finally figured out how to open a text message on this thing! I don't know why they make them so complicated now."

He doesn't say anything, as though a young person who doesn't know how to use an iPhone is the saddest thing he's ever seen.

"Can you drop me at Yarralumla shops instead?" I say, now that his defences are down again. "That was my dad saying he wants me to help him with the shopping."

His eyes flick to mine like he's about to disagree, but he stops himself. Good. My fingers are itching for a cigarette, and I want to assert who's boss again. He pulls into a parking space next to a van outside the local shops, then turns to look at me.

"I understand that you want all this to be over," he says, the car still idling, "but it won't really be over until we catch the person responsible."

They never will. Whoever did it is long gone.

"Tomorrow I'd like to start retracing your steps on the day you went missing. Your walk from the bus stop home, the bus ride, leaving work. There has to be something you remember. I want you to try, okay? For me."

"Okay," I say, looking up at him with wide eyes, lips slightly parted. "For you."

I catch him hesitating on my white cotton skirt and bare legs. He looks away quickly. I wonder how many Hail Marys he'll have to do for whatever impure thought he had in his head just then.

"See you tomorrow," I say, jumping out of the car and slamming the door behind me.

I chain-smoke my way back home, not knowing when I'll get another chance. Inhaling slowly, I feel each muscle soften. The sun is out but the air is fresh. Goose bumps are rising on the backs of my legs but I don't mind. It's good to have a few minutes without being watched. I stare at my new phone and let the little blue arrow guide me to Bec's house.

I look over my shoulder at the sound of tires moving slowly behind me. A black van. It must be going way under the speed limit. There was a black van next to Andopolis's car when we parked at the shops. Had it been following me then? I shrug it off. Andopolis has gotten me freaked. I turn off onto Rebecca's street and the van rolls past me. I laugh at my own paranoia and suck hard on the cigarette. Maybe I should have bought some breath mints, too. Precious little Rebecca probably wasn't a smoker.

My phone dings. I really do have a message. I open it, expecting it to be from the mom, asking when I'm coming home. But it's not.

Get Out. That's all it says.

The squeal of tires and suddenly the van has come back

around and is tailing me again, heading up my street. My heart hammers. It's definitely following me. I drop the cigarette and start to run. The van accelerates. Pushing myself to go as fast as I can, I run up our driveway and through the front door. I slam it behind me and stand with my back against it, gasping for breath.

"Is that you, honey?" I hear the mother call from the kitchen.

"Yes!" I call back.

For a moment I consider telling her about the message and the van. But of course she'd call Andopolis straightaway and I didn't want that. I didn't want to give him any more reason to keep pursuing the case. I look through the mottled pane of glass in the door; the street is empty.

I turn my back to the kitchen, making sure the mother can't see me, and call the number that sent the message.

"The number you have called is switched off or unavailable. Please check the number and try again," a woman's voice tells me. I slide my phone back into my pocket and walk into the living room.

Andrew and Paul are sitting with the dad, who is still staring into the middle distance. The news is on television, but again, no one seems to be watching.

"How did it go?" the mom asks, coming into the lounge room, her rubber gloves back on.

"Has Vince burst that vein in his temple yet?" says Andrew.

"It was fine," I say, sitting down on an empty chair. The cat, Hector, jumps up onto my lap. He curls up into a ball and I stroke him behind the ears. My heart is starting to slow now, but I still feel panicky. It's good to be doing something with my hands.

"Anything come back to you?" Paul asks.

"Not really," I say.

We stare at the news. The new prime minister comes on for a press conference. He's lit unflatteringly from behind, exaggerating the pink of his large ears. They cut to children and their moms being led off a little boat by men in army uniforms with big guns.

"Who is that?" I say, realizing the opportunity.

"Who?"

"Him," I say, when the prime minister comes back on screen.

"You don't know who Tony Abbott is?" says one of them—Andrew, I think.

I look down, pretending to be embarrassed.

"It's our prime minister," says the dad.

He is still staring at the screen. Paul and Andrew are looking at me, but their expressions are all wrong. They look surprised and confused, when I was going for pity. I realize I need to keep the brothers talking. Usually people like you more if you manage to get them to confide in you.

"Do you remember the last time you both saw me? It might help to piece it back together."

"You can't remember?"

"Not really. It's all a bit blurry." Already I wish I had asked them something else. The past was dangerous territory.

"Well," says the one I think is Andrew, "I have to say... you were a bit of a bitch!"

All three of us laugh, the tension broken. I give myself a mental pat on the back.

"No, I wasn't!" I say, just because it seems like the right thing.

"You kind of were, Becky. You said you would take us to the pool, remember? Then you freaked cos you found a dirty magazine in my backpack," Paul says.

"Then we never saw you again," says Andrew. "Way to give us a complex about sex!"

We laugh again, although I notice the one I'm pretty sure is Paul watching me carefully. It's like he's expecting me to say something. I almost jump out of my skin when there's a knock on the door. I hear the mom go over and open it.

"It's for you, Bec," she calls almost immediately.

I walk over, imagining a man, the black van behind him waiting to take me away. He can't take me from here, not with all these people around. But the woman standing on the steps looks corporate and successful, wearing a dark green blazer and matching skirt and shiny sheer stockings. Her blonde hair is swept off her face in a bun. She's staring at me like I'm a ghost, her mouth open and her eyes wide.

"Bec?" she says, and then, just before she lunges toward me, pulling me into a tight hug, I recognize her from the video.

She pulls away from me, crying, snot streaming down her face.

"Lizzie."

6

Bec had an early shift that morning. It didn't matter; she hadn't really been able to sleep. The chair was wedged firmly under her door handle, but in the back of her mind she knew if it really was something paranormal then it probably wouldn't make much difference. Plus, it was so hot and stuffy in her room. Even with the air conditioning, she could feel the heat pushing its way in through the bricks and glass of the house. It was going to be forty-three degrees today.

Bec lay still and listened to the sounds of her mom and dad moving around downstairs: the clinks of her mother rinsing out their cereal bowls, the beep as she pulled open the dishwasher. Her dad's voice was a deep mumble, but she couldn't hear her mom speaking at all. She waited until she heard the front door shutting, then the motor of the car running outside, to get up, pulling off her sweaty sheets and going straight downstairs to get some water.

Her mom had a way of erasing any signs of her presence from a room. The kitchen looked, as always, like a set. Not a place where they all lived and breathed and ate. Even the sink was totally dry, not even a drop of water. She smiled to herself, knowing once the twins woke up it would look very different. Walking past the kitchen table, she ran her fingers across the warm wood. There was a moment at dinner last night where she had considered telling her mom about the specter. But, as usual, her mom was so focused on her brothers she barely even looked at her. Sometimes it was as though her mom forgot she had a daughter, as well. If Bec were honest with herself, she knew there was no way her mom would believe her anyway. She'd think Bec was either lying or going mad.

Bec heard a bang. Before she even thought about it, she was on the floor, cheek pressed against the kitchen tiles. Then she heard it again. It wasn't a gunshot; in fact, it didn't sound anything like one. She got up and peered through the sheer kitchen curtains. Max, the neighbour, was nailing down the loose paling in the fence. Bec took a breath. Of course it wasn't a gun. That was silly. But the sleek shine of the shotgun came into her head without her being able to stop it. She'd been in her parents' closet a few months back, intending to try on her mom's new black leather heels. Just to see if she could walk in them. It was wedged right up the back, behind the hangers. It looked new. The dark ebony of the handle was spotless; the long barrels gleamed. She had never seen a gun before. It definitely hadn't been there last time she'd looked. When she'd reached out to touch it, the steel felt cold and smooth under her fingertips.

Running water into the glass, she took a big gulp and almost spat it back out. The water from the cold tap was running so hot, it burnt her throat. Holding her hand underneath, she waited for the water to turn back to cold. It didn't. The pipes outside must have heated up in the morning sun. She put the glass down, very purposefully right in the middle of the empty bench top, and went upstairs to get ready for work.

As Bec walked down to the bus stop she felt that now-familiar crawling feeling on the back of her neck. She clenched the muscles in her shoulders, trying to make the feeling go away. It was in her head; it must be. But then, out of the corner of her eye, she saw a shape move. She whirled around. It was just a kid, staring at her. He was about ten and had been sticking up posters on trees. He was wearing tiny short shorts with pictures of footballs on them. The sun lit up the downy white hair on his legs.

"Have you seen him?" he asked.

Bec looked at the paper in the boy's hand. It was a missing poster for a white Maltese terrier. The boy had put one on every tree. He looked at her hopefully, eyes red and blotchy.

"No—sorry."

He turned before she could see his face fall. Poor kid.

"I'll keep an eye out!" she called, and he smiled at her sadly over his shoulder as he started ripping tape to stick a poster to the next tree.

She remembered when her parents had put signs like this out for their cat Molly. They'd left them up only a week before they brought a surprise home: a tiny little black-and-white kitten. Hector. It made her sad how replaceable they thought Molly was. It was like they thought that she wouldn't even notice the difference. It was stupid, she thought as she sat down at the bus stop. No one could really disappear. You always still existed somewhere.

Through the glass, Bec watched Luke as he filled up the deep fryer. His eyes were blank, his thoughts focused inward. She liked that she never knew exactly what he was thinking. His eyes changed when they looked at her, though; she liked that the most. They always softened and crinkled in the corners. She wondered how he must see her. He probably thought she just woke up like this, with perfect skin and hair. That she was young and pretty and found life so easy. She wondered if he ever thought bad things about her, if he ever thought she was silly or naive.

When she knocked on the door and he looked up, a melted pleasant ripple went through her. "Let me in!" she called. "I'm cooking out here!"

"What's the magic word?" he asked, walking toward her.

"Is it *dickhead*?" she called back.

He laughed and bent down to unlock the door. Looking down at him squatting at her feet sent a strange pleasurable jolt through her body. If the glass wasn't between them she could have reached out and pulled his head toward her. He got up and pulled the door open and she felt her face flush for a moment, embarrassed.

"On time for once," he said.

"Only for you," she replied, walking straight past him and hoping he wouldn't notice her burning cheeks. She dropped her bag in the back, waiting to come back to the front counter until she was sure the blush was gone.

"Do you think it will be busy today?" Bec asked him, as she clipped the nozzles onto the Coke machine.

"Well, personally, I can't imagine anything more disgusting than eating deep-fried food on a forty-degree day."

When they opened the doors there was a small group of people waiting. Matty came running into the kitchen, tying his apron on as he went.

"Sorry, mate," he said to Luke.

"You know I don't care," Luke replied.

"Hot cakes," barked a middle-aged man, "maple on the side."

"Sure, that will be three dollars and seventy-five cents." Bec tried to smile.

When they'd served the first wave of customers it got quiet again. The people all sat alone, shoveling food into their mouths.

"Why does he always ask for maple on the side?" Bec said quietly to Luke. "He comes here every morning. He knows that we serve it prepackaged."

"It's cos he's a snob." Luke didn't lower his voice. "Cos we're in this suburb, people like to pretend to be ritzy even if they are eating at fucking Macca's."

She'd never thought about it like that before. Bec watched as a mother quietly scolded her child as he threw fries at her, looking around to see if anyone was watching. The woman didn't look at the counter, though. Bec realized that the woman probably didn't care if she saw. Because she worked at McDonald's, she didn't count as someone to be embarrassed in front of. Luke was right; these people thought they were better than her and better than where she worked, even though they were choosing to come here. The thought brought with it a powerful wish to succeed, to do something amazing and put them all in their place. She wasn't sure what exactly. She was reasonably good at most things at school, but not really great at anything specific. Sometimes she and Lizzie talked about starting a styling company. It started off as a bit of a joke. They would sit at Gus's Café and carefully watch people pass, then discuss how they'd re-dress that person if they could. They'd decide on what styles would suit their body types, what colours would suit their complexion. It had started off kind of bitchy, but now they both took it really seriously.

Luke and Matty joked around next to the stove, making dirty jokes that she couldn't quite understand. She desperately wanted to be part of the conversation, but didn't want to act like an annoying little sister. Bec wondered how they could be happy still working here. Luke was twenty and Matty must be at least twenty-seven. Matty had told her once that he'd studied creative writing at uni. He'd written a few short stories that had gotten published in magazines and even written a novel once, but that it had never gone anywhere, so he'd just stopped writing. That made her sad. Just giving up on your dream that way. But Luke was worse. He was really smart but he never even went to uni. Sometimes it felt to Bec like he was just bowing out of life. Bec was sure when they finally got together that she could help him, though, make him see that his life could be amazing if he just tried a little.

"I always wonder what you're thinking so hard about," Luke said. He was staring at her. *Do not blush, do not blush,* she thought.

"Your arse," she said slowly. "I just can't stop thinking about your arse."

"You're so filthy!" he said.

Matty howled with laughter from the kitchen, but before Luke quickly turned away to lift the chips out of the oil, she saw the beginning of redness on his cheeks.

The day wore on and it only got hotter. Matty sweated onto the burgers, offering inputs every so often to her and Luke's conversation. She liked Matty but she kind of wished he wasn't there. It made Bec feel like she had to watch what she said and try not to be too flirty or obvious about how she felt. Still, working with Luke always left her feeling elated. Both of them talked to her as if she was an adult, like she was just as smart as them and not some dumb kid who had no idea what they were talking about, even though that was how she sometimes felt. It didn't bother her, though; just knowing that they saw her as an equal was enough. She made a mental note of some of the things they were saying. She would look them up on the internet when she got home.

Bec noticed a backpack under one of the tables. Black and nondescript, it was bulging full. She tried to ignore it; someone had probably just forgotten it. Instead she played a game of "Spot the bad tattoo" with Luke. Since it was such a hot day, people who didn't usually bare flesh suddenly had no choice and all of a sudden you saw all the wrinkly barbed wire on arms and the faded dolphins on ankles. After half an hour, though, the backpack was still there. Bec imagined the force of the blow as it exploded; she imagined the bits of their bodies lying in a blackened, mangled mess.

She pointed the backpack out to Luke, but when he went to get it, she stopped him.

"What's wrong?" he asked.

"I dunno. I don't want to sound stupid. It just freaks me out seeing it there by itself."

"If you see something, say something!" Matty called from the kitchen, doing his best impression of the television ad.

"No, it's not that. It's just…" She trailed off. She was quickly feeling a bit stupid. Maybe she'd just seen too many news reports. They'd watched them all day at school during the terrorist attacks.

Matty came out of the kitchen, mopping his brow. He was looking at her in a strange way. His large stature seemed imposing again all of a sudden.

"Come on, don't be an idiot. Those ads are just plain racism," he said.

"What do you mean?" she asked. "It could happen. It did happen!"

Matty took a deep breath and leaned hands against the front counter. He looked angry.

"We try to breed out the Aborigines, we send people looking for refuge to that Villawood concentration camp, and the ones that finally get through we set up for bashings with that racist propaganda. It's like White Australia all over again."

Bec really did feel like a dumb kid now. She didn't really understand what he was saying.

"If you believed in a Day of Reckoning," he continued, "all of us would be goners. We'd be wiped out, sucked into the ocean. What we are doing is disgusting and it's only getting worse."

"Or eaten by a giant whale maybe?" Luke said.

"Moby Dick!" exclaimed Bec and they both started laughing.

Matty said nothing and went back into the kitchen. Again,

Bec wished that he wasn't there. He'd scared her a little bit, calling everyone racists and saying they were going to be wiped out. It almost seemed like he was including her in that. She'd seen him go on rants like this before. Calling John Howard a bigot and a homophobe and all kinds of things. Her parents weren't too fond of the prime minister either. No one seemed to be. But Matty was so extreme about it.

A man came in then, all sweaty and sunburnt. He breathed an audible sigh of relief and holstered the backpack onto his shoulders. Luke made a face at her and Bec felt silly then. She hated when things were awkward at work. Going to stand next to Matty, she rested her head against his shoulder.

"I'm sorry," she said. "Those ads just got me freaked out. I was being dumb."

He put one of his thick arms around her and pushed her cheek against his chest.

"Don't say sorry, Becky. Now I feel bad! Sometimes I just forget you're a kid cos you're so smart."

She wasn't sure if that was a compliment or not, but it was nice being squished into him like that, so she left it. She felt so protected, breathing in his warm sweaty smell. As though nothing bad could ever happen to her.

"Hey, what about me?" she heard Luke say and she felt more arms reach around them both.

"Get back to work, both of you," said Matty, pushing them off. "It's too hot for this!"

Bec went back to the counter, but she was smiling. At work, she could be a different person, warm and unaffected. It was so different to being at home.

"It's my birthday next month, you know," she said to Luke. "What are you going to get me?"

Seventeen, she would be seventeen, which meant he could ask her on a date. That would be the most amazing gift of all.

"Actually, I've got something for you now," he replied. "One second."

Her head had just begun to spin with ideas when he came back with the mop.

"Happy early birthday! Apparently the ladies' is flooding."

She tried to think of something witty to say, but nothing came, so she just grabbed the mop and stormed off into the ladies' bathroom.

Opening the door, she saw the water was already about a centimeter deep. One of the taps had been left running and the water was overflowing from the sink. She waded over and quickly turned it off. She realized that not only had someone left the tap on but someone else must have seen it and gone to complain to Luke, without even trying to help. It was going to take her forever to mop it all up. It smelt gross in there, too, and the air conditioning didn't venture that far.

Listening to the slowing drips of water falling from the sink, she spent an hour mopping the floor, interrupted every so often by a customer looking to use the bathroom. When she'd tell them it was flooded they'd look her up and down with a disgusted expression and then walk out like it was all her fault. She hated that, the way she must look. So pathetic and dirty. She had started sweating, too. It wasn't the way she wanted to see herself. If there really was a camera on the other side of the mirror, she hoped that they weren't filming now, that it was a commercial break or something. This was one of those uncommon moments when she truly hated her job.

Eventually the floor was dry enough. She checked herself

in the mirror before she left the bathroom, wiping off the eyeliner that had slid down under her eyes and practicing a few smiles. She still looked pretty good, not quite as fresh as before, but definitely not like she'd been mopping a dirty wet toilet floor for an hour. Opening the door, she could hear Lizzie's voice; she must have started her shift. That meant her time on the counter with just Luke was already over. She put the mop back and came around to the counter. The three stopped talking and looked at her.

"What?" she said. "Do I smell like pee?"

Luke looked at Lizzie uneasily.

"I'm sorry, babe," Lizzie said. "I thought you would have told them about the specter."

"Liz!" Bec said, realizing why they were all looking at her. She'd been thinking about Luke so much that, strangely enough, the specter had been completely wiped from her mind.

"Are you all right?" Luke asked. "Seriously, that sounds horrible."

"I'm fine," she said.

"Are you sure it wasn't a trick of the light or a dream or something?" asked Matty.

"I'm sure," she said. "You don't have to believe me, but I know what I saw."

They must think she was crazy. Trust Lizzie to go babbling about all her secrets; this was why Bec had to be careful what she told her.

"I believe you," said Luke. "If you're sure, then I'm sure."

Her insides swelled.

"Really?"

"Of course," he said. Lizzie turned away from them and Bec hoped it was because she was feeling guilty.

Just then, a family came in, all red-faced and arguing. Worst timing, of course. Luke started keying in their order and Matty went back to the grill. More people started piling in for the afternoon rush. Lizzie caught her eye from behind Luke.

"Sorry," she mouthed and Bec knew she meant it.

Later on, when it quieted down and Bec's shift was almost over, they got a chance to talk again.

"I had an idea last night. It might be dumb but it's worth a shot," said Lizzie.

"What is it?" Bec asked.

"Well, I was thinking. What do people in the movies do when things like this happen?"

Bec knew exactly what she was about to say.

"We should have an exorcism!"

Bec heard Matty groan from the kitchen. He'd never said he believed her.

"I'm not sure," said Bec.

"Why not? If it doesn't work it doesn't matter."

"I think we should do it," said Luke.

This surprised Bec, as she'd always thought of him as more of a skeptic.

"Really I just want to see inside your bedroom, though," he continued.

"Oh, shut up!" she said, hitting him softly, but she was smiling.

"Well, think about it," said Lizzie.

"Okay, if something else happens, then we'll do it," Bec said slowly, "but fingers crossed it won't."

Lizzie raised crossed fingers in the air. Bec didn't want to think about something happening again. She couldn't even imagine feeling that scared for a second time. She tried to hide a shiver as it snaked down her spine. Looking at the clock, Bec realized her shift was over.

"I'm done. Do you still want to see a movie later?" she asked Lizzie.

"*Catch Me If You Can*? Yes!"

"I bet you two are just seeing that because of Leo," Luke said, leaning against the counter.

"No!" said Bec right at the same time as Lizzie squealed "Yes!"

"Bec!" said Liz. "Don't pretend you didn't have an *I love Leo* shrine in your room. I saw it!"

"Shut up! It's just meant to be a really good film, all right."

Luke raised his eyebrows at her. For a second she wondered if she could get away with inviting him. No, that could be weird. She'd wait for him to ask her on a proper date. She went around the back, changed into a summer dress and grabbed her handbag.

"'Bye, guys!" she called, wishing she didn't have to open the glass door and go back out into the blazing hot afternoon.

7

There's an iciness to the air, even though the sun is out. The street is silent except for the faint rustle of the breeze through the drying autumn leaves and the crunch of my shoes against the gravel. If I listen carefully I can also hear the purr of Andopolis's car tailing me as I re-create Bec's last walk home, but I try to ignore it and enjoy the moment. It's colder than yesterday. I keep my pink fingers jammed into my jacket pockets.

The mother had wanted to throw my jacket away. The lining was still stained with the dark plum of my blood. Rebecca's old coat was hanging, waiting, in the cupboard, baby blue with fake fur around the hood. The girl really had the tackiest taste in clothes, although perhaps it was fashionable back then. I couldn't remember. It shouldn't have made much of a difference wearing her coat—I was already wearing her clothes right down to my underwear—but it felt nice to still have something with me that was mine. Although, really, this jacket wasn't mine. It was Peter's.

He'd been a good boyfriend for a while, with his sun-bleached mop of hair and constant enthusiasm. We were both unemployed, so we'd spend every sunny day at the beach. It was when I was in my surfer phase last year. My wardrobe was filled with Roxy board shorts and flip-flops. Although we girls didn't really surf; we were expected just to sit on the beach and watch our boyfriends. The other girls seemed to like it. They wore bikinis and worked on their tans. I got sick of that quickly. I bought a board and tried to get Peter to teach me, but he got frustrated and impatient. He'd loaned me the jacket because I was cold at a beach bonfire. Then I caught him making out with one of the bikini girls. I kept the jacket not to remember him, but because I knew he didn't have enough money to buy another one. Every chilly winter's day it would keep me warm to know he was cold.

I wrap it around myself, breathing in the sweet smell of rose gardens and mown lawn. It's exhilarating being someone else, but also exhausting. I enjoy the rare moment of not pretending.

"Stop there!" Andopolis calls from the car.

He pulls in onto the curb and comes walking toward me.

"Did anything come back to you?" he calls.

I am halfway up the hill of Rebecca's street, about five doors down from her house. I wait until he's closer before I speak.

"I remember the fear."

"What else?" he says quietly.

"I thought I was alone."

"But you weren't?"

I think about the black van yesterday. "I remember the sound of a car accelerating."

"Go on," he says, his voice hushed now. He's excited.

"The squeal of tires."

"And then?"

"Darkness."

"And after that?"

"That's all."

"Do you remember the car? The make and model? Even the colour?"

For a moment I consider saying it was a black van but decide against it. I was trying not to think about the text message. The person driving the van must have written it. Was it possible it was the person who took Bec?

I'm torn. If I give Andopolis the number the text came from he'll find the driver, but he may also find the truth—about Bec but also about me.

"No," I say in the end, "nothing."

"Are you sure?"

"Yes."

He looks at me again in that penetrating way, like he's trying to find a clue from the squint of my eyes or the bend of my mouth. Almost like he thinks I'm lying.

"How did you know it happened in this spot?" I ask.

"We traced your phone and found it here." He pointed to the rosebush to my right. "It was under that bush."

So this was where it happened, right where I was standing. I imagine how this street would look in the dark, the quickening of Bec's heart when a car pulled up next to her, the struggle. She'd been so close to home.

It's as if history was trying to repeat itself. I force myself to believe the van wasn't even following me. It was probably just going the same way and the driver had laughed when

I started running like that. And the text might have been a wrong number. It had to be. No one even knew Bec was home. They couldn't be connected. I was being paranoid.

"Get in and I'll drive you home," he says.

"But my house is just there," I say.

"Get in, Bec."

I walk to his car obediently and get into the passenger seat. He sits in the driver's seat and closes the door but doesn't start the engine.

"I know you aren't interested in seeing a counselor."

I say nothing. Not this shit again.

"So I've made an appointment with a hypnotist. She has the potential to really help with your memory loss."

A hypnotist would be the worst possible thing. I had to think of something quick. If they really did hypnotize me I would probably confess in an instant. I took a deep breath.

"It's so good to be home," I say, letting my voice wobble. "When I think about it…it's just like a big black hole filled with fear and pain but that's all. Thinking about it is like going back there."

He looks at me, his eyes searching for something that isn't there.

"Are you saying you don't want to know what happened?"

"No! It's just…" I could think straight if he'd just stop staring. "…I think right now it would be too painful. I'm only just holding on as it is."

He says nothing. Just stares. I wonder if this is the way he looked at Lizzie all that time ago in the interrogation room.

"I used to think I might know your face better than I knew my own. I've spent so long looking at photographs of you. Looking into your eyes and trying to understand the secrets you must have held. Knowing if I could just find you everything would be revealed. But now I'm looking right at you and it's like I don't know your face at all."

Fuck. His voice is low, but it makes the hairs on my arms rise. I can hear in it a festering rage that is barely being restrained. I'd feel less scared if he had yelled.

"But you didn't find me, did you?" I say. "I waited but no one ever came to save me. I had to save myself. Now just leave me alone."

"I'm sorry, Rebecca, but I just can't do that," he says, "not until I know who you are protecting."

"No one!" I yell. But now it really is a lie and I wonder if he can tell. I might really be protecting Rebecca's killer.

I get out of the car and run to the house. I can feel my anger flare. Not just because he saw through me somehow but because he won't let it go. He cared more about finding the answer then he did about Bec. He wasn't just a good guy plagued by guilt. I'd massively underestimated him. There was a wretchedness to the way he spoke. I couldn't tell if it was himself or me that he was so angry with. Perhaps both. It didn't matter. This case had somehow sent him over the edge, and for whatever reason, he seemed to think solving it would be the only way back. I'd never believed in redemption, but he did. He wanted it from me but I could never give it to him.

The only thing I had on my side was the DNA test, the absolute proof that I was Rebecca. If I didn't have that, I think he might have seen through me a while ago.

I climb up the stairs two at a time. He was so selfish. I hated him, but I couldn't show it. Somehow, I had to get him back on my side. If he thought I was protecting someone, he might start digging. Asking questions I didn't have answers to.

I throw open my bedroom door. The mother is standing inside, her back to me, and she jumps.

"What are you doing?" I ask, angry with *her* now. Why is she in my room? Has she found the cigarettes under my bed? Does she doubt me now, too?

"I was just cleaning up for you, honey," she says, turning. Behind her I see my bed is made. "I'm sorry."

"Oh, sorry. It's just…" I don't know what to say.

"No, you're right. I should ask first." She looks down, almost cowering, like she thinks I might hit her. I lean in to hug her and I feel her body tense.

"I appreciate you cleaning my room. You're the best mom ever." Her body loosens slightly. "I just snapped because my arm is hurting again."

"Oh, Becky, you should have said." She pulls away and takes my arm, looking at the bandaged section carefully. "You have your appointment at the hospital tomorrow. Maybe I can call them and make it today instead?"

"No, that's okay. I can wait until tomorrow." I'd forgotten about the appointment. I was meant to be getting the bandages reapplied, but I really didn't want to see how bad the wound was.

"Okay, well, I'll get you some ibuprofen and brew some tea before you go and see Lizzie."

"Okay, thanks, Mom."

She leaves my room and closes the door softly behind her. I feel bad for talking to her like that, although it seemed to upset her so disproportionately, like when she dropped the mug in the kitchen.

Now that I had this new life, I desperately didn't want to let it go. I'd felt so lost and lonely for so long it had begun to seem normal. I'd thought freedom and protection was what I wanted out of this game, but it had begun to feel like more than that. Having a family around felt so amazing; having a mother again was so much better than I'd imagined. Despite myself, I was really starting to care about her. But now I know to use anger if I ever need to control her, although I hope I won't have to do that.

I get down on my hands and knees and look under the bed. My packet of cigarettes is still there. I'd have to find a better place to hide them. I hid condoms in my paired socks when I was a teenager—maybe I'd try that. I open Bec's underwear drawer and pull out a pair of knee-high school socks. Unpairing them, something heavy falls out onto the floor. For a moment after I pick it up I don't know what it is, and then I realize. It's an ink tag. The kind stores put on clothes; the kind where if you try to pull it off it sprays ink everywhere. There's a small circle of fabric around the clip, cut so perfectly it makes me smile. I put it back in the socks and scour the undie drawer to see if I can find anything else. Right in the back corner is a photograph, folded up into a tiny square. It's a close-up picture of Bec's face, younger and smiling broadly. She's holding a brown tabby, pressing her cheek against the top of its head.

I sit down on the bed, still looking at the photograph. The cat isn't Hector, who is black-and-white. It must have been an older pet. I can see its collar around its neck, the name *Molly* engraved into it. What a strange thing for Bec to hide. I put the photo down, a feeling of grief coming over me. I had just enacted this girl's final steps. If Bec really was plucked off the street like that, then she is most likely dead. Her family thinks she's back with them, but she'll never be back. I wonder for a moment if her body is nearby, a little stack of bones buried somewhere in this town. I shiver; it's better not to think about it.

Dialing the number that sent me the text again, I get the same "turned off or unavailable" message. I spin the phone in my palm, considering sending a message back to them. In the end I decide it's better not to stoke the fire. Whoever it is, I don't want to make this person angry.

What I really need to be thinking about is Andopolis. He's getting impatient with me. More than that, he's starting to doubt me. The man driving that van couldn't get me with the safety of police and family all around, but one wrong move and Andopolis could put me in jail for a very long time. I needed to give him something, some kind of detail that would put his attention elsewhere.

I type Rebecca's name into the search engine of the phone. Pages and pages of results come up. I click on one at random: Police Fear Rebecca Winter's Body Incinerated and May Never Be Recovered. The link loads and a picture of Andopolis heads the article. His hair is jet black and the droopiness has gone from his face, although he looks tired. He stands behind a podium, mouth open in midspeech. I scan the article.

Senior Investigator Vincent Andopolis today announced that police fear that Rebecca Winter's body may have been incinerated in the Canberra Bushfires of January 18.

"Whether Rebecca left on her own accord or she met with foul play is still being investigated," he said. "However, the proximity of the fires to the Winter home and the timing of her disappearance

lead the ACT Police to consider the possibility her remains may
never be recovered."

My head fills with the image of her face, which looked
so much like my own, covered in flame. Burning. I don't
want to imagine it.

"I have made a promise to the Winter family that if their daugh-
ter is still alive, I will find her."

Senior Investigator Andopolis did not take questions on whether
there are any suspects in the case at this time.

All I want to do is stay at home. Hang out with the mom,
maybe even cook something together. I feel worn out, tired
beyond tired, and my arm really is hurting again. But it's
time to go see Lizzie. She hadn't stayed long when she came
by yesterday. She'd stood in the doorway crying and hiccup-
ing and saying she had to get back to work but not leaving.
Eventually she made me promise to come over and see her
today, texting me the address with a smiley face. It's the last
thing I want to do but everyone seems to think I should
be eager to see Liz. She was Rebecca's best friend, after all.
Avoiding her would be suspicious.

I dress quickly, finding the most adult dress I can in Bec's
closet. Lizzie had looked so well-groomed yesterday, despite
the snot; it would feel weird to turn up in a child's clothes.
I decide to just bring the cigarettes with me; it's easier than
hiding them and means I might even get a chance to sneak
one if I have a minute to myself. When I go downstairs the
tea is waiting for me on the kitchen table, next to a packet
of ibuprofen.

"We're going to take you to Lizzie's instead of Mom, okay?"
says one of the twins, walking into the kitchen.

"We've barely spent any time with you!" the other calls from the lounge room.

"Are you sure it's not too much hassle?" I ask. I was hoping to use the undoubtedly silent car ride with the mother to come up with a game plan for my time with Lizzie.

"No, it's on our way," the first twin says, leaning against the kitchen doorway. "I'm going to visit some mates from med school who work at the hospital here."

That one must be Andrew, then.

"Okay, thanks." I quickly down the painkillers with a glass of water and leave the tea untouched. Walking out the front door, I notice the mom dusting the spotless shelves in the lounge room.

"'Bye, Mom," I say.

"'Bye," she says, but doesn't turn to look at me. I linger for a moment but she keeps dusting like I'm not there.

"Come on," says Paul from behind me. I turn away from her and walk down the path to the car. Andrew lets me sit in the front seat with Paul while he sits in the back. I wish I could have a cigarette.

Paul leans forward and carefully touches the remnants of the yellow bruise on the side of my face. "Does it hurt?"

"Nah," I say. It's basically gone now.

Paul smiles at me. "Good."

"Does it feel strange being back?" Andrew asks as Paul pulls out of the driveway.

"It's great," I say, turning to look at him. He has his hair brushed forward, where Paul's hair is slicked back. I'll have to remember that—otherwise they seem to be the same right down to their freckles.

"We really missed you," he says. I'm struck again by how

attractive he is. How attractive they both are. I almost blush as I turn back around. I'm meant to be their sister.

"I missed you, too," I say.

"Good," says Paul. "We don't want you to leave again."

I stare at his profile. What a strange thing for him to say. It's like he thought Bec chose to leave. Then I finally get it; I understand why they've been so distant with me. Deep down, they must believe Bec ran away. They must think that she abandoned them.

"I didn't want to leave you," I say softly. "I had no choice."

They don't say anything.

"I love both of you more than anything," I say, trying to fill my voice with as much pain and love as possible.

"We know," says Paul. "We love you, too."

"Come here!" says Andrew and he pulls himself forward and throws his arms around me from behind the seat.

"That got mushy so quickly!" he says into my ear. I can feel my skin tingle where he touches me and I try not to focus on it.

"Yeah, I thought Andrew would start the waterworks any second."

"What about you? I remember you crying about Bec all night when we were little," Andrew says and they both laugh. That seems a little harsh to me but I laugh along with them, not wanting to lose this newfound solidarity.

Paul pulls up outside a small white brick house.

"See you later, alligator!" he says. I guess this must be Lizzie's house.

"'Bye, guys!" I say as I get out of the car, equal parts relieved to leave that situation and dreading what's coming next.

I try to think about what role Lizzie would like from me

as I nervously walk up to her front door. I remember those girls at school who had close-knit best friends. Always skipping around together with linked arms and in-jokes. How could I possibly fake that?

In the video Andopolis showed me, Liz had said she and Bec were so close she'd even noticed her posture changing. I had the decade of separation to my advantage, but still. This is going to be really hard. I wonder if I would have time to sneak a cigarette outside her house before I go in, but she opens the door before I even knock.

"Hey, babe! Thought I heard you walking up the path. Come in."

She doesn't look at me as she talks, then turns abruptly on her heel. I follow her into the house. It's beautifully decorated, with simple furniture and paintings all over the walls.

"I thought we could sit outside but it's a bit cold, so I set us up in the lounge room instead."

"That's fine," I say, sitting down on the sofa. A bottle of red sits in the middle of the coffee table, with two wineglasses next to it. She goes to sit down in the chair across from me, but then stops.

"Do you prefer white? I have white wine in the fridge if you prefer that."

"Red is fine."

"Okay, good," she says, sitting down. There's a split second of silence and then she jumps back up.

"I'll go get the cheese."

She's nervous and has made a huge effort. I'm glad now I got changed into something more adult before I came. She comes bustling back in with an elaborate cheese plank and sets it on the table between us before she sits down again, then leans forward to rearrange it. I grab her hand.

"Lizzie," I say, looking at her, "stop it. It's me."

For a moment we stare at each other in silence. Then she starts to laugh, slightly hysterically.

"Fuck, I'm sorry," she says. "This is just so crazy I don't even know how to act."

"Open the wine, then," I say.

"Good idea."

Lizzie picks up the bottle, pierces the foil and starts turning the corkscrew. I notice her hands are shaking as she tries to pull out the cork. She starts laughing again, not being able to get it out.

"Do you want me to try?" I ask.

She looks up at me. Her eyes well up and she puts a hand over her mouth.

"Where have you been, Bec?" she whispers. "What happened?"

"I can't remember," I say, quietly. For the first time, I feel terrible for saying it. Lizzie so desperately wants answers and I can't give them to her. I look at my lap as she cries, waiting for her to stop. And as I sit there something niggles at my mind. Something my subconscious knows is important, but I can't quite put my finger on.

"I'm sorry," she says, interrupting my thought. "I'm so sorry. I didn't mean to do that."

"It's okay." I wish people would stop apologizing to me. It was starting to make me feel guilty. She puts the bottle down and gets up to get some tissues. I take it off the table and pull the cork out. It makes a dull little popping noise. I fill up both glasses and then, while her back is turned, quickly gulp mine down and then refill it to the same level. Lizzie sits back down across from me, her face blotchy and her mascara slightly smudged, as the heat of the alcohol trickles through my body.

"Cheers," I say, holding out the glass.

"Cheers," she says and clinks hers to mine.

"Your house is beautiful, by the way," I say, trying to get the conversation into safer territory.

"Thanks."

"Do you live here by yourself?"

"Yes. I just bought the place last year. I'm a bit of a home-body these days."

"Well, it works for me to stay inside. I'm trying to keep everything low-key for a while." I lean forward and load up a cracker with cheese.

"That makes sense," she says. "Pity, though. We could have gone to Gus's, had some eggs."

"Bit late for breakfast, isn't it?" I say, laughing. I bite into the cheese, and it's perfectly rich and gooey. Looking up, I realize she's looking at me strangely. I must have said something wrong. I take my jacket off, hoping seeing my bandaged arm will distract her.

"I remember when we got that!" she says, looking at the teal Scanlan & Theodore dress I'm wearing.

"Me, too," I say. "It cost me about fifty hours of wrapping Big Macs."

She looks at me strangely again. Then there's a knock on her door.

"Who's that?" I ask.

"I don't know, wasn't expecting anyone." She gets up, giving me another funny look.

I remember the ink tag in Bec's drawer. Idiot. Of course

she must have stolen it. I try to think of something to fix my mistake but she's already at the front door.

"Now's not a good time," I hear her say.

"Don't be mad at me." It's a guy's voice. "I hate it when you're mad at me."

"Well, don't do it, then."

"Come on, let me in. We can talk about it properly."

"It's really not a good time."

"You're being a dick."

"I'm not!"

"What's the big secret, then?" I hear footsteps.

"Jack! Stop it!"

I look behind me and a tall shaggy-haired guy stands in the doorway. When he sees me his eyes widen and his mouth opens. It was a look I was becoming all too used to: shock and disbelief, like I'm the walking dead.

"Hi," I say.

"Come in here!" demands Liz, pulling him into the kitchen. He lets her lead him, staring at me until he's out of the room.

"What the fuck?" I hear him whisper.

"She's back," Lizzie whispers.

"Where was she?"

"I don't know. She's got amnesia or something."

A moment of silence. I smile. Amnesia sounds so ridiculous.

"Why didn't you tell me she was back?" His voice rises. "I'm your brother!"

"I only just found out myself!"

"Still! You should have called me."

"I had to be careful. We don't want the media finding out."

"Oh, come on, that's not it. You know I wouldn't spread it."

"It's really important! Plus, I was still pissed off at you."

"Well, now I'm pissed off at you!"

He marches out of the kitchen and comes back into the lounge room.

"Hi, Bec," he says to me. "Sorry about staring. I didn't know."

"That's okay," I say, feeling strange sitting while they're both standing on the other side of the room, looking at me.

"I guess I should go," Jack says, looking at his shoes, his brown fringe covering his face.

"Do you mind giving me a lift home? I'm feeling pretty tired now," I say to Liz. Really I'm afraid I might put my foot in it again. Talking to Liz is like a minefield; she knew Bec too well.

"Already? That's okay. Of course."

"Yes. No, I mean, yep. That's fine," he says, stumbling over his words. I get up and put my jacket back on.

"Thanks for everything, Liz. It's so amazing to see you."

"You, too," she says, but she looks hurt and confused.

Jack and I walk out to his car, which is parked on the other side of the street. He keeps looking at me out of the corner of his eye, but every time I look at him he looks away.

"Careful," I say. "You're going to walk into something."

He laughs. "I guess I'm in shock," he says, unlocking his car. He gets in and slides across to unlock my door. His car is rickety and old, the fabric on the seats ripped. He looks too tall for it. He has to bend his head slightly to prevent it from touching the roof. I catch him eyeing me again as

I clip in my seat belt. I wonder how well he and Bec knew each other.

"So are you just going to keep staring at me, or do I get a hug?" I ask.

"I'm sorry. I'm being a weirdo," he says, leaning forward and pulling me against him softly. Unexpectedly, my skin tingles under his touch.

He starts the ignition and pulls out from the curb. If I can get him on my side, I can use him to convince Liz for me. I know I messed up a bit today. I need to do some damage control.

"I can't believe she didn't tell me!" he yells suddenly.

"She said she was pissed off at you," I say.

"You heard that?"

"You're not the best whisperers."

"Sorry. But still, she should have told me."

"I agree—she should have." People like it when you're on their side.

"Thank you," he says, stopping at the traffic light. He turns to look at me again, but it's different this time. The shock is gone; instead he is smiling warmly. Looking at me in awe, like I'm some kind of beautiful mystical being. He fancied Bec. He fancies me.

"You should get my number off Liz," I say. "It would be cool to hang out."

"Oh. Yes. It would, um, you know, be cool." He blushes, and then the car behind us beeps and he jumps and turns. The traffic light has turned green and the cars that were in front of us are already around the bend.

"Fuck. Shit. Whoops, sorry," he says, changing gears. I laugh. Maybe I fancy him a bit, too.

I look behind us at the angry traffic. Then I see it and my heart drops. A few cars behind, the black van. I turn back as we accelerate, but the sun reflects off its tinted windows. The driver's face is hidden.

8

Bec, 13 January 2003

There was something in her mouth, something stopping her from breathing. She woke with a start, heaving in air. Something soft and hot smeared over her fingers when she scrubbed at her face. Lizzie screamed with laughter.

Bec looked down at her hand. It was covered in melted chocolate.

"You fucking bitch!" she shrieked.

Lizzie had done this once before when Bec had slept over, stacked chocolate buds on top of Bec's lips to see how high the tower could get before it woke her. She jumped on top of Lizzie, wiping the chocolate all over her face. Lizzie tried to push her off, hitting her with the pillow and squealing.

The bedroom door opened and Lizzie's dad poked his shiny, balding head in.

"You two girls okay?" he asked and then eyed them slowly. "I'm not interrupting anything, am I?"

Bec realized how it must look—she was barely dressed

and straddling Lizzie in the bed. She got off her and pulled the blanket over her tiny singlet.

"Shut up, Dad!" Lizzie groaned. He raised his eyebrows at them and closed the door again.

"God, he's so annoying sometimes!" she said.

"He's not that bad. At least he's got a sense of humor," Bec replied.

"I guess." Liz tried to rub the chocolate off her cheeks.

"Bags first shower!" Bec said, jumping out of bed before Lizzie could stop her.

She had a quick, cold shower. Just long enough to get rid of the melted chocolate and the sleepy feeling.

Bec was glad she'd stayed over. They'd had such a fun time watching *Catch Me If You Can* in Manuka and the idea of going home and having to worry about whatever had been in her room that night seemed silly. She really was ready to just forget all about it.

Running back into Lizzie's bedroom with her towel wrapped around her, she could hear Jack's metal music start up in his room. What a weird thing to listen to first thing in the morning. She closed Lizzie's door so she didn't have to hear it and watched for a moment as Lizzie flicked through her clothes. She was softly singing along to the radio and wriggling her butt.

Bec couldn't help but jump in.

"I say, it's got so hot in here, so take off all your gear," Bec pretended to rap. Lizzie whirled around laughing.

"That's not even right!"

Bec jumped onto the bed, dancing mock suggestively in her towel.

"I am so sweaty, I smell like hot spaghetti," she sang in a high-pitched voice, trying to follow the tune.

"Ew!" said Lizzie, laughing and flicking Bec with the towel she had over her shoulder.

She loved the way this looked. It could be right out of a movie.

"Ohmegawd, you are so hot!" she said to Lizzie in an over-the-top Aussie accent.

"Holy boly moley canoley, you are tooo sexy!" Lizzie said, giggling wildly as she walked out to the bathroom, leaving the door open a crack. Bec sat down on the bed, panting. So much for the shower—she was already beginning to sweat. Pulling on her undies and bra, she hoped for a moment that Jack would come past and see her. He didn't, so she put yesterday's summer dress back on and wandered out to his doorway.

Jack was lying on his bed fully dressed. She leaned in the doorway in what she hoped looked like a relaxed and unintentionally sexy position.

"Hey," she said. He looked up and went white, then quickly sat up.

"Hey." He pulled his fringe out of his eyes and looked at her intensely. She remembered the way Jack used to be: a rosy-cheeked older boy always happy to play with them. Now with his metal T-shirts and dirty jeans, he just looked a little bit greasy.

"Why do you listen to this first thing in the morning?" she asked.

"I dunno. I like it," he said.

Bec looked around his room. It was really messy. There were clothes strewn all over the floor and it smelt like a mix of sweat and spray deodorant. His walls were covered with metal posters; a huge silver-and-purple Black Sabbath one taking pride of place.

"Better than Nelly," he said. He'd heard her singing. That was so embarrassing. He grinned, and for a moment he looked the way he used to look. If you ignored the bad skin and terrible clothes, he was actually pretty cute.

"Nothing's better than Nelly," she said, not being able to help but grin back.

"Hey, um, sorry about the other day," he said. She wasn't sure what he meant for a second. Then she realized he meant running into her in her bikini.

"Oh, no, you don't have to apologize for that." She wished he hadn't said anything.

"Nah. I know. It's just… You know. I don't want you to think I'm perving or whatever."

"I don't think that," she said. He was so different to Luke. Why was he making it weird? If this were Luke he'd make some joke about wank banks, they'd laugh and everything would be normal again. The sound of Lizzie's shower stopped.

"See ya, pervert!" she said, smiling again and going back to Lizzie's room before he could react.

Lizzie's dad was making pancakes downstairs.

"Hungry?" he asked them.

"Okay, you officially have the best dad ever!" she said to Liz.

"He only does this when you're here," grumbled Lizzie.

"Actually, I was hoping to blackmail you both to my side in the little debate I'm having with your brother, Liz."

Bec took a seat next to Jack. His dyed-black hair flopped down in front of his face as he looked at his empty plate. He was doing his best to look moody but Bec was pretty sure he was just trying to hide his acne from her. Bec couldn't believe she used to have a crush on him. Although, if she were completely honest with herself, she still did just a little bit. Hopefully he got that she was joking when she called him a pervert.

"Is it about his music again?" asked Lizzie.

"At least it's not that teenybopper shit you listen to," Jack retorted, not looking up.

"Hello! I was just about to defend you, dickhead!" Liz said.

"Language," her father quickly interjected.

"Oh, come on, Dad. Your language is the worst of all of us," she replied.

"She's right," Jack agreed.

"Piss off, both of you," Lizzie's dad said and they all laughed.

"What was the disagreement?" Bec asked, enjoying being an honorary member of their family. It all felt so comfortable and easy.

"Liz was right. It's the music." He flipped a pancake over and then quickly added, "Not all of the music, though. Just that awful Ozzy Osbourne."

"It's Black Sabbath, Dad. They're a classic," Jack said into his plate.

"Yes, I remember. But really he's just disgusting now. And that reality show about his family is putrid."

"I like that show. It's funny!" said Lizzie.

"Well, that worries me, too. I thought you were growing up to be smarter than that," he said.

Lizzie groaned but looked slightly hurt.

"If you're going to play his record on repeat, can you just

do it when I'm at work?" Lizzie's dad put the last pancake onto the stack and turned off the stove.

"I know why you don't like him," said Jack.

"Why?"

"It's cos he bites the heads off bats and doves on stage."

"That's just a stunt!" Lizzie said.

"No, it's not!"

"Eat your pancakes before they get cold," said their dad.

Bec watched as Jack sliced into his pancake. Her stomach twisted and she felt a little faint, cold sweat building up on her forehead. She kept imagining that old man she'd seen on the show biting a head off a little bat—the poor thing squirming to get away, the blood squirting from its lifeless body. How could they laugh about it like it was no big deal? She tried to push the image out of her head but it kept looping like a video.

"Don't tell me you're worried about your figure?"

"Leave her alone."

The shriek of their knives against the breakfast dishes mixed with the little bat's squeal. She imagined Ozzy, black hair and eyes, spitting blood out of his mouth, smiling. There was blood everywhere. It came back into her nostrils clearly, like she was smelling it again for real. Metallic and sour, so strong she could almost taste it.

There had been so much blood.

"Is she all right?"

The loop stopped and Bec realized they were all looking at her.

"You guys just killed my appetite," she said, but her words sounded strange.

"You look pale. I thought you said you two guys just watched a movie last night?"

"We did!"

"I'm going to go," Bec said, her voice sounding more normal. "I just remembered I was meant to have breakfast with Mom. She's going to kill me!"

As soon as she was out of Lizzie's house she started feeling better. *Breathe in through the nose, out through the mouth.* That's what her mom had taught her to do when she felt sick. It was working. The air was still thick with heat, which was strangely calming. It took away the cold shiver in her body. She knew she had embarrassed herself. Lizzie and her family were no doubt talking about her right now. But she didn't care; something had just felt so wrong and she'd had to get out. A little voice in the back of her mind was telling her she was acting strangely. Just like a crazy person. Bec breathed deeply again and smiled before the images from last summer could flood back in.

She wasn't crazy. Anyone who saw her right now would think she was just a young woman going home. Which was exactly what she was. Nothing strange about that.

The tar on the road had started to melt. A few little stones were stuck to the bottom of her sandals. She tried to push them off as she walked instead of stopping, keenly aware that she hadn't put sunscreen on again. She didn't mind her freckles, but she didn't really want any more of them. There was a girl in her primary school who had so many little orange freckles that they joined together on her cheeks, making her look like she had some kind of weird rash. No, she definitely didn't want that.

Maybe she'd go past work before home. It was only another ten minutes' walk away. She could tell Luke her parents were going grocery shopping nearby and she was waiting for them to finish. Or maybe even say she was the one going grocery shopping; that sounded much more adult. Then she got that feeling again. That feeling like someone was watching her.

Bec bent her head down and kept walking past the bus stop and through the little park area toward Manuka. She liked this park; it was like a little pocket of respite from the cruel summer day. The shade of the trees cooled her and blocked the reflection from the road so she could stop squinting for a few moments. She wouldn't look around. No. She was not going to let the stupid feeling get the best of her. She was not crazy. Then she heard footsteps. Real, solid footsteps. Running toward her. She was about to turn when the world turned white.

It felt like she was floating. Her limbs were suddenly weightless. Her mind was flailing, trying to grip on to consciousness but nauseatingly unable to do so.

She opened her eyes. All she could see in front of her was blood cells. Her tiny blood cells swaying slightly in the wind.

"Can you hear me?"

She wanted to reply but couldn't quite open her mouth.

"Her eyes are open."

"I'm okay," she managed to say and tried to sit up.

Strong female hands forced her back down.

She blinked again and swallowed. Her limbs felt heavy; the floating had stopped. Now they felt like dead hunks of meat that didn't belong to her.

She could feel the rasping dead leaves under her fingers,

and looking up, she realized that it wasn't blood cells she was seeing but the speckled light coming through the trees. Turning her head slightly, she saw a middle-aged man's face hovering in front of her.

"What happened?" she said.

"I think you fainted from the heat. We heard the noise when you fell."

"Do you feel all right, honey?" A woman's voice, from the other side.

"Um…yep, I'm fine." Bec tried to sit up again and this time the woman didn't stop her. She felt pretty woozy, but refused to let herself lie down again. Tentatively, she pressed down on the back of her head, and a sharp pain blasted all the way down her spine. Her fingertips came back red with blood.

"I think someone knocked me out," she said.

The woman and man exchanged glances.

"I don't think so," the man said. "We came straightaway. There wasn't anyone dodgy around."

"You must have hit your head when you fell, sweetheart. Do you want to use my phone to call your mom?"

"I've got a phone," Bec said.

Bec tried to open her handbag, but her hands started shaking as she fumbled with the clasp. The woman bent over and unclipped it for her.

"Thank you," she said, and all of a sudden she wanted to cry.

Swallowing, she brought up her dad's number. It almost rang out before he answered.

"Hi, Becky," he said, his voice barely audible over the noise in the background.

"Dad," she said, trying to stop her voice from cracking, "I fainted."

"Oh, no, Becky, you poor thing. It must be the heat. Today's a shocker." He sounded weirdly overexcited and his words were running together slightly.

"Um...can you come get me? I don't feel very well."

A long silence. Bec could hear the clinking of glasses. He was in a bar.

"Now's not really a great time, sweetheart. Can you call Mom?"

"Okay."

Her face was burning as she hung up.

Bec rested her head against the car window as they drove home. Her mom was still talking, but she'd stopped listening. She had barely asked if Bec was okay before she began talking about the twins. Worrying about whether they were getting bored at home, if she should take some time off work so that she could take them out. The thing was, Bec wasn't sure if she was okay. She felt strangely cold and her hands were still shaking. Part of her wanted to shout at her mother. Scream and yell that she needed her. Tell her that she was starting to feel scared. But it wouldn't make any difference. Her parents were always more focused on the boys. That's just the way it was.

She'd had to wait half an hour for her mom to get there, and the couple, Tony and Fiona, refused to leave her. Tony got her a Coke, which made her feel way better, even though she usually hated the stuff. But after a while she'd wished they'd go. Bec couldn't get her head around exactly what had happened. She was sure she remembered hearing footsteps before she'd fainted, but they'd said no one dodgy was around. Bec had felt pretty strange already that morning; it could have been heatstroke. She'd waited around in Manuka for Lizzie to finish work for two hours yesterday and it was crazy hot. Her phone beeped.

Been thinking of you today. Hope everything is all right.

It was like he knew. Like Luke could feel her hurting from all that distance away. She started feeling a little better.

The car pulled into the driveway and Bec got out on wobbly legs, the front door seeming very far away. A solid arm came around her.

"Are you sure you're okay?" her mom said, her attention finally focusing on Bec.

"I think my head might be bleeding," Bec replied.

"Oh, Becky, you duffer! You're a sensitive little petal sometimes, aren't you?" She smiled down at Bec, who couldn't help but smile back, all her annoyance disappearing.

As they walked up to the front door, she was beginning to feel a lot more like herself, even though she almost tripped on her brothers' bikes. Opening the front door, she laughed at Paul and Andrew, who were sitting on the steps in their swimmers.

"Why are you wearing your swimmers at home, you losers?" she said.

"Bec!" her mom warned.

"Oh, they know I'm just joking, don't you?"

But the boys didn't say anything; they just stared up at Bec. Their identical faces were blank. Then she remembered. She was meant to take them to the pool.

"You said we were going to spend the whole day together but you didn't even sleep here!" yelled Paul.

They said nothing else, just looked at her with hate in their eyes. It made her want to cry. She couldn't believe she'd forgotten. They would have been waiting all morning, all ready to go, slowly realizing it wasn't going to happen.

"Oh, no, I'm sorry."

"You'll take them another day. Won't you?" The warmth had gone out of her mom's voice.

"Yes. I promise."

"Good. Now let's have a look at your head."

Bec allowed herself to be led up to the bathroom. Her mom turned the heat lights on and looked carefully through her hair. She wet a cotton wool ball and started dabbing, making Bec wince.

"You're right—it is bleeding. It's not too bad, though, just a cut. You must have fallen on something."

"I don't know if I did. What if someone knocked me out?"

"Don't be silly."

Bec wished her mom would turn the heat lights off; they were making her head throb. Her mother looked at her closely in the mirror.

"You're not feeling dizzy, are you?"

"No," Bec lied.

"What about blurry vision?"

"I'm fine," Bec said, but in truth all she wanted was to lie down on the cold tiles. Her reflection was starting to sway in front of her.

"Good," said her mom. "You don't look well. I thought you might have a concussion. Tell me if you start feeling

nauseous or anything, okay? Concussions can be really serious."

"It's just the heat."

"Maybe you should go and lie down for a while?"

"Thanks, Mom." Without making the conscious choice
to do it, she was hugging her mother tight.

Bec wished she could tell her mom everything, all the
things she was worried about, but she knew she couldn't.
Her mom gave her a quick squeeze and left the room. She
had never been much of a hugger. It always seemed to make
her uncomfortable. Bec looked at her face closely in the mirror. Under the heat lamps her pupils looked like they were
slightly different sizes. Weird.

Bec was desperately tired and feeling more and more light-
headed. She needed to get into bed, but first she knocked
on the door next to hers.

"Can I come in?"

"Go away! No girls allowed."

"Especially not shithead girls like you!"

Bec opened the door.

"If Mom hears you using that word you're going to be
in big trouble."

"Well, you are a shithead," said Paul. They were splayed
out on the floor, looking so much like angsty teenagers that
she had to stop herself from smiling.

"I know I am. Biggest shithead in the world."

"Biggest shithead in the whole universe," muttered Andrew, but the corners of his mouth were twitching.

Bec sat down on the floor between them.

"I know you guys are really bored. It must suck."

They didn't say anything.

"If you forgive me, then I'll tell you my idea of where I'm going to take you to make up for it."

They looked at each other, trying to decide whether it was worth it or not, and Bec remembered how left out she used to feel. They had this little world together that she'd only ever be on the sidelines of. Her mom told her that they took a year longer than most kids to talk. It was like they had a way of communicating just with each other and it was all that they needed.

"Okay," Paul said eventually.

"How about... Big Splash!" she said.

Big Splash was the huge water-slide park out in Macquarie. Even Bec loved it. The smell of chlorine and sunscreen, the constant sounds of kids screaming in equal measures of joy and terror, eating salty hot chips with tomato sauce all day. It was awesome.

"Well, I'll just let you decide whether you forgive me or not," she said, walking toward the door.

"We forgive you!" yelled Paul.

"Thought you might. We'll go on Tuesday. Don't forget!" she said, closing the door quickly before they could throw anything.

Bec got into bed, smiling. The sun was still out, but she didn't care. She felt dizzy and crazy tired. Pulling her blinds down and slipping between the sheets, she realized she had one more person to talk to before she could go to sleep. She dialed Lizzie's number, letting the phone rest between her cheek and the pillow. She closed her eyes, still feeling incredibly nauseated.

"Hey, psycho," said Lizzie.

"Hi, bitch," she replied. They both laughed.

"I'm sorry," she said, after a pause. "I don't know why I was being so weird. I think I got heatstroke or something."

"Don't say sorry—I'm just glad you're okay," Lizzie said. "I've been worried about you. We all were. My dad even went out to look for you after you left."

"That's so embarrassing!" said Bec. The idea of Lizzie's dad driving around looking for her made Bec feel weird. It made her not want to tell Liz what had happened.

"Don't worry about it. As long as you're fine."

"I am."

9

Someone is knocking on my bedroom door.

"What?" I call out.

"We've got to get going. Our appointment is at ten."

The hospital. I had forgotten again. I look at my phone. It's already nine thirty.

"Fuck! Why didn't you tell me sooner?" I yell, annoyed. Silence from the other side of the door.

"I'm sorry," she says, her voice cracking.

Sighing, I rub my eyes. When I open the bedroom door, she takes a step back.

"Sorry, Mom. I'll be quick. Thanks for telling me."

I smile at her, and hesitantly, she smiles back. I've been awake only thirty seconds and already I feel like I've messed things up. I take a deep breath, promising myself to think more carefully before I speak to her from now on.

It isn't just upsetting the mom that is making me feel rattled. I've been having nightmares. Well, one nightmare really. Again and again. In the dream I watch Bec walk down her street, alone and afraid. Then the black van pulls up next to her. Bec turns, smiling, not knowing what's coming. The window winds down. Inside, the driver's skin bubbles and twists; his face is a shadow. Bec screams as he reaches for her.

My jacket is still on the chair I left it on last night and Hector is curled up asleep on top of it. I pull it out from under him, and he gives me a dirty look and stalks out of the room. He's left a thin carpet of cat fur on my jacket. I try to shake it off, but most of it stays.

"I'm ready!" I call.

"Took your sweet time," says Andrew, coming out of the kitchen with the mom. He's smiling when he says it. Last night the three of us had watched TV together after dinner. After my car ride with them, a lot of the tension was gone. Plus, I could finally tell them apart. We laughed together and made fun of the people on the show we were watching. I could still feel a very slight hesitation, though. If only there was some way I could mention something unique they had shared with Bec. Something that would remind them that I really was their sister and I wasn't going anywhere.

We all get into their car, the mother driving and the father next to her. In the back, I sit in the middle between the two twins. We look like the perfect happy family.

"Are you two coming to the hospital, too?" I ask.

"Nah, we're just getting a lift into town," says Paul.

I check the time. There's no way we'll get there by ten if we drop them on the way.

"Relax, sis," says Andrew, nudging me. "Doctors are always late, trust me."

"Yeah, relax," says Paul, nudging me from the other side. The car turns off our street.

"Corners!" yells Andrew, pressing all his weight into me, squishing me into Paul, who is already flattened against the window.

"Hey!" I say, holding my arm out so it won't get hurt.

"Left bend coming up!" yells Paul, and he pushes me the other way as we turn.

They both start laughing madly and I can't help but laugh, too. I haven't played Corners since primary school.

"Roundabout!" they both yell at the same time.

"Oh, no!" I squeal as I'm pushed from one side to the other. Watching them giggling like this, I can imagine how they must have been as little kids. I'm suddenly much fonder of them.

"Poor Becky is getting squashed," says Andrew, still laughing.

"I've got my own revenge, though," I say. "Cat fur."

"Ah, shit," he says. The sleeve of his black woolen coat is covered in white fur, transferred from mine when he pressed against me. He tries to brush it off.

"Bloody Hector," he says under his breath.

I remember the picture in Bec's drawer, the one of the other cat.

"I still miss Molly sometimes," I say.

Jackpot. He looks up at me, his eyes suddenly charged with emotion. I turn to Paul, and he's looking at me in the same way. I take Paul's hand and lean on his shoulder. Andrew takes my other hand. We sit together like this the whole way to the city.

Finally, I had them. I could relax at home. I'd wanted them to leave, but now I'm happy to still have a few more days with them.

Andrew was right. Even though we were ten minutes late to the hospital, we are still waiting. Hospitals are the worst places in the world. Across from us a woman coughs wetly, sounding like she's about to puke out her lungs. A disgusting teenage boy keeps scratching himself under his shirt, his nails making a horrible scraping sound. The particles of whatever nasty skin condition he has are probably becoming airborne. I shiver involuntarily. The mother takes my hand and squeezes it. She must think I'm worried about the doctor. Maybe she's right. I rub the bandage on my arm lightly, the gauze rough under my hand. It's been irritating me, but still I don't want them to take it off. I'm scared to see how bad my arm is going to look. I keep remembering the glass cutting through my skin.

In the corner of my eye I see a black shadow. It's here. The van. I grip the mother's hand tighter. How did it know where we were going?

I'm about to point it out to the parents. I know it's the wrong thing to do, but I have an overwhelming urge to share my fear. Then I hear the clip-clop of nurses' shoes coming toward us.

"Rebecca Winter? The doctor is ready for you."

The father smiles at me as I swing my legs, waiting as the doctor takes out all his instruments. I feel like a toddler sitting up here. The room is slightly too small for us all, the doctor bending over next to me, the nurse at his side and both of the parents hovering near the door. I wonder if it's normal for the parents to come in when their child is in their midtwenties.

There is a collective intake of breath as the doctor unwraps the bandage. The last layer of it sticks to the wound. It's disgusting. Shiny and weirdly lumpy, it's about the size of a fifty-cent coin. The bandage pulls open the scab and it begins to bleed again. I look away, feeling queasy.

"Is it bad?" the father asks the doctor, who also looks mildly ill.

"No, no. It's only a flesh wound," the doctor says. I feel his hot breath against my arm as he speaks.

"Are you okay?" says the mother, staring intently at my face.

"Fine," I say.

I wince as the doctor squirts on thick antiseptic. He applies a clear plastic bandage and then covers the wound in gauze again.

"Okay, we'll just take your blood and you can go."

"Why do you have to take my blood?"

"We received an order from the police department for a blood test. You were meant to do it when you were here last," he says, not quite looking at me. I guess he thinks I might be embarrassed about sobbing and pulling out my own hair.

"From Andopolis?" I ask. He looks at the file.

"Yes, Vincent Andopolis," he says, reading.

"But why? What are you testing for?"

"Everything, really. A test for infection or disease. A tox screen, too." Then he mutters grumpily, "Although that would have been much more conclusive if we'd done it when you first arrived."

I'm screwed. Now that I'm not giving him what he wants, Andopolis really does doubt me. He's changed so quickly from that dopey, snoring man asleep at the hospital. I realize the nurse is preparing a syringe. Looking down, I see Bec's file open on the desk. *Blood type: A+.* They'll know it's not me by the end of the day. Everything is about to blow up in my face. I'm going to go to jail. I'll lose the mom forever.

The nurse walks toward me, the syringe in her hand.

"I don't want you to do that!" I say.

"It's okay, honey. We're here," the mom says.

Horrible, jittery panic rises up in me. The nurse holds my uninjured arm out, rubbing at the veins at the crook of my elbow with her white-gloved finger. I can't let her put that needle in. I could pretend to faint. Maybe that's what I should do. But no, then they could take blood while they think I'm unconscious. The needle hovers for a second over my skin. I don't have a choice. I smack the syringe out of the nurse's hand. It clatters to the floor, the only sound in a shocked silence. All eyes are on me.

"Rebecca," the doctor says, clearly shocked, "if you are going to be violent I'm going to have to have you restrained." The doctor's words are steady and even, but I can hear the anger underneath them.

"I don't want you to take my blood," I say.

The mother takes a step forward and puts her arms around me.

"Don't be scared," she says. "It will just hurt for a second."

"No one is listening to me. I'm saying no!"

The doctor's face has gone tight. "This is a police order, Rebecca. Now, we can get security in here to restrain you, we can have you arrested, or you can just let me take your blood. It's up to you."

The doctor takes my wrist this time, his grip a lot firmer than the nurse's. I look over at the father, who is staring down at the linoleum, shoulders around his ears. He's my last chance.

"Daddy!" I say, letting the tears roll over. "Please."

His eyes snap up to meet mine and he springs into action.

"You get your hands off my daughter!" he says to the doctor and takes a step forward. He looks taller now, somehow. The doctor must notice it, too, because he lets go immediately.

"I'm sorry, sir, but Rebecca really needs to cooperate. I only have her well-being in mind—"

"My daughter is traumatized, and you threaten to restrain her? I'm taking her home. Right now."

I slip down from the hospital bed onto my feet and beam at the father. I didn't think he had it in him.

I've dodged a bullet. I know it. Andopolis is asserting himself. He is taking back every bit of control I thought I had. It's more than just frustration—he doubts me. He doubts my story, my motives. I just have to hope that he doesn't doubt the DNA test, but even that's looking possible.

The drive back from the hospital is quiet. I can't help but look behind me at every turn, scanning for the van. It's a relief to get back home, to lock the door on the outside world. Between Andopolis and the van, I feel like I'd be happy to never leave. I'm being hunted. Stalked on every angle. Home is the only safe place left.

Sitting on the couch, I try to breathe. Feeling helpless will get me nowhere. Fear will get me nowhere. I try to swallow it back down.

The parents don't want me to go out with Andopolis later that day. The father calls him to cancel, but I know it won't be that easy.

Right on time, his car pulls into the drive. I could ask the father to go out and tell him I'm not coming. Somehow, I'm sure that pushing Andopolis is not the key. He's probably used to that. He'll just push back, harder.

Yesterday, he told me to bring something to cover my face, that we'd be riding Bec's bus route home from Mc-Donald's. I pull a hat on and walk out the front door to meet him. Game on.

Andopolis and I ride the bus in silence. I am so angry at him, I can't even speak. To go above my head like that, to try to take away my rights to my own body. He was playing dirty, getting real. He had no idea what he was in for. I watch the suburbs slip past the window, fuming. Around me, people chatter with each other and on mobile phones.

"Not got much on your mind today, then?" he says.

I clench my hands into fists; I could hit him. I stare out the window, trying to keep my calm although I am not see-ing anything anymore. Giving in to anger would only take away more of my power.

"I've been thinking maybe we should hold a press con-ference," I whisper.

This surprises him. Good.

"I don't think that's a good idea," he says, looking around to make sure no one is listening.

"I do. I think people should know that I escaped. It'll be inspiring for other victims."

It will also make him look terrible. What was it that he

said back then? That if Bec was alive, he'd find her. Well, he didn't.

"I'd like to tell my story," I continue. "I think people will want to know about that horrible long drive in the police car when I almost bled to death. And how great you've been with helping me try to remember, except for today when I was told I had to choose between being restrained and arrested."

His jaw sets. "You know who'd like to hear your story? Me. That's all I want."

I say nothing. He should know that he's not the only one who loves a victim. I imagine the headlines: police misconduct, a decade of stuff-ups, senior investigator disgraced. Photographs of poor little old me and big brutish Andopolis.

I'm bluffing, of course. Going to the press would be far more damning for me than it would for him.

"So this isn't jogging your memory, then?" he snaps.

Asshole. My anger surges.

"Please, leave me alone!" I scream, letting my voice sound slightly hysterical.

The bus goes silent; people glare at him.

"Calm down, Rebecca," he mutters, looking around.

"Get away from me, please!" I scream.

"Hey, mate," says the man in a baseball cap in front of us, turning around, "leave the girl alone."

Andopolis pulls out his wallet and flashes his badge.

"Stay out of it," he says. The man looks at me and then turns quickly back around. I notice something when Andopolis flashes his badge, though—his fingernails are splintered at the end. They didn't look like that before. He's started biting them.

"Stop it, now," Andopolis says to me, his voice low, almost a growl. I wish I could just get off this bus and run home, but I'm too afraid to be by myself now. The van is probably following this bus right now, biding its time.

Eventually we get to Bec's stop. Andopolis stands, presses the button, then grabs my arm and marches me off the bus.

"What the hell was that?" he asks, as we stand on the street.

"Let go of me!"

"Stop it, Bec!"

"You're hurting me!" I scream, though he isn't. He lets go, as though my arm is charged with electricity. I march up the street, hating him but hoping he'll follow until I'm closer to my house. He does.

"So no memories coming back to you, I suppose?" He almost has to jog to keep up with me. His stomach jiggles up and down.

"Do you know what I remember? I remember the asshole doctor you ordered to take my blood threatening to strap me to a hospital bed." I don't even care that I swore.

"If you go to the press, we're done."

"Good!"

He groans in frustration. "I'm just trying to help you, even if you don't want me to."

"So threatening a traumatized abduction victim is helping them, is it?" I ask. I'm angry, so angry, but I know now is the time for tears. I've made my point; I've shown him what I can do. So I stop on the street and look down, biting the inside of my cheek so hard I taste blood. But tears come, too.

"I thought I could trust you," I say.

He looks down at me, conflicted.

"I'm sorry," he says finally, but it comes out a little tersely.

I look around; the street is empty. So I run away from him, up the street to Bec's house.

The next morning I lie on the couch on my stomach, waiting for the sound of Andopolis's car. It is long past the time he usually arrives. I must have done it, I realize, pushed him far enough that he doesn't want to come back. He must have bought my threat that I'd go to the media. If that's true it means Bec's life is officially mine. I wouldn't need to worry anymore; it would be over.

I play with Hector, who sits on the carpet beneath me chasing an old shoelace I swing back and forth. I'm not sure what I'm going to do all day now. The mother took the twins shopping, saying she'd bring me back some clothes since I was meant to be with Andopolis. I wish I'd taken Jack's number rather than telling him to get mine—I could have asked him to come and pick me up. But then again, it might look weird for an abduction victim to be pursuing a guy. Hector rolls onto his back, all four pink paws up in the air as he tries to catch the shoelace. I rub his belly and he looks shocked, jumping back onto his front and backing away like he's being attacked.

I hear something then. The sound of someone crying. It's soft, only just audible. For a crazy moment I think perhaps it is Bec, finally home and realizing she has been replaced. As I walk toward the stairs, the crying is louder. It's definitely real. Someone is in the house crying. It's deep—a man. I get to the foot of the stairs. The sound is coming from my left, the parents' room. Their door is shut, so I knock softly. There is no answer but the crying stops. I consider going back upstairs to my room; part of me doesn't want to see the father cry. He's family now, though, I tell myself. He saved me at the hospital yesterday. I push the door open. The father sits heavily on the side of the immaculately made bed. It's the only piece of furniture in the room except for the spotless bedside tables. The blinds are down, blocking out the sun. His hands are over his face and his shoulders heave, a black silhouette in the grey room.

"Dad?"

He looks up at me, his face grey and creased.

"Oh, God," he says quietly. He begins crying again. It sounds painful, like each sob is ripping through his insides.

"What's wrong, Daddy?"

"I'm fine," he whispers.

"Why are you whispering?" I ask loudly.

When he looks at me, his wet eyes are panicked. He puts a finger to his lips.

"There's no one else here," I say.

"Go!" he whispers, urgently.

He turns away from me, looking down as though he is waiting for me to leave. The hairs on my arms rise up. How can this be the same man who'd been so commanding yesterday? What could have happened between then and now?

"Please don't be upset." My voice sounds so forced, but I can't leave him there like this. "I love you, Dad. You saved me yesterday."

His whisper is so faint I have to lean in to hear it. "No. It's too late. It's already too late."

I don't know what he means, but he's starting to scare me. My heart is beating painfully fast as I close the door and go up to my room.

I can still hear the sobs from there.

10

Bec, 14 January 2003

At first Bec thought the screaming was in her dream. It was a nasty dream, the worst kind. Its sweaty, festering images lived for a moment when she woke and then recoiled back into her subconscious. But the screaming remained. She listened to it for a moment impassively. It was definitely real. It could be her mother or her father or one of her brothers.

Pulling herself out of bed, she tried to walk toward the door but it swayed and danced in front of her. The doorknob winked. She reached out until her fingertips brushed against its cold plastic and then she pulled it toward her. She held herself up by the wall until she got to the stairs, where she sat at the top, surveying the abyss. The muffled cry came again, strangled and panicked. Pulling herself up onto all fours, she shakily crawled backward down the stairs. She couldn't quite get to her feet at the bottom, so she continued crawling toward the noise.

The inside of the laundry quivered with a strange energy as she crawled toward it. The noise was coming from beyond, though. On the other side of the door. In the garage. Pulling herself onto the tiles, she forced herself to stand. She reached for the door handle, the noise suddenly loud. Too loud. Crackling painfully in her ears. Her hand slipped off the handle. It was wet. Her fingers glistened red.

She woke early, her room shining with the pale morning glow. The wind outside sounding like waves crashing into the shore. For a moment she imagined she was at the beach. That she lived alone in a little weatherboard house and spent every day sitting with an easel on her front porch and painting the horizon. But she was a terrible painter. Bec pulled herself out of bed unsteadily, her forearms trembling under her body's weight. She'd had horrible nightmares. The worst in a while. She blinked away the images of blood and torture.

Weirdly, she couldn't really remember going to bed last night. Lizzie's house, leaving and making a fool of herself and falling in the park were all clear. But after that it was all a bit hazy. There were fragments there: her brothers being angry with her, her mom looking at her head in the bathroom, but they were murky and confused. It was like she was trying to remember what had happened years ago, not just last night. She looked down at herself, realizing she'd slept in her clothes. Smears of dark red ran down her dress; it looked like blood. She clapped a hand over her mouth to stop herself from screeching. There was more blood in the bed when she pulled back the sheets. And her hands, it was all over her hands. Her palms were red. She lifted her dress with shaking hands, expecting for a moment to see some shiny, gaping wound underneath it. But her skin was unmarked. The blood hadn't come from her.

Bec pulled the dress off over her head and ran into the bathroom, jumping straight into the shower in her undies and turning it on full. She felt sick, so entirely disgusted. Bile swam up her throat and she was kneeling in the shower, vomiting onto the tiles.

There were little red stains on the carpet leading to her bed, she noticed, when she was scrubbed clean and wrapped in a towel. She quickly pulled off the sheets and left them as a tangled heap on the floor. It was her fault. She had fallen asleep without putting the chair under the door. It was the specter. It must have come into her room and dripped blood all over her. She closed her eyes and forced the thought out. The idea of it made her want to be sick again.

Dressed, she went down to the kitchen to make a coffee. She didn't want to be in her room at the moment. She couldn't stand looking at those tiny red dots on the carpet.

"You're up early," her dad said. He was sitting at the kitchen table eating breakfast.

"So are you," she said, turning on the kettle.

"I always get up this early. You're just never awake to see it."

She continued making her coffee, not really wanting to talk to him.

"I'm sorry about yesterday, Becky. I was really tied up with something at the office. How are you feeling today?"

"I'm okay. I think it was just heatstroke."

"Well, take it easy today, all right?"

"Okay," she said, sitting down at the table.

"Mom told me you forgot to take the boys to the pool."

"I said sorry!" He'd barely finished his apology and he was already talking about her brothers.

"I know. But try and make it up to them, okay?"

Bec just ignored him. How sick would she have to be for them to focus on her rather than the twins? The paper was open on the table to a large picture of smoke and flames. It was hard for her to imagine that there was a fire burning right now, not even that far away. Her father finished his breakfast and took his plate to the sink; he never really had much to say to her. As he walked across the tiles, she noticed his feet. They were pallid and hairless, his toenails slightly too long. She looked away quickly, her coffee threatening to come back up.

Upstairs, she heard the water of her mother's shower turn off. She picked up her mug and went quickly back to her room, wondering when it had become so weird with her dad. She remembered when she was younger he'd bring a puzzle home every Friday night after work. He'd come through the door and shake it at her triumphantly and she'd be allowed to stay up as late as it took to finish it. It was something special they had, just her and him. But then one Friday he brought home a puzzle with horses on it. Did he really think she was one of the horsey girls? The girls who came to school wearing jodhpurs and somehow never got in trouble even though it wasn't part of the uniform? They'd swap cards with pictures of horses on them and imagine their school chairs were trotting ponies, pretending to ride them then giggling madly. Bec couldn't understand how her dad could think she was one of those girls. She'd refused to do the puzzle on principle.

Well, mostly on principle, and also partly because all the rest of her friends had started being allowed to go to the movies together on Friday evenings. She could still remember the look on his face. He never brought any more puzzles home after that.

Later, when her parents had left for work, she hauled the bundle of bloody sheets and the dress downstairs. She felt like a shameful bed wetter trying to hide the evidence. Bec shoved it all into the washing machine, dousing it in bleach. The lid clicked closed and the machine began its cycle. She watched them for a while, going around and around in circles. For a moment she wished she could climb in there with them. Be bleached clean and perfect again.

Leaving the laundry, she noticed the door to the garage was open. She pulled it shut and a sudden unexplained sense of panic shot through her body. Last night's dream threatened to resurface. She quickly grabbed the bleach and a sponge and went upstairs to scrub the carpet.

By the time she got to work she felt like herself again. The itchy polyester of her uniform and the smell of sizzling meat seemed to calm her in some strange way. It was busy, so she started serving straightaway. Ellen was on the till to the left of her and Luke was on her right. She could hear Matty banging around in the kitchen behind her and Lizzie's voice through the speaker from the drive-through. They didn't speak to each other directly, but they were so used to moving in synchronicity it was like a dance. She felt protected, like nothing bad could ever happen to her when she had these people all around her. They were like a family.

As the crowd died down, Luke flung an arm around her shoulders. She felt slightly dizzy again, being engulfed completely in his scent.

"How're you going?" he said.

"It happened again," she told him.

It felt good to tell the story. Bec thought she might be embarrassed, but she wasn't. It felt like she wasn't alone anymore.

"How much blood exactly?" Ellen asked.

"Quite a bit. There were dry smears of it everywhere." She left out the bits about blood on her hands.

"Could it have come from you?" asked Luke.

"He means do you have your period!" said Lizzie.

"No! That's not what I meant!" Luke shoved her lightly.

"I don't have my period, you weirdo," Bec said to him, watching his colour rise.

"I meant from a cut or something," he said.

"Sure you did," she said, "pervert."

"Oh, shut up!" he said, grabbing her and ruffling her hair.

Bec squealed and pushed him off. Looking around, the laugh died in her throat. Ellen was looking at her carefully and Matty was unusually quiet in the kitchen. They didn't believe her. Of course they wouldn't, not if she was mucking around and laughing. It was just hard for her to be anything but happy when she was with Luke. She could never be scared or upset when he was there, especially when he was touching her.

But it was true. She wasn't trying to get attention or anything like that. It was true and she would show them.

"I want to do the exorcism," she said.

"Yes!" said Lizzie. "I'll bring the Ouija board."

"Maybe tomorrow. Will you guys come?"

"I'll be there," said Luke.

Ignoring the glowing feeling in her chest, she turned to Ellen, looking her square in the face.

"Will you come?"

Ellen didn't meet her eye. Bec wasn't sure why it was so important to her that her boss be there.

"We can't all go, Bec. Someone has to work."

"We'll do it after close."

"Creepy!" said Liz.

"Won't your parents have a problem with that?"

"We'll just be quiet."

"Why don't we do it in your garage?" asked Lizzie. "It's kind of blocked off from the rest of the house. There's no way they'd hear us."

That unexplainable panic rose through her again, but Bec ignored it.

"Let me think about it, okay?" Ellen said.

Later on, after Ellen had left and the sky was dimming, Luke came over and put an arm around her again. Bec stopped scooping the fries and just stood, breathing him in.

"Are you sure you're okay?" he asked.

"Yes. I feel better now we're doing something about it."

It wasn't entirely true, but it sounded like the right thing to say. She didn't like the idea of doing the exorcism in the garage, but Lizzie was right. It was the only place where they wouldn't wake her parents.

"I think what you need is to take your mind off it. A friend of mine is having a house party tonight. You should come."

She could feel herself blushing.

"I'd love to," she said.

"Cool. I'll text you the address."

He squeezed her shoulder and went back to the counter. That Scanlan & Theodore dress would be perfect. She watched herself walking in through the door of the party wearing it, casually chatting to Luke on the couch. Meeting all his friends like she were their equal. Luke holding her hand again.

"Oi, bitch, wake up!" said Liz, smacking her on the butt.

"Um, excuse me. That's workplace sexual harassment," Bec said.

"What about this?" Lizzie poked her in the boob.

"Ouch!" Bec laughed.

"So do you want to get ready together before the party?"

Bec's heart slipped.

"What party?"

"Um...didn't Luke invite you? Awkward!" said Liz.

"He did. I just thought it was a cool party for cool people and not losers like you."

"Wow, catty. I love it!"

"Let's get ready at my house. I still have supplies under my bed."

"Great—I get to see the haunted house with my own eyes."

Lizzie made ghost noises as she went to sit back in the drive-through window. The heat light was on over the fries. She stared into it until green shapes flashed in front of her eyes like jelly beans.

Perhaps it wasn't so bad that Lizzie was coming with her, she decided. She couldn't imagine walking into a party alone. Lizzie had chatted endlessly as they approached her house, then abruptly gone silent as Bec started fishing in her bag for her keys.

"Are you scared of my house now?" Bec asked her.

"I just haven't been here in ages. I think I'd started imagining gargoyles and a moat or something."

Bec rolled her eyes and unlocked the door. It creaked open, the hallway eerily silent.

"After you," said Bec.

Lizzie took a small step inside and then suddenly the twins jumped out in front of her.

"Boo!" they yelled.

Lizzie's scream was bloodcurdling.

"You little shits!" she yelled at them, lunging for Paul.

He ducked underneath her and they both ran up the stairs, giggling madly.

"Did you plan this?" she said to Bec.

"No! That is just what they're like." Bec was laughing, too.

"I swear to God, I'm so glad I don't have little brothers," she said, a hand over her face.

"Calm down. They're just kids." Bec laughed as they walked up the stairs.

"Yeah, but they're weird. Remember that dead beetle collection you found in their wardrobe?"

"That was ages ago!"

Bec swallowed the anger that always flared up if someone other than her said something bad about her brothers. Lizzie was just stalling, though, so Bec let it lie. She was standing still in Bec's bedroom doorway, looking into the dark space. Bec flicked the lights on and she felt Lizzie's body tense ever so slightly next to her.

"It's okay," she said, looking under the bed. "No monsters, only vodka."

She pulled out the half-empty bottle of vanilla vodka from

the tube of her bed frame. Lizzie only smiled weakly and stared at the carpet. Bec realized she was looking at the tiny stains. She had scrubbed at them twice that morning, but she could only get them to fade to a pale pink.

"Bec, this is genuinely freaking me out. I don't understand what's going on."

"It's okay. We'll figure it out tomorrow."

Liz still hesitated, as if she felt crossing the threshold would change her somehow.

"Who knows? Maybe it was just my period."

"Really?" A real smile was starting to tug at the corners of Lizzie's mouth.

"Probably."

"You filthy bitch! I'm not stepping on it!" Lizzie hopped over the stains and sat next to Bec, taking the vanilla vodka out of her hand and taking a swig.

"Oh, Jesus, this stuff is nasty!" Her voice was hoarse. "Next time let's just get the regular kind, okay?"

"Let's go for gin next time. Apparently that's really good." Bec felt so relieved to be laughing again in her room, for it to be just *hers* again, not some horror scene.

"My dad said gin just makes you cry."

"Yeah, but your dad's a pussy."

Lizzie threw a pillow at her and she jumped to her feet to get out of the way.

"My dad is not a pussy!" Lizzie cried.

"Then why does he cry when he drinks gin?" Bec asked. "Anyway, let's get ready. I want to look hot tonight! This has been a shit week."

Bec pulled out the teal dress as Lizzie jumped up and started flicking through Bec's closet with one hand, still holding the bottle of vodka in the other.

"You better have something good that will fit over my honkas."

"Yeah, I've stolen tons of stuff that doesn't even fit me."

"Like this?" Lizzie pulled out a hideous shapeless dress that looked like it had been made from a faded old gingham tea towel.

"Oh, put it away! It hurts my eyes."

"Why do you have it?"

"My mom bought it for me. She gets really hurt that I don't wear it."

"Don't wear it." Liz looked at her seriously. "Even if it hurts her feelings. Never wear it."

"I'd sooner die." Bec sat down in front of the mirror and began smearing new makeup over the old.

"I might wear this," said Lizzie, holding out a black leather skirt. "Going to go for the dominatrix look!"

"Ha, I've never been able to bring myself to wear it."

"Why not? It's so slutty I love it!" She laughed, putting it back in the drawer.

Bec turned back to focus on her makeup. She was going to look amazing tonight. Her phone buzzed. It was Luke texting her the address, with a little *x* at the end. Like a kiss. Bec watched the goofy smile unfold across her face in the mirror.

"It's in Deakin."

"Should we walk?"

"Nah, I want to wear heels. I'll ask my mom to drive us."

The liner spread perfectly across the orb of her closed eyelid. The mascara pulled tight and didn't leave any lumps.

Her left eye looked perfect. She held a hand over her right side and then swapped it, looking at how much better her face looked with makeup on. The room felt strangely quiet. It was Lizzie. Bec was so used to her constant chatter that the silence made her feel uneasy. She was staring into the wardrobe, a strange look on her face.

"What's wrong?"

"Can you get your dad to drive us instead?"

"Why?"

"I don't know. Your mom makes me feel weird sometimes."

"Like how?"

"I don't know."

She looked into Lizzie's face, trying to find the answer. It wasn't there.

"All right, I'll ask my dad. He owes me."

She jumped up and ran down the stairs. Her parents were sitting on the sofa, watching the news.

"Dad, can you drive me and Lizzie to Deakin?"

They looked up at her, their faces looking alien in the light from the television. Their eyes looked red and tired and there was strangeness between them, like she'd interrupted some silent argument.

"Okay, honey," he said, and they turned back to the news.

Later, as the silent car drifted into the next lane again, Bec wished she'd asked her mother. She wanted to bend down and strap on her heels, but she was beginning to feel the faint nausea of carsickness. It was like her dad was half-asleep. His eyes were glazed over and he was hunched strangely over the wheel. He indicated to get off the main road, the click filling the car like a heartbeat.

The moment he was off Adelaide Avenue, Lizzie yelled out, "We'll walk from here!"

"I get it—no parents allowed?" he said, pulling over.

"Thanks for the lift!" said Bec, sliding over so Lizzie could get out her side.

"Yep, thanks, Mr. Winter!" Lizzie slammed the door shut and he pulled back out on the road unsteadily, like a toddler just learning to walk.

"Wow, your dad sucks at driving!" Lizzie said. "I think even I could do better."

"I know. I feel sick." Bec held her forehead, feeling the queasiness begin to subside.

"The vanilla vodka probably didn't help," said Lizzie. "Come on, let's go. It's only ten minutes away anyway."

"Oh, shit," said Bec, looking down. "I left my shoes in the car!"

"Oh, no. Should we call him?"

"Nah. Fuck it. I can't walk in those things anyway."

They laughed and walked toward the party. The streets were deserted, even though it was only nine thirty. After a while, they could hear the beat of the music permeating the calm. As they got closer they could see a mill of people outside one of the houses.

Ducking through the crowd, they went down the side gate toward the pumping bass. The backyard was crammed full of figures. Some dancing, some sitting on the stoop talking; couples making out against the shadowy back fence. They had fairy lights all through the trees, like tiny ice-blue stars. Bec spotted Luke through the crowd; he looked up at them at the same moment. He walked toward them, his eyes reflecting all the tiny blue lights. Pleasure fizzed through her veins.

11

My phone rings with an unknown number.

"Hello?"

"Hey, how are you?" It's a guy's voice.

"Who is this?" I ask, smiling with relief. I had been sitting in the quiet house for hours and it was starting to get creepy.

"Oh, sorry. It's me. Fuck, I mean, it's Jack."

"I know it's you, dumbass," I say and he laughs. I hear the sound of a car outside and look out the window. Luckily it's the mom's, not Andopolis's.

"So, um, how are you going?" he says.

"I'm all right. Do you want to do something? I'm feeling a little cooped up here."

"Oh, sure. When?"

"Why not now?" I ask, as the mother comes into the room, puts a bag at the end of my bed and then scampers back out.

"Now? Okay, sure."

"Can you pick me up?" I ask.

"No worries. I'm on my way."

"Awesome," I say, then hang up.

I smile; this day is looking up. The bag of clothes sits on the end of my bed like gifts from Santa. I can't help but look inside. The smell of brand-new fabric, everything wrapped neatly in tissue paper, is intoxicating. Something about it always felt so good to me; too good. I remembered when my stepmom had found the bags under my bed back home. Packages and shoe boxes from the most expensive boutiques in Perth. She thought I must have had a secret rich boyfriend and I could see she was happy. She smiled at me, one hand on her pregnant stomach, glad to know I might be gone by the time her baby came.

Really, I had no boyfriend, just a drawer full of her friends' credit cards. She'd looked so surprised when I started offering to take people's bags and coats at every pathetic little dinner party. I hadn't known you could go to jail for something like that.

"Are you going out?" the mother says, turning off the vacuum cleaner.

"Just for a couple of hours, with Jack," I say. "Is that okay?"

"Yes, of course, honey. Lizzie's brother, Jack?" she asks.

"Yep," I say. Before she can turn the vacuum cleaner back on I give her a quick tight hug, breathing in her vanilla smell. If Andopolis has dropped the case it means she really is mine, for good.

I go outside to wait for Jack, my packet of cigarettes in my bag. But Paul is already there, leaning against a tree and smoking.

"You caught me," he says.

"I won't tell if I can have one."

"Becky! Never thought I'd see the day." He flicks the bottom of the cigarette box so that one sticks out and offers it to me.

"Smooth," I say, though it really was.

He raises an eyebrow and lights my cigarette for me. We both take a puff of our smokes. I feel like I'm a little closer to Paul than Andrew. It's nice to have some time with just him. Sometimes the two of them seem too close, so that it's almost impossible for me to get to know either of them as individuals. A station wagon pulls into the driveway next door and a tribe of screaming kids gets out, following a very harassed-looking mother into the house.

"Max left a few years after you did," Paul says, as though that was what I was thinking.

"I was wondering," I lie. He must have meant the neighbour who had lived in the house when Bec was still here.

"He had another episode, screaming and yelling all night. Then he just wandered off one day and never came back. He must have gone off his meds."

"Oh, no," I say, not sure how upset I should pretend to be. Paul just shrugs. I flick my ash into the grass.

"How'd it go with Vince this morning?" he asks.

"He didn't show."

"Really? Why?"

"I don't know."

"Do you think he's going to back off a bit?" he asks.

"I'm sure he won't," I say, after a moment. I don't want to upset him. "I think something just came up."

I see Jack's rickety old car climbing the hill. I put my cigarette out against the trunk of the tree. Paul looks at the car and then raises an eyebrow at me.

"Shut up!" I say and walk down toward it.

Jack takes me to Glebe Park. I know I'm not really meant to be seen in public yet, but I can't say no. I'd almost forgotten how tall he is. I only come up to his shoulder. We buy some coffees and pastries at a café nearby and sit on the grass. Sitting cross-legged, he looks almost comical, as though his limbs are too long to know what to do with. I want to curl up against him, but I don't. I need him to feel like he's got to earn it.

It's a nice, sunny day for autumn. Kids are laughing and squealing on the play equipment, some throwing heaps of orange leaves. Mothers sit on the surrounding benches, some gossiping to one another, others just watching their children serenely. A few public servants are out for a late lunch, eating sandwiches out of cling film and looking over paperwork. I close my eyes and force myself to enjoy the moment; the creaminess of my latte and the sour sweetness of the raspberries and custard of my Danish. The warmth in the air and the smell of wood and cut grass. Opening them, I see Jack is staring at me intently. I hadn't noticed that his eyes are a striking shade of green, with little golden flecks around the edges. They are really pretty. In fact, all of him is really nice-looking. His arms are thin but strong. His messy hair. That goofy smile. If I were being me, I probably would have kissed him already. But I'm Bec now, and I can't forget my real reason for being here with him.

"So have you forgiven Lizzie yet?" I ask.

"I guess so. She's a hard person to stay mad at, you know?"

"Yep."

I give it a few moments.

"Actually," I say, as though I've been stewing on it, "I kind of want to ask you something about her, but I don't want to put you in an awkward position."

"You can ask me. What is it?" He looks at me carefully, cocking his head.

"It's just… When I saw her the other day I got a weird vibe from her. Like… I don't know, like she was mad at me or something. It was just…" I trail off and look at the ground. It's hard to lie to those beautiful eyes.

"Just what?"

"I'm sorry. I shouldn't really be talking to you about her. It's not fair."

"Bec," he says, pushing my shoulder lightly, "just tell me what's on your mind. I might be able to help."

"It's just that I was so incredibly happy to see her, but I felt like she didn't feel the same way. I felt like she was quizzing me or something, almost like she didn't believe it was really me. It upset me."

It never hurts to sound a bit pathetic. Jack looks at me sadly and squeezes my knee, his wide palm warm. He takes his hand away, but I wish he would leave it. A few moments pass before he speaks.

"It was really hard for Lizzie when you were gone, really hard," he says finally. "Everyone saw her as the missing girl's best friend after that. Either they felt too awkward to talk to her or they would just sort of pump her for information about you."

"That's awful."

"I know. I guess it just really changed her. I don't know if she told you, but she's doing amazingly well for herself now."

"No, she didn't tell me," I say, quietly.

"She is. I'm really proud of her. She climbed the public-service ladder. She's the boss to some of your school friends' parents now, I think. It's all part of it, though. She was very lonely back then. She withdrew for quite a few years and just completely focused on school."

I don't know what to say. He's staring out at nothing, misty-eyed, drifting into thought. My plan is backfiring; I need Jack on my side. I wait for him to continue. If I bring the conversation back to me now I'll look selfish. The breeze pushes against some new plantings, bending their thin trunks.

"My dad didn't help either," he says. "He made her feel so bad that she wasn't there when you came over on the day you...well, you know. He kept saying he was sure you'd just run away. It made her feel like she could have stopped it all from happening."

"Nothing could have stopped what happened to me," I say, seizing the opportunity.

The mist clears from his eyes.

"Shit. I'm sorry, Bec."

"No, I brought it up. I'm glad I know. Poor Lizzie. It must have been horrible."

"You're so selfless," he says, his smile warm. "Yes, she had a bad time. But it was hardly your fault."

"I still feel bad," I say, playing it up.

"No, don't feel bad. Lizzie shouldn't blame it on you. That's ridiculous."

"Maybe you could talk to her?"

"No worries."

"Thanks," I say, putting my hand on top of his on the grass. He looks at it and then looks at me, smiling. Usually when people are this easy to fool it makes me see them as weak. Stupid, even. But for some reason, it was only making me like him more.

"So why is she mad at you, anyway?"

He groans.

"She thinks I'm getting too involved in something I shouldn't."

I'm really curious now. "What is it?" I push, trying to get him to confide.

"I'll show you," he says, standing up and brushing the dirt from the back of his jeans.

At Jack's house, I follow him inside and up the stairs, wishing I wasn't wearing Bec's kiddie underwear. His house is modern and large, much bigger than Bec's and almost as big as mine back in Perth. His bedroom is a bit messy, but it's warm and sun-filled. His bed is in the middle, with a desk and computer covered in Post-its. A large stack of cardboard leans against the wall. Looking out his window, I notice the gleaming oblong of blue water. A swimming pool.

"Don't judge me for still living at home!" he says. "I moved out for a while but then I had…"

"I'm not judging you," I say, cutting him off.

"At least I'm out of my metal phase, though, right?"

"Yep, that is a relief." I remember my own metal phase.

Jack sees me looking at the pictures on the cardboard. They're children's drawings, blown up to poster size.

"They're pictures made by kids who live in Australian detention centres. A Save the Children worker smuggled them out before they were banned from going there," he says. "We put them on placards for a demonstration I was part of a few months ago."

I flick through the pictures. Simple drawings of children, big sad faces and tears down their cheeks. They have drawn cages around themselves. One of them has a giant sun with an evil face. Another has a drawing of a man under a tree. It takes me a moment to realize that he has hung himself. "Melika, 6" is written in the corner.

I return the placards to their place. They are too hard to look at.

"It's awful," I say.

"I know." He sits down on the computer chair. "Look, I'll show you…"

He opens a blog and scrolls through the content. It seems to be an activist page about asylum seekers. There're blurry photographs of white politicians smoking cigars and having dinner in fancy restaurants, and next to them a photograph of an Arabic teenager with his lips sewn together, a little African girl pressed up against a fence.

"This was before the blackout."

"Um," I say, "I'm not so up to date with politics." Being abducted is a great excuse for being ignorant about the world.

"Sorry!" he says. "I didn't forget. It's just—"

"No, it's okay. I want to understand. Explain it to me."

"Well," he says, stopping for a moment to think, "stop me if you know this, okay? I don't want to patronize you."

"I don't think you will. Go on." I really didn't know much about this sort of thing. Politics has never really interested me.

"Well, unlike other countries, Australia sends asylum seekers to detention centres. When we were young there was

Woomera and Villawood, remember? They were out in the middle of the desert."

I nod. His eyes were blazing. He was really passionate about this.

"Well, now we changed the law to be even worse. Now we send them to Nauru and Manus Island, in the Pacific. The conditions there are horrifying—they're literally living in tents and it's incredibly hot.

"The new government has ordered a media blackout on detention centres. It's really dangerous to try to find out what's going on in there. The government doesn't want us to know. We've got this picture, though. It was taken from a helicopter."

He shows me a photograph of a camp of tents and dirt with a tall wire fence around it. People are holding up signs, but they're too far away to be legible.

"They are being held there for years, kids, too. It's costing us billions to keep these places open, and yet we have no idea what's going on in there. A few things have leaked, though. A guy died there from a treatable infection. He just had a cut on his foot. And the guards are sexually assaulting the asylum seekers on a mass scale. Even kids, Bec, but nothing is being done about it. There are kids there who've tried to kill themselves."

He swallows and looks at the picture. "Everyone is so scared of these people being monsters, they don't realize that *we've* become the monsters."

I don't know what to say to him. I feel terrible for not knowing about any of this, about turning off the news when it came on because I thought it was just politics rather than people's lives. Feeling guilty isn't going to help my present situation, though, so I try to change the subject.

"But what's it got to do with Lizzie being mad at you?"

He looks at me carefully.

"The guy who runs this blog, he calls himself Kingsley but no one knows his real name. I guess you'd call him a guerilla journalist. He's the one who organized the protest, little good it did."

"Why does he have to be anonymous?" I'd imagine someone would want the glory if they were putting so much work into something like this.

"There was another guy he used to work with. Used his real name. He was proud, defiant. No one's heard from him for about a year. One day—" he clicks his fingers "—vanished. Kingsley needs to be anonymous to do what he wants to do next. He wants to go further now and he needs my help."

"Your help? Is it dangerous?"

His eyes suddenly soften.

"Nah, of course not!" he says. "Anyway, I should get you home. I've got to go to work."

"Okay," I say, disappointed. I'm not quite ready to go home yet. I try to think of some reason to make him stay, but he's already picked up his keys and walked out the door. I follow him down the stairs.

"See ya," I hear him call. Swinging around, I realize there's a man sitting in the lounge room. He looks up from the iPad on his lap with a slight sneer on his face. Although he looks close to fifty, his thin hair is slicked back and his clothes are new and fashionable. I can see Jack in his nose, Lizzie in his eyes. He must be their father.

"Hi," I say, waiting for the inevitable shocked look of recognition. I'm starting to get used to it.

"Hi, Bec," he says, but the sneer doesn't drop. He looks back down to his iPad, as if the sight of me means nothing at all.

Jack pulls out of the drive and heads toward my house. Something about his father rattled me, but I try to shake it off and focus on Jack. His air has shifted slightly and he was a bit cagey back up in his room. I don't think it's to do with me, though. He's hiding something, but it's too early to ask him.

"Your dad didn't seem surprised to see me," I blurt out.

"No. I have to admit you were all I've been talking about these past few days."

"Really?" I ask.

"Of course. And also—" he pauses for a moment "—I guess he hasn't quite forgotten what you said to Lizzie about him."

"What did I say?"

He looks at me closely. This must be something I should know.

"It doesn't matter."

"So," I say, hoping to get him talking about himself again, "where do you work, anyway?"

"Red Cross," he says, pulling the corner of a red vest out from underneath his hoodie. "Got the night shift tonight."

"Really? Jesus, Jack!" I say.

"What?"

"It's like you're a bloody saint or something!"

"No, I'm not." But he's blushing slightly; he likes the idea that I think of him like that.

"You're so nice I don't even know what to do with you."

"I'm not that nice," he says, trying to sound tough.

"Don't even try!" I say, hitting his shoulder playfully. He laughs, clearly embarrassed. It surprises me that he was into metal in high school. He's so goofy. I imagine him more as the nervous nerdy boy too afraid to ask you to be his partner in dance class.

Jack takes my hand from my lap and holds it in his as he drives with the other. He runs his finger across my knuckles, and the feeling sparkles through my body. Maybe he wasn't that nerdy kid after all. The sun shines through the windscreen as we drive back to my house. In that moment I don't think about Andopolis, I don't think about the text message, and I don't think about the dad sobbing by himself in his bedroom. All I think about is the feeling of Jack's fingers lacing between mine. Then I see it.

"Pull over," I say.

He lets go of my hand.

"Sorry!"

"No, it's not that. Just pull over."

He puts his indicator on and pulls up onto the curb. The van does the same, lurking behind some parked cars.

"That van. It's been following me."

"What?" says Jack. "For how long?"

"I've been seeing it since I've been back."

"You don't think it's…" He trails off, staring at it in the rearview mirror.

"I don't know," I say, and then I feel a new resolve. "Let's find out."

I unclip my seat belt and get out of the car. With Jack here, I don't feel as vulnerable, and I'm sick and tired of being afraid. I hear him get out of the car, too.

"Bec!" he says. But I ignore him, even though my heart is beating fast.

Approaching the van, I try to see through the windows, but they're tinted. Jack catches up to me and moves to block my path.

"We should call the police."

"No." I try to pass him, but he steps to the side, blocking me again.

"We have to! This could be dangerous! I've...we've lost you once already."

He takes his phone out of his pocket to call the police. I put a hand on his shoulder until he stops and looks up at me. I can't let him call them.

"Will you come with me? I won't be in danger with you there, too."

Jack pauses, staring at me, his finger hovering over the call button.

"I'm tired of being scared, Jack. I need to do this."

He takes my hand and holds it tight.

"Okay."

Every part of my body wants to turn and run as we get closer to the van. The faceless man from my dream flashes through my mind and I start feeling myself shake. I stop walking when we are close to the driver's door window but still far enough away to run.

"Hey, fucker!" I yell. "Why are you following me?"

Nothing. All I can see is my own pale reflection in the glass.

"I've got your plate numbers and I'm calling the cops in ten seconds."

I hear a shuffle from inside the car.

"Ten, nine, eight." And then the window starts sliding down. I feel every part of my body tense, waiting to see a monster.

But it's not a monster. It's a fat, bespectacled guy who looks back at me through the open window.

"C'mon, don't call the cops," he says, his voice whiny.

"Why are you following me?" I say.

"Rebecca?" he asks, looking at me carefully.

"Who's asking?" Jack says, before I can answer.

The man clears his throat.

"Jason Borka, Channel Eight. Are you Rebecca Winter?"

"Why don't you answer her question first?" says Jack.

"Isn't it obvious? I needed to be sure," the man says in his annoying voice, looking me up and down, "and you've convinced me. If you give me an exclusive I can offer you a very generous deal."

A few months ago, I might have been tempted by something like that. But now I don't even hesitate.

"I'm not Rebecca," I say. It feels so good to say the truth out loud.

He looks at me dubiously.

"I'm her cousin," I add.

"I don't believe you," he says, piggy eyes narrowed.

"Believe what you want, asshole. If you come anywhere near me again, if you text me again, I'll have the cops on you like that." I click my fingers and turn on my heel. Jack follows.

"Last chance!" calls the guy. "I can get you on *A Current Affair*!"

Getting back into Jack's car, I can feel the endorphins rush through my system. I couldn't believe that little rat had gotten me so scared. Hiding behind tinted windows and anonymous text messages—what a coward.

"Wow, Bec," says Jack, sliding in next to me, "I didn't know you were so kick-ass!"

I lean over and look at him closely. He stares back at me with surprise. Then, very carefully, his hand reaches up and touches the side of my face. I kiss him slowly. His mouth is soft and warm as his stubble rasps against my cheek. My muscles dissolve into tingles and butterflies. He pulls me closer and the world around us disappears.

12

Bec, 15 January 2003

It was one of those amazing parties where time seems to move in fast-forward. Blue lights made faces glow like full moons and the throbbing music was like a pulse as Bec jumped up and down on the dance floor. She was dipped by Luke and then Lizzie and then Luke again until the world whirled and twirled.

They talked slowly on the balcony. Lizzie lying on her lap. Bec's head resting on Luke's shoulder. Existing together in a perfect moment that felt like it could last forever. Watching as the sky brightened and air hushed until it was 5:00 a.m. and she and Lizzie were walking home, the soles of Bec's feet turning black.

When Bec woke, she didn't know what time it was, what day it was or what had happened the night before. All she knew was her mouth was dry and her head was throbbing. She lay still, staring at the grey bulb on her ceiling. The sound of a plane flying overhead got louder and louder until, sure it was about to smash into her house, she gripped the blanket, closed her eyes and waited for her own death, images of crumpled bodies and carnage flashing in front of her eyes. Then the plane only got quieter until the noise had gone completely and she was left feeling silly while her heart still hammered.

"Are you awake?" The blanket shifted and Lizzie turned around to face her.

"Sort of."

"Remember how Lisa used to wake up and cook us a massive breakfast when we stayed at her house?"

"Yeah."

"Best hangover cure ever, right?"

"Yeah."

"We need to call Lisa."

"I think she's away. Isn't she away?"

"I don't know."

"Me either."

"Call her."

"You call her."

"Okay."

The mattress heaved again as Lizzie turned back over, her breathing slowing almost instantly as she went back to sleep. Slowly, images from the night before began to dribble back. Reliving each moment and listening to the rhythmic sound of Lizzie's breathing, Bec felt truly and deeply happy.

Later, when Lizzie had gone but her headache remained, Bec sat in the middle of her unmade bed deciding how to spend the day. She had a fashion magazine open on her lap, a strong coffee billowing steam from her bedside table and Justin Timberlake blaring from her speakers. Ideally, she could spend the whole day doing exactly what she was doing now.

But there were two things, two equally important things that weighed on her mind. Tonight was the exorcism and Luke was coming over. She'd already decided she'd ask him to come at eleven and tell everyone else midnight. He was going to be in her bedroom. Looking around and seeing her things through his eyes made her both giddy with excitement and cringe with embarrassment. He would be on her bed, though, sitting right where she was now. What would happen in the hour before everyone else arrived?

She imagined him sitting next to her, stroking her leg, touching her hair. It was too much. Bec put the magazine over her face and let out a squeal of anticipation. She had to decide how far she was going to let him go. She knew she wanted to do *it* with him. To have sex. But then, if she did it straightaway, there was probably no reason for him to ask her out.

She remembered the last time she'd gotten close. Her boyfriend last year had wanted to do it. She'd thought she wanted to as well but then when he was on top of her, breathing his hot-dog breath into her ear and fumbling around with her undies, she realized it was the last thing she wanted to do. He'd gotten so angry that she had dumped him on the spot, all the desire she had felt replaced with revulsion. It would be different with Luke, though. Her phone buzzed and she blushed, knowing it was him. Last night was amazing.

I know. I had the best time, she wrote. As soon as she sent it she wished she had asked him a question. If he didn't respond, she would have to text him again about tonight and then she would look crazy. But before she could get too annoyed, her phone buzzed again.

Is tonight still on?

Yep, do you want to come at 11 and help set up?

She held her breath and crossed her fingers.

Sure. Still just want to see what your bedroom looks like.

The magazine went back over her face as she squealed again. She sent him her address and then put the phone under her pillow, unable to look at it again just in case he changed his mind.

She smiled to herself, wondering how she was ever going to fill the time between now and eleven o'clock. First thing first, she had to get out of her room. If she sat in there all day she'd drive herself mad, end up texting him again and then feel dumb. Putting the magazine down, she pushed off from her bed and walked out of her room. The twins' door was wide open but they weren't in there. It was rare for her to have a chance to go in their room alone, so she did. For a moment she considered looking under their pillows. She remembered how she used to be in charge of putting her brothers to bed when they were still little. Andrew had shown her his new toy, a tiny little plastic robot he must have gotten out of a Kinder Surprise.

"This one goes under my pillow. Like a tooth."

"Except the tooth fairy isn't coming," Paul had added.

"Because it's not a tooth?" she'd said.

"No, because she's not real. It's Mommy."

"Is it?" she'd asked.

"Yes! Don't you know?" Andrew had said.

Both of them were staring at her as if she was the biggest idiot in the world.

"How do you know it's Mom?" she had asked.

"We saw her."

She hadn't known what to say to that. Bec was only about twelve herself then, so she'd gotten up to turn off the light. She was afraid they might bring up Santa.

"We hate Mom," one of them had said while her back was turned; she hadn't been sure which.

"What? Why do you hate Mom?" she'd said, her own voice still young and childish.

"Because she's not real. Me and Paul are the only real ones."

She could still see their soft little faces, smell the clean child smell of their hair, as though it had happened just this week. But she wasn't standing in a child's room now, and if she looked under Andrew's pillow she didn't think she'd find a tiny little toy or a tooth.

Going out into the front yard, she carefully propped the door open. Her hands were a little shaky; the alcohol was still pumping around her body. Their bikes were gone from where they usually lay, upturned and entangled, at the top of the driveway. They'd be in big trouble if they weren't back soon.

The sun was at full force, making her squint as she stared down the empty street. It was making the air shimmer. Looking up into the mountains, she noticed smoke billowing up and, if she looked very closely, a hair-thin line of red. She felt her hand come over her mouth; the fires were so close.

"They're under control."

Her neighbour was standing out the front, too, leaning

against the gate looking at her. Max's eyes looked more alert than usual. She wondered if this meant he was getting better. Or getting worse.

"They look so close," she said.

"I wouldn't worry too much. What you can't see are all the firemen up there. There are helicopters and back burning. They've done it a hundred times before."

"That's good," she said.

She suddenly wanted to ask what it felt like to go mad. If part of you knew what was happening, or if you were oblivious until you were drugged up in pyjamas in some facility somewhere. Surely if you worried about it, it meant that it wasn't happening. Max's pale brown eyes were still set on her. For a moment she felt like she could see the madness there, glinting under the surface.

"I've lived next to your family a long time, you know." Max's eyes didn't leave hers for a second. As though he wasn't even blinking.

"Yeah, I know."

"It's not just you. I see it, too."

The sweat was coming thickly now, squeezing through the pores on Bec's back. Her whole body getting grimy and wet. He could see her madness.

"I don't want to be out of line," Max continued, "but if you ever want someone to talk to, I'm here."

He wouldn't stop staring at her, his eyes set on hers like magnets. Hot anger began boiling inside her. She was about to say something, anything, to make him stop, when she heard the glide of bikes coming up the drive.

They clattered down loudly as her brothers threw them onto the concrete.

"Where were you guys?"

"At the shops."

"We're allowed to go to the shops!"

"Yeah, well, you're not allowed to ride without helmets, are you?"

She looked back over the fence, but Max was gone, the screen door swinging shut behind him.

"Are you going to tell on us?" asked Paul.

"Maybe!" she said, her voice coming out strange now. The neighbour's words were still humming in her ears.

"Fine!" said Andrew. "Then we're going to tell Mom you're having friends over tonight."

"What? How did you know?"

"ESP!" screamed Andrew, and the boys ran back inside.

Later that night, when the rest of her family had gone to bed, Bec was putting the final touches to her room. She was bluetacking photographs that made her look sexy and fun, and hiding teddy bears and pink things in the back of her closet. She'd blackmailed the twins to keep their mouths shut. The deal was that she wouldn't tell her mom about the helmets and she would buy them as many hot chips and lolly snakes as they wanted at Big Splash tomorrow. They would probably end up vomiting, but that would be their own fault.

It had taken her a long time to decide what to wear. The hard part was looking like she wasn't trying. After all, she was in her own house. She'd chosen a simple smock dress that came to just above the knees and no shoes. She hoped it looked like this was what she always wore when she hung out at home, when really it was her ratty old kitten pyjama pants. She promised herself to never wear them again.

Her phone lit up. He was here. Bec felt giddy all of a sudden. She sat down on the carpet and put her head between her knees. She wasn't sure if she could do this. Rocking herself back and forth, she took a few deep breaths and then leapt to her feet and tiptoed down to the front door. She could see the shape of him through the mottled glass. His wide shoulders, the curve of his jaw. He was here just to see her. She threw the door open, her fingers to her lips and her heart beating fast. It was strange to see him there. The image of him was so familiar; she'd thought of him so often. But to have him in her own doorway, smiling at her and stepping from her doormat onto the floorboards of the entrance hall, felt wrong somehow. He existed in a different world to this one.

Motioning for him to follow, she walked quietly up the stairs. His feet made the same squeaking sounds on her stairs as hers did. His hands were running up her banister.

She closed her door behind him. There he was, standing in the middle of her bedroom. Her heart was beating so fast she was worried he might hear it. She'd just left her desk lamp on, so the light in her room was dim and golden.

"So, this is my room," she whispered. "Was it what you expected?"

"I guess. Where's Liz?"

She realized then how uncomfortable he looked. His shoulders were set a little high and his hands were deep in the pockets of his bomber jacket.

"Not here yet, I guess."

She sat down on the bed, but he stayed standing. She patted the mattress next to her. He sat, but still wouldn't look at her. His profile shone. The slight bump in his nose, the bend of his chin; the little lump of his Adam's apple. She could stare at him all day.

"So how do you feel? Hangover gone?" she asked.

She wished she could put music on, but she didn't want to risk her parents' waking.

"No, I feel ratshit. Old men like me don't bounce back so easily."

She wished he would take his jacket off. It seemed odd that he was wearing it at all, when it was still sticky and hot outside.

"You can put your jacket on my chair if you want."

"I'm fine."

"Okay."

The hemline of her dress was riding up a bit now that she was sitting. She didn't pull it back down. She willed him to lean over, put one warm palm on the exposed flesh of her thigh. Look at her closely. Kiss her. Hands sliding around her legs and gripping on to her butt, squeezing her and pulling her toward him. Forcing her legs apart with his stomach; hip bones against hip bones, her skin electric.

But he did nothing but stare down at his knees. Shoulders sloping forward, hands still in pockets. Silent. All of a sudden Bec got the overwhelming urge to pee. She jumped to her feet.

"Be back in a sec."

She raced into the bathroom, pulled down her knickers and started peeing straightaway. Looking at herself in the adjacent mirror, she caught the pathetic look on her face. She forced on a smile. This was not how it was meant to go. It was just a false start. After she was finished, she closed her eyes, willed the negativity away, smiled again and went back into her bedroom. He liked her, she was sure. He was looking into his phone when she opened the door.

"Lizzie's here," he said.

"At the door?"

"Yeah."

Forcing the smile to stay wrapped across her face, she turned on her heel and went back down the stairs. She had told Lizzie midnight; she was sure of it. Pulling the door open, she half hoped there would be no one there. But no, Lizzie was standing out front holding a shoe box and smiling genuinely.

"Is everything okay?" Her smile faltered slightly as she took in Bec's face.

"Of course. Come in."

She couldn't believe that her time with Luke was over already. The disappointment dropped slowly in her body, a lead weight.

"You're early," she whispered to Lizzie as they climbed the stairs.

"Am I? Luke texted me when he was on his way from work."

"I guess you both are." Bec tried to cover, but Lizzie was already bounding into her bedroom.

"Hey, perv, sorry to interrupt," she said to Luke, who was still sitting awkwardly on the bed. "Thought you'd be going through her undie drawer by now."

"I already put some samples in my bag for later," he said and Bec noticed his face soften and his shoulders drop. The lead weight got bigger, filling up her throat now.

"Can't wait to show you guys what I got!" Lizzie held up the box in front of her. "Why are we up here, anyway? Shouldn't we be down in the garage?"

"I was just waiting for you to get here, didn't want to fight off the spiders alone," Bec said, her smile real now.

Lizzie hated spiders. Bec watched as she began unconsciously rubbing the back of her neck and itching her hair, as though millions of spiders were already crawling all over her.

"Let's go, then!" Bec said, not looking at Luke.

If she caught his eye the tears might come.

Bec was glad that Lizzie was walking in front of her when they got to the laundry. Averting her eyes, she heard Lizzie turn the handle and step into the garage like it was nothing. Just another room in the house. Her heart was beating fast, sending tremors down to her fingertips. This was so stupid; she wished she could just go to bed.

"Come on, slow coach," said Luke's voice from behind her, pushing her slightly. She turned and he was smiling at her again, the awkwardness from before completely gone. She didn't understand him.

Staring into the gloom framed by the doorway like a portrait, she clenched her hands into fists and forced herself to step right into it.

13

As I step through the front door, an unexpected anxiety comes over me. I'd had a great day in spite of the weird incident with the father in the morning. Now that I didn't need to worry about the black van, I should be able to relax. Everything was all falling into place. Perhaps that was why I felt anxious. When things were going well, I usually did something to stuff them up. Not this time, though.

"How was your afternoon with Jack?" the mom says, holding a basket of laundry.

"Good," I say, and it was good. It was great. He was an unbelievable kisser. Perhaps it was the endorphins leaking out of me after the confrontation with the journalist that had started it, but I didn't care.

"What was I like as a kid?" I ask. The thought coming into my head and out my mouth at the same moment. "Was I naughty? Or shy? I can't really remember."

"You were… Well, I want to say you were perfect." She laughed. I realized it was the first time I'd heard it. "But you were a bit bossy. Dressing up your little brothers like they were dolls and making them do fashion parades."

"Really?" I try to imagine Paul and Andrew doing that. I can't.

"You don't remember that? I'm sure I've got some photos of it somewhere."

"I wouldn't mind seeing them," I say.

"Of course, honey. Do you need any clothes washed?" she asks.

"No, I'm okay," I say. "Thank you, though."

She hurries back into the laundry and I sit down on the sofa. I don't really want to be in Bec's room right now, surrounded by all the remnants of her life. That journalist had really gotten to me; I couldn't believe such a pathetic man had made me feel so scared. He didn't care about Bec; he just saw the opportunity to further his career, to take his slice of the profits from her tragedy. How could he just see her as a paycheck rather than a real person? He thought something awful had happened to her, but that didn't stop him from texting her, hounding her. Hounding me.

I can't help but look up her name on my phone again, and this time I search for videos. I'm not sure why, but I want to see her moving, see her talking. I want to see her looking more alive than in just those static photographs.

There is only one video, and Bec isn't in it. It's titled City Mourns Missing Girl at Candlelight Vigil. Hundreds of people are standing in a city square, with a raised stage at the front. The camera weaves between the people, all holding glowing orange lanterns. Some of them are crying. There are large placards of Bec's smiling face with Come Home written across them. I notice a young Lizzie in the crowd, her eyes darting around and her mouth gaping, like she can't believe it. A lanky guy a bit older has his arm around her, but I can't see his face. Bec's father stands in front with a microphone.

"Please," he manages to say, and then he puts a hand over his face and begins to cry.

People have put objects and photographs all over the steps. All of these pictures that could be of me. My chest feels a little tight. The camera focuses on a teenage girl dropping a bag of candy onto the pile. In the shadows behind her I see Lizzie's dad dropping a McDonald's cap. Bec's mom walks slowly over to the microphone. She looks so different. This could be thirty years ago, rather than eleven, she's aged so much since then. As she reaches the podium, she is not crying and her hands aren't shaking.

"What are you watching?" Paul asks, sitting down next to me.

"Nothing," I say, turning the phone off quickly. "Just mucking around on YouTube."

He puts his arm around me.

"Do you want to do something tonight?" he asks. "Maybe go out for dinner?"

He strokes my hair, slipping it behind my ear. For a moment I wonder if he's asking me on a date, which is ridiculous.

"That would be nice," I say.

"Don't want you getting cabin fever," he says.

His body is so close to mine I can feel the heat radiating from it. I close my eyes for a second, feeling his fingers stroking my hair. I clench my fists and push him off. I can't feel this way.

"Oi, stop it! You're messing up my hair!" I force myself to say.

"Can't get much messier!" he says, laughing. "I don't know how to tell you this, sis, but you need a haircut."

"I do not!" I say, mocking offense. This is better. I'll have to stay in safe territory of childishness and teasing until I can get my feelings in check.

A squeak as a car pulls up in front of the house and the slamming of doors.

"Who's that?" I ask.

"I dunno. Vince?"

"Nah," I say.

He gets up and strange flashes of light cross his face as he pulls open the front door.

"Andrew? Paul?" a voice says.

Paul slams the door shut with so much force I almost jump.

"Fucking leeches!" he yells.

"What?" I ask. He looks so angry, his face has flushed red.

"Looks like dinner's off," he says and marches upstairs.

I get up and peer through the curtains. Three men stand out the front, one holding a microphone and the other two shouldering video recorders, still cameras with huge zoom lenses around their necks.

I guess I wasn't as convincing as I'd thought.

By the time the sun goes down, there are eight vans out the front of the house. I sit with the family in the lounge room. No one speaks, but the room is filled with the sounds of excited chattering from outside. Every so often there's a bang at the door or the window. Sometimes they yell Rebecca's name. I desperately wish I could take back my confrontation with the journalist. Although this probably would have happened anyway. My phone buzzes. It's Jack. *Are you okay? There was a story about you on TV.*

I hadn't thought it could be this fast. I switch on the television, moving channels until I find the program. The host appears in midspeech.

"—eleven years ago, when walking home from her local bus stop.

"Missing Persons Senior Investigator Vincent Andopolis had little to say on the matter."

Andopolis appears on the screen. His face is drawn and tired, but still, he looks livid.

"That is something I can neither confirm nor deny at this time," he says into the multiple microphones pushing toward his face. "On behalf of the police department, and the Winter family, I request that the investigation be given the space and respect needed at this time."

The screen flicks back to the host's smug face. "However, if Rebecca Winter has in fact been alive all of this time, it calls into question the integrity of Detective Andopolis's investigation as well as raising the possibility of gross police negligence."

A new image appears on the screen. A still photograph. It's from the day I walked home smoking. That reporter must have taken it while I fumbled with my house keys. The picture is pixelated and blurry, as though he took it through his windscreen. I'm pressed against the front door, slightly turned as though I'm just about to look over my shoulder. You can see only a fraction of my face. Just the edge of my cheek and the corner of my eye. It might be enough. For someone who really knew me, who could recognize the shape of my shoulders, the way I held myself. It might be enough for my dad.

"Turn it off," Andrew says.

When the police arrive the next morning, I wonder for a moment if they're coming for me. The blue and red lights fill the silent house. But they don't even come inside. I hear them talking to the journalists who are camped out the front.

"What are they doing?" I ask the dad, who is eating his breakfast next to me in the kitchen. I'm too afraid to go and look out the window myself and I can't let them get another photo of me.

"I called them early this morning. I need to get to work and those vans are blocking the street."

"Will they really leave just because the cops tell them to?" I spin my cereal around in circles. I don't feel like eating right now.

"Probably not. They'll have to put a barrier at the end of the road," he says. "This is exactly what happened before. They left eventually, when they got bored enough."

The room goes back to silence. Eventually the dad gets up, tightens his tie and picks up his briefcase before walking out the front door. I hear the swell of noise as he leaves, questions being asked on top of each other, the cameras clicking.

I sit next to Paul on the couch. He's wearing just cotton boxers and a tight white singlet and watching cartoons. I force myself to stare at the television instead of his amazing body. An animated tiger is wearing a red hooded jumper and riding a tram with his tiger family. I try to pay attention to the story, but really, I'm starting to panic. Now that the media had unknowingly called my bluff, had carried out the threat that I never had any intention to act on, the only leverage I had left with Andopolis was gone. He was going to be really angry with me and I had no idea how that would affect his next move. Plus, the house was now surrounded with cameras. I was literally trapped. Stuck inside my own lie with no room to move. I tried to take a deep breath; panic wouldn't help me right now.

"Don't think so hard," Paul says, smiling. "You're getting wrinkles."

I hadn't realized he'd been looking at me.

"Shut up!" I say, glad for a distraction.

"Sorry, sis. Just trying to look out for you."

"You should look out for yourself," I say. "I can see a nasty one appearing just there."

I flick him right between the eyes. He looks at me, calmly, then jumps on top of me, pinning me to the couch.

"I can see lots right here," he says and licks my forehead.

"Yuck!" I scream. "I can't believe you just did that!"

"Believe it," he says and starts tickling me under the arms.

"Stop it!" I squeal with laughter, writhing around underneath him. But he's strong and I can't move much. His hot weight is against me. Breathing in his sweaty sleep smell, I push against his chest with my hands and can't help but notice the hard muscle underneath. My skin feels sparkly and sensitive. This is wrong. I try to pull myself out, but he only tickles me harder, his stomach pressed against mine.

He dips a spitball out of his mouth and lets it hover above my face.

"Don't you fucking dare!" I scream, but still I can't help shrieking and cackling like a little kid. My body is singing for his. He sucks it back up and grins at me, and for a moment

I desperately want to kiss him. I desperately want to put my arm around his neck and pull him toward me. I want to feel his hot mouth on mine, his hands touching me.

"Hurry up, Andrew," a voice says.

"Coming!" He pushes off me.

I look around. Paul is walking down the stairs, fully dressed. It was Andrew who I was just mucking around with, not Paul. His hair was unstyled, so I hadn't noticed. How could that be? I pull myself up into a sitting position, feeling like I've just been caught out doing something disgusting. Andrew jogs up the stairs to get dressed. I feel tricked somehow, even though there was no way he would have thought I could barely tell them apart. Guilt swirls in my stomach.

Bec would hate me if she knew I was lusting over her little brothers. Although she would probably already hate me by now regardless. Plus, I can't help but think of Jack.

After a few hours I begin to feel trapped. Andopolis didn't turn up, and I can't go outside. Andrew and Paul went out somewhere a few hours ago and they're not back yet. I watch daytime television and lie on the couch, letting the mom bring me plates of food. I text Jack, asking him to come over. If I have to stay here, at least Jack would be a distraction. He might momentarily stop the feeling of the walls closing in around me. He texts back: I'm at work. Wish I wasn't. Frustration washes over me. I'm about to throw my phone away when it dings, Jack again. I can't stop thinking about kissing you.

I flick through the channels until *The Young and the Restless* comes on. I pick up on the storylines again quickly. Right after I dropped out of uni, it was the highlight of my day. I'd

never miss an episode. I'd started the first semester being sure
I was going to make something of myself, but it didn't last.
I'd still get dressed every morning and leave home just before
Dad did, my bag full of textbooks. Then I'd just go down to
the bakery on the corner and sit in the back eating sour cherry
custard tarts and flipping through their trashy magazines with
my sticky fingers. When I was sure he'd have left for work,
I'd go home and lie on the couch until he got home.

When I was at university it was suddenly okay for me to not
have a job and to still live at home. I knew Dad was proud of
me. He looked at me like he really did love me. If I told him
I'd quit I knew that would change. He'd ask me what I was
planning to do with my life and I wouldn't have an answer.

Eventually the three o'clock news comes on. The top story:
Has Rebecca Winter Returned? They feature the same blurry
photograph of me, zooming in to the side of my face. I turn
it off. I can't watch this.

"I hope this isn't upsetting you, honey," says the mom,
hovering in the doorway.

"I'm fine," I say, getting up and trying to smile at her.

In Bec's room, the wall of photographs of Bec and her
friends stretches out in front of me, like she couldn't possibly
have a care in the world. Andopolis's words come back to
me. What had he said? Something about looking at a photo.

*I'd look into your eyes and try to understand the secrets you
must have held.*

I look closely at the pictures of her. She's sitting on the
grass with a group of girls, all wearing the same ugly school
uniform. A photo of her and Lizzie pouting for the camera,
both wearing a huge amount of makeup. One of Bec smiling sweetly, the sun illuminating her from behind. I look

into her eyes, the eyes that look so much like my own. He's right. There's a sadness there, something that doesn't match the smile. Maybe she did have secrets.

I whip open the closet, happy to have finally found something to do. I know the cops have probably done all this before. But somehow I feel like I might be able to find something they didn't. They had missed that weird seance spell that had been in Bec's pocket. Maybe there was more they'd been too incompetent to find. It's more than just that, though. I feel like she might have left something, just for me.

I look through the pockets of all her clothes. Nothing but a few dirty tissues. I find a handbag hanging on the inside door. It's got her student ID, makeup and a scrunched-up ticket stub for *Catch Me If You Can*. I pull off the pillowslips, remembering hiding unsent love notes in there when I was her age. Nothing. I pull the mattress up, seeing if there is anything slid between it and the slats. Nothing. I stop and look at it. If this was my room, where would I hide something?

Of course. The bed. The frame is made from white iron tubes, sealed on each side with black plastic plugs. I take one off and look inside. Nothing. But the other holds something, right at the bottom. Something circular and shiny. I sit down on the carpet and put my arm in as far as it reaches. I realize what it is before I pull it the whole way out. A bottle of vodka. It's half-empty. I open the lid and take a sip, and it burns down my throat.

What did Andopolis mean when he talked about secrets? When he'd said it I had been too distracted, thinking he might be on to me. But now I think about it, he'd said he thought she was hiding something before he'd even met me. I didn't understand—why did it matter if she had secrets if she'd been plucked from the street like he'd said? That was completely random. She was just a victim of chance. And why was he asking me about the summer before she went missing? Why did he seem to think I was protecting someone? It didn't make sense. I look at the photo again, the one where she is smiling but her eyes are sad. Had she known somehow? Did she know she was marked for tragedy? I raise the bottle to her before I take another swig.

My mouth is parched when I wake up, my tongue like a dried-up sponge. The room is dark, but there's an outline of white around the closed blinds: it's morning. The room spins as I try to open my eyes, and I'm suddenly sure I am going to be sick. I shift to the edge of the bed, so that if I vomit it will go over the edge. When I move, the blanket stays in place; there's something heavy holding it down. I roll onto my back and open my eyes. The mom is sitting on the bed staring at me.

"They told me I should pack your room up. Use it for storage or something. But I couldn't. I knew you'd come back."

She pats my ankle through the blanket. I don't know what to say to her. It's been so long since I've had a mother, I'm not sure if it's normal for them to watch you sleep.

It feels weird, though.

"The boys are heading back to Melbourne on Sunday," she says, smiling. "It'll be just us after that."

"Great," I croak. Sunday is the day after tomorrow. It seems strange that she would be happy to have her sons leave. She looks at me carefully. I wish she'd go away.

"Vince called," she says finally. "He wanted you to know he's sorry for missing yesterday. There was some kind of an emergency. He said he'll be here soon."

The urge to vomit has subsided, but my head is throbbing.

"I'll let you get ready." She gets up and goes to the window, where she opens the blind halfway, letting some light in. "I might see if I can dig up that photo for you, the one of the fashion parade."

"Can you open the window before you go?" Some fresh air would really help right now. But it seems like she doesn't hear me, not responding as she walks out and closes my door behind her. The sun hurts my eyes for a second, but it helps me to feel more awake.

I force myself up and go straight to the shower. Standing under the lukewarm water, I need to hold both arms against the glass, I feel so dizzy. It was so stupid to drink all that vodka by myself. If the brothers or parents had come up to talk to me I could have so easily slipped. And now Andopolis was coming back. The investigation wasn't over at all. I was so tired of him and his self-serving guilt. And I was done playing defenceless victim, too; he was just lapping it up.

As the hot water slips down my body, taking some of the nasty dizzy feeling with it, I try to think of a new plan. A new way to make Andopolis leave me alone for good. Men like him never saw young women as people, just as objects that played into their macho fantasies. Well, if the victim role wasn't working I'd have to take the risk and go to the other extreme.

When I get out of the shower I take another look through Bec's closet. Every sixteen-year-old owned something slutty, and I was sure she would be no different.

I peek through the window next to the front door. The street is empty. Right down the bottom, I can see some glowing yellow plastic traffic blockers set up. In the kitchen the mother has left two slices of peanut butter toast waiting for me on a plate on the table. She's cut them into triangles, like you do for little kids. I wonder if she'll start cutting the crusts off, too. I'm glad for the breakfast, though. I swallow quickly, barely tasting it, hoping the bread might soak up some of the alcohol. I hear the sound of tires pulling into the drive. Andopolis must be here already. I pick up the last triangle and go looking for the mom to say goodbye. There's no response at her bedroom door, but I can hear movement coming from the laundry. Going in, I see the door to the garage is half-open. I realize I've never gone in there before.

Pushing the door open, I get a slight chill; it's much colder in here. I step down the three narrow steps to the cement garage floor. It smells a bit, like mould and rot. The room is crammed with boxes and bookcases, old child-size bikes and a dirty white sheet scrunched up in the corner. It seems odd she'd let it get so bad. She seems to be constantly cleaning the rest of the house, even when it is already immaculate. The light is dim, but I hear rustling from behind one of the bookcases.

"Mom?"

There's a bang and she pops out from behind the books, holding a photo album.

"Go back inside!" she says sharply. "There are spiders in here."

She's looking at me strangely, like she's afraid of me somehow. Her eyes flick between me and the wall behind me. I turn to see what she's looking at, but there's nothing but boxes.

"Okay, just saying goodbye," I say defensively.

"'Bye," she says, disappearing back behind the shelf.

★ ★ ★

I get in the car next to Andopolis, enjoying the way his eyes look like they're going to pop out of his head when he sees what I'm wearing. It was the best I could find in Bec's wardrobe—a tiny black leather skirt and a little black singlet. I'm freezing cold and I long to pull my jacket around me. But I leave it gaping open, letting Andopolis's eyes feast on his little victim's pale legs.

"Why are you looking at me like that?" I say.

"Like what?" He turns away quickly, starting the ignition and pulling out of the drive. "You better cover your face when we pass," he says, clearing his throat.

Bending forward, I put my arms round my knees and pull the jacket over my head. I don't want them seeing any of me. Once the sounds of them have died down, I sit back up.

"When will they leave?" I ask him.

"They won't stick around for too long. As long as you don't give them anything to see." His eyes flick to my legs again.

He drives the rest of the way in silence. I notice his hands on the steering wheel. His nails are bitten down to the quick now. Some of them even have little flecks of dried blood on the side. I'm definitely getting to him. We park out the front of McDonald's and watch the poor staff flip burgers and mop floors. Bec must have hated this job. After a while, I realize one of the workers is a bit familiar. I squint, trying to remember where I've seen him. He's older than the rest of them; he leans against the counter, laughing with one of the girls. Then it hits me. He was in one of the photos of the McDonald's staff of 2003, Lucas.

"Aren't we going to go inside?" I ask.

"Too likely you'll get recognized," he says, looking me up and down again. He probably just doesn't want to walk in there with me, afraid people might mistake me for a hooker or something. I notice his hand instinctively coming to his mouth; he notices and manages to stop himself before he puts a fingernail between his teeth. But I know I'm close now. He's almost at breaking point. I've nearly done it; I've nearly won.

"But you took me on the bus," I say.

"Yes, but that was before you went to the press."

"I didn't go to the press."

"Right."

We sit in silence for a while.

"You're really starting to tire me out." There is a plea in his voice as he continues. "All I want to do is help you."

"Well, maybe I don't want your help. Maybe I'm just fine the way I am."

Andopolis bangs his hand on the steering wheel, making me jump.

"God damn it, Bec! Who is it? Who are you protecting?"

"No one!"

He groans in frustration and turns the ignition, reversing out of the parking lot too quickly.

"How could you possibly think I'm protecting someone?" I say. "You think I don't hate the person who stole my life?"

It was me who had stolen Bec's life.

"No, I don't think you hate them."

"I do! I hate them more than anything! You're acting like this is all my fault, like I knew that I was going to get snatched. How the hell would I know that was going to happen?"

I realize I'm really asking him.

"If that's what happened," he says under his breath, driving a little too fast.

"What do you mean?" I ask. He says nothing.

It's like he is talking in riddles. How could he think Bec wouldn't hate her captor? Why wouldn't she hate them?

"You don't think I hate them." I'm thinking out loud. "You think I like them?"

He says nothing.

"You think I love them?" It comes out sounding like an accusation, but he doesn't flinch. That is what he thinks.

And then, finally, it clicks; it all falls into place. The way he looked at me like I was lying when we were standing at the place Bec was grabbed. That was when he really started doubting me.

"You think it was someone who knew...me," I say, almost saying the word *her* out loud. He says nothing, just keeps driving. That's as good as admitting it.

"What about the phone?" I ask. "If your theory is right, how did it get there?"

"Planted," he says. So final, like it was a fact.

"That's crazy!"

"What's crazy is to think that a girl could be accosted in such a quiet area without anyone, not even the insomniac across the street, hearing anything," he barks.

There's only silence as his words hang in the air between us. He's right. How could I have not seen it sooner? After a while, I notice we are driving back the way we came.

"Are you taking me home?"

"Unless you can remember anywhere else you went that day, this is it."

But there was somewhere else. Jack had said Bec went to

see Lizzie but she'd been out. Somehow, Andopolis didn't know about that.

"Same time tomorrow?" I ask, as he pulls into my driveway.

"I have real victims, who need and want my help, to spend my time on."

"So that's it?"

"That's it, Rebecca."

I know I should feel happy. I finally have what I wanted; Andopolis is done with me. But I don't. It's not just that whoever had done it might still be lurking in my life now, although that did terrify me. No, it was what he'd said about victims. Bec was a real victim and because of me the truth would never be discovered. There would never be justice for what happened to her.

I don't want to think about Bec anymore. I feel suddenly as though she's taking me over. Like the line between us is getting fainter. That I really am Bec Winter, except I am a faded version, not as bright and loved as the original.

Inside, the television blares from the lounge room.

"...missing in 2003 on her way home from work. Police are yet to make a formal statement to whether Rebecca Winter has in fact been found after a decade-long disappearance."

"Hey, Bec," says Andrew as I walk into the lounge room, "how did it go with Vince?"

He and Paul sit on the couch, staring intently at the screen.

"Fine," I say. I don't want to talk about it. I don't want to tell them that whoever is responsible for their sister's absence will never be caught. I don't want to tell them that it's all my fault. That I've botched up the investigation so badly that the person responsible for taking their sister away will never know justice. I desperately just want to run away from everything. I feel like I haven't breathed fresh air in forever. But I can't get out without a car. So instead I go up the stairs to my room, pull on a much more modest dress and call Jack. He's the only one who can make me feel better right now.

We lie in his bed, the last of the day's light making the room glow. We kiss passionately and softly. It feels like it could last forever.

"I can't believe this is happening," he says, carefully touching my hair.

"I know," I say. I'm so into him.

"If someone told me a week ago I would be making out with Bec Winter right now, I would think they were mad. Completely insane."

I smile at him, but part of me is a little hurt. I hate hearing him call me by her name. I wish I could tell him the truth.

"You look sad," he says. "What's going on in that head of yours?"

"I wish we could be completely honest with each other," I say and for a moment I feel I could say it, I could tell him. But he moves away from me and rolls onto his back.

"You're right," he says. "I'm sorry. Was it that obvious I was lying?"

I realize he must mean about the new mission with Kingsley, when I asked him if it was going to be dangerous.

"I'm just really good at seeing through people," I say.

"I'm not. I'm terrible at it," he says. *I know*, I almost say.

"You don't have to tell me if you don't want to," I say. I don't want to talk about it anymore. I just want him to kiss me again. To let myself just enjoy him without having to think too hard about it.

"No, you're right. I think you might be someone who can understand." He turns back and looks at me closely. "You're the most selfless person I've ever met."

I don't know what to say, so I say nothing.

"The Red Cross are allowed in to the detention camps. I've been angling for the assignment for ages—that's why I got a job with them. Finally they've given it to me. I'm going to Manus Island in two weeks and I'm going to bring a hidden camera."

I stare at him, shocked. That's not what I was expecting him to say.

"I'm going to live-stream it to the blog," he continues. "I think people have a right to know what's going on."

"But if you get found out you'll be in so much trouble! Shouldn't he be the one doing it?"

"Who?"

"Kingsley!" I half yell. I don't want Jack to do this.

He looks at me carefully, as though he is slightly confused. When he does speak, it's slowly and evenly.

"You know, you might not be as good at reading people as you thought," he says. "I'm Kingsley."

"Fuck" is all I can say. He's too far in; there's no way I can convince him not to do this. He laughs at me.

"That's a pretty good reaction." He stares at me, running his thumb over my eyebrow softly. "You know, it was you that changed me. I used to be so interested in death and pain, I loved heavy metal and gory movies and all that. And then after you disappeared I saw things differently. I couldn't take all the violence and horror. It was like it was taking over the world. I wanted to be part of something positive."

I slide my hand around his neck and pull him toward me, kissing him, making him stop talking about Bec and what happened to her. I kiss him deeper and put my hand down to undo his fly. He jerks away from me.

"What's wrong?" I say.

"I don't know. Is this what you want?"

"Yes. Is it what you want?"

"I guess I've just thought about it too much," he says.

"Stop thinking," I say, pushing him lightly onto his back.

I pull myself on top and rock gently against him. I try kissing him again, and this time he kisses me back hard. I sit back on top of him and pull my dress over my head.

"Is this what you imagined?" I ask.

"Yes," he says quietly.

I take off my bra and slide off my underwear.

"Is this?" I ask. I'm sitting on top of him completely naked now, and he is fully dressed. He pulls me back toward him. His hands move everywhere, over my back, my breasts and finally to the place I want them. I groan then, relinquishing control. He turns me over so that he is on top and quickly slides off his clothes and pulls on a condom from his drawer.

He looks at me for a second, naked on his bed.

"You're so beautiful," he says and closes the space between us.

The feeling is amazing. He leans over and kisses me, moving faster and faster. Our sweaty stomachs pressing together. He slides his fingers into my hair; I grip his back and pull him deeper.

"I love you, Bec," he whispers. "I always have."
He groans and collapses on top of me.

After a while, Jack falls asleep, holding me tightly against
him as though I am special and precious. I feel sick, disgusted, although I'm not sure if it's with him or myself. I
was so stupid to think this began when we met at Lizzie's.
Of course it was about Bec. It was all about Bec. I'm ach-
ingly jealous of her, which makes me hate myself. For the
first time I wish I'd run into the dark that night. I wish I'd
never come here and I could still be me.

I can't stay here anymore. I push his arm off me and grab
my phone from my bag next to the bed and dial for a taxi.
I say the address to the operator and hear Jack stir behind
me; I must have woken him. The operator tells me that a
cab is on its way.

"Who was that?" asks Jack.

"My mom," I lie. "She's worried. I've got to go home."

I get up and look around for my clothes.

"Right now?" he asks, and I can hear the hurt in his voice
already.

"Yep. She wants me back for dinner." I can't bring myself to look at him. I find my underwear and quickly hike
them back on. I can't find my bra. I look all over the floor.

"Is something wrong?" he asks.

"No," I say, getting down on my hands and knees. It's
not under the bed.

"Are you sure?"

I find it under his shirt. I clip it back on quickly and pull
my dress on, too. I force myself to look at him. He looks so
vulnerable, sitting on the bed naked, the sheet pulled up to

his waist, his skinny chest exposed. I felt like every asshole who's jumped out of my bed the moment after the deed was done. Every asshole who called me pet names and said he would call but never did.

"Everything is fine." And then, hating myself for it but not knowing what else to say: "I'll call you later."

I know I should at least kiss him before I leave, but I can't bring myself to go to him. So I just smile at him weakly and half run down the stairs to wait for the cab.

It's when I'm waiting, already feeling guilty, the wind whipping my hair around, the last of the light turning everything silver, that I get the message. My phone beeps and I think it must be Jack, asking what went wrong. But it's not. It's from that number I don't know.

Leave now or it will happen again.

14

Bec, 16 January 2003

Lizzie took a folded white sheet out of her bag and laid it out for them to sit on. It was hot in the garage, the air conditioning didn't go that far, and it stunk of mould and stale air. The hot water tank hummed in the corner. They didn't have to whisper anymore. You could never hear anything from in here.

"Ellen's still coming, isn't she?" Liz asked.

"She said she would stop by after she closes. Matty didn't reply to me, though."

"That's okay," Liz said. "We only really need four to do the spell."

"The spell? Wow, you've really gone all voodoo on us now," Bec said.

"Fuck off!" she said, but her eyes sparkled. She was excited.

They sat on the sheet cross-legged. Bec noticed how close her knee was to Luke's. The hairs on his leg were almost touching her. It gave her goose bumps. She wondered if he even noticed. Perhaps it was all in her head after all; she'd just exposed herself as a dumb girl with a dumb crush. She felt so stupid.

They watched as Lizzie unpacked the box slowly, taking out one item at a time. Two thick church candles. A small metal dish with a rose engraved at its base, a lighter, some sage still in its supermarket packaging and a pair of silver scissors. She placed them carefully on the sheet in the centre of their triangle, the dish in the middle and the candles on each side. Finally, she revealed four copies of a spell that she had printed from the internet and passed the scissors to Bec.

"What?"

"We need a lock of hair."

"What!"

"Oh, come on, Bec, don't be chickenshit," said Luke.

Usually she would have smiled when he said something like that but this time it stung. Usually she would have chopped off a piece of hair and laughed about it like it was no big deal. But right now, she didn't want to. She felt somehow like she had to keep what was hers. As if everything that made her herself was slipping away too quickly. But she hated the way they were both looking at her, so she picked up the scissors and held them to a piece of hair behind her ear and snipped. A little strip of orange lay on her palm, lifeless like a dead goldfish. She held it out to Liz, who picked it up between her thumb and forefinger and carefully placed it in the metal bowl.

Bec eyed the spell in front of her. It was ridiculous. Half the words were in Latin and some of it even rhymed. This was so idiotic.

"Ellen's going to hate this," she said.

"Why?" Lizzie looked hurt, which made Bec feel unexpectedly happy.

"Cos it's dumb. You've just printed any old thing off the internet."

"No, I didn't! I researched for ages!"

"Calm down, ladies," Luke said.

"We aren't fighting!" she said to him.

"Sure seems like it to me."

There was a moment of awkward silence and Bec felt stupid and angry again.

Lizzie wouldn't look at her. "Well, we'll just see what Ellen thinks when she gets here."

Right on cue, Bec's phone lit up. Ellen was at the front door. She jumped up to let her in, happy for an excuse to get out of there, even for a moment. As she walked to the garage door, she stepped on something, and a tiny jingling noise sounded as she did. She looked down. The little silver bell rolled out from under her foot. She kicked it out of the way and kept walking, pushing it out of her head.

Ellen looked at her dubiously when she opened the door, but Bec didn't even care anymore. When they got back, Luke and Lizzie were talking quietly, their faces close together, his smile broad and real.

"So is Matty coming?" Liz asked Ellen when she noticed her.

"He said he had a friend's birthday to go to." The lie was so obvious, no one even needed to say it.

"Oh, well," said Liz, "here's your copy of the spell."

Ellen looked it over and Bec knew what she must be thinking. She didn't say anything, though, and Liz looked at her and raised her eyebrows like she was right. Bec wondered why it was that Lizzie was taking control of this; it was her house and her haunting.

"How do you know this isn't just going to make it angry?" Bec asked.

Lizzie looked at her strangely. "What do you mean?"

"We don't know why it's here or what it wants. It's violent, though. We know that from the blood."

"I agree with you, Bec. I don't really believe in these things, but if there's any chance this is real then I don't know if we should be playing around with it," Ellen said.

Bec raised her eyebrows right back at Liz.

"But it's not real," Liz said.

"It is!" Bec could feel the hurt showing on her face.

"You said it yourself, Bec. You said the blood came from you. I thought we were just mucking around to make you feel better."

"I didn't say that!" But Bec remembered she had said it, before the party the previous night. She'd said it to make Lizzie come into her room, and the lie came through in her voice.

A moment of silence, all of them staring at her. Then Ellen stood.

"Don't go already!" Bec said, her throat tightening.

"For fuck's sake. What's your problem? I was so worried about you, Bec. I thought there was something going on here, something awful. But all you want is attention. It's the middle of the fucking night and I'm not a fucking teenager!"

A red blotchy rash crept up Ellen's neck and onto her cheeks as she spoke. She never raised her voice, but her words were so sharp they were like a slap across the face. She turned on her heel and walked straight out of the garage. Luke got up to follow.

"I should make sure she's all right." He didn't look at Bec as he walked out.

The piece of her hair blew out of the bowl as the door opened and shut. She supposed Lizzie had intended to burn it. She leaned forward and picked it up, and it felt so soft and light, she was suddenly glad she hadn't had to watch it turn black. Exhaustion flooded through her body.

"I'm so sorry, Bec. I didn't mean it to go like this."

"If you go now you'll catch up to them."

"I thought I was going to sleep over."

Bec stared at the lock of hair in her hand.

"No," she said quietly.

"What's with you? You're acting so crazy!"

Bec's hand clenched around the hair. When she looked up her eyes were blistering, but she didn't raise her voice.

"I'm not crazy. I'm just sick of having a moron for a best friend."

"Bec!" Lizzie looked like she'd been slapped.

Bec almost smiled. "I'm sorry, but it's true. You're a complete idiot. Your brother's a loser and your dad's a pervert."

"He is not!"

Lizzie didn't look hurt anymore; she was looking at Bec like she hated her.

"Take it back," Lizzie pushed, her voice cold.

She couldn't look at Lizzie. If she did she would have to say sorry, because she already was. If she apologized then Lizzie would stay, and Bec just wanted to be alone now. Perhaps forever. So instead she just listened. She listened as Liz put everything back into the box, the swish of her skirt as she rose to her feet, the whisper of her footsteps through the laundry and the quiet thud of the front door as she closed it softly behind her.

Then, as Bec sat alone on the white sheet that glowed like a ghost from the light coming from the laundry, she hated everyone.

In the morning, Bec's pillow was wet. Splotches of damp on the bleached white cotton. She couldn't remember her dreams, but they must have made her cry. Maybe they weren't dreams at all, but the events of last night played in a loop. She had never fought with Lizzie before, never in almost five years of friendship. Looking at her phone, she expected to see messages of apology from her, maybe one from Luke asking how she was. But her screen was blank. They all thought she was a liar.

Pushing off the sheets before she could let the painful thought take hold, she got out of bed and left her bedroom. It was Big Splash day and there was no getting out of it. Walking past the twins' room, she looked in. They were standing next to Paul's bed, looking into his backpack. "Don't forget sunscreen," she said.

They jumped at the sound of her voice and turned around quickly, blocking what was behind them.

"You're such a nagger," Andrew said.

"Well, you don't want any more freckles, do you?"

They rolled their eyes at her. She looked at them suspiciously for a moment and then kept walking to the bathroom. Maybe this would be a good thing to do today. Just hang out with kids in the sun and scare herself on water slides.

She showered, put her swimmers on, lathered herself in

sunscreen, tossed a dress on over the top and rolled up a towel to put in her bag. It felt good to do something, even if her body still felt hollow. The boys were waiting for her in the kitchen.

"I'll just have a coffee and then we can go, okay?"

They smiled at each other, clearly excited. Putting the kettle on, she realized how happy she was to be taking them out. Soon they'd be teenagers and they wouldn't need her anymore. They might not even like her. They'd stink and have deep voices and maybe even girlfriends. The idea seemed ludicrous. Sitting down with her coffee, she tried to imagine them without their full cheeks and puppy fat. She couldn't.

"Hang on," she said, realizing. "You've both forgotten your towels!"

They looked at each other and Paul smacked his head with over-the-top exasperation.

"Silly old fool!" he said, and they both burst out laughing.

"Go get them, then!" she said.

They jumped to their feet, but just before he ran out of the room, she noticed Paul's eyes slide to his backpack as he got up. Like he was thinking of taking it with him. There was something in there he didn't want her to see.

Part of her didn't want to look. Just wanted to let the day be golden. But she had to.

In the first pocket: just his Discman, his scruffy Velcro surf wallet and house keys. She zipped it back up, feeling slightly guilty, then opened the other one. Supplies for a booby trap. Her body went cold. She could already picture it, see the water of the swimming pool turning pink. Her insides twisted.

Not bothering to zip the bag back up, she got up and

walked straight out of the house, slamming the door shut behind her. Part of her knew it was her duty as big sister to stay and talk to them about what was in there. To make them understand that actions had consequences. To explain to them what it meant to hurt someone, that it wasn't a game, that it wasn't funny. But it was just too much for her. It was that house. That house made everything inside it ugly and warped. She needed to put as much distance between her and the house as possible. This was meant to be her golden day of innocence and fun.

Bec walked and walked, not sure where she was going. The towel stuck out of her bag at an awkward angle, banging against her back with every step. Her cheeks were hot and wet, from tears or sweat she wasn't sure.

She was almost there before she realized her feet were taking her to Luke's house. Some unconscious part of her brain knew that she had to tell him that she wasn't a liar. Part of her wanted to tell him everything. To open that part of her mind that hurt to touch and let all the poison out.

From the road, it was just a wide driveway and some eucalypts, blocking the building from view. Once you took a few steps up the drive you rounded the corner to the squat brown brick apartment building. Not very remarkable in any way, but knowing it was where Luke lived gave it some kind of breathtaking mystique to her. It could have been the Notre Dame or the Taj Mahal. It looked about four levels high, with two economic cement balconies protruding from each level. But she knew he lived on the ground level. He'd told her once about how his friend used to bash on his window to wake him up. Matty had given them all a lift one night and they'd dropped him off; she'd memorized the address instantly.

It felt peaceful, with the shade from the trees, the humming cicadas and the sting of the eucalypt smell in her nostrils. It would be a nice place to live. She went up to the door and knocked, her heart hammering. She waited for a few moments, leaning like a rag doll against the letterboxes. Looking around, she noticed the buzzers and felt instantly embarrassed, even though there was no one around. How stupid to knock on an apartment building. The buzzers had only numbers, though, not names. The choice seemed to be between sitting out the front like a stalker or pressing the buttons one at a time until she lucked out. But that might get him into trouble with the other tenants.

There was nowhere else to go. She couldn't go home; she couldn't go to Lizzie's. Pushing her fingernails into her palms, she tried to force herself not to cry. The only thing worse than him finding her sitting on his doorstep would be for him to find her sitting on his doorstep weeping like a crazy person.

Ducking under the low-hanging branches, she crept around the side of the building. If she could figure out which apartment he was in then it would all be okay. She peeked into the first window. The room was dim. It took a moment for her eyes to adjust. She gasped and ducked back down. Inside was a middle-aged man with a huge bulbous stomach sleeping naked in bed. A hysterical laugh almost escaped her, but she took some deep breaths and shuffled through the dead leaves to the next window.

There would be three apartments on the bottom level at most, so she crossed her fingers there would be no more gross naked men and straightened up to look inside. There was no one there. Just an unmade bed across from an old desktop computer, with a dividing wall from the kitchen and an open door where the carpet turned to cracked white tiles. The bathroom, she guessed. And on the floor was a scrunched-up McDonald's shirt. The window she was looking through was wide open. He was clearly not home, though. Without really thinking about it, she hoisted herself up onto the window ledge and jumped down onto his bed.

Standing in the middle of his room, Bec couldn't believe what she had just done. But she didn't leave. No, instead she lay down on the bed and took a big breath in of his smell. Stretching out on the bed, she felt the warmth of his pillow, the soft cotton of his sheets, imagining him coming home from work and slipping into them. Swinging to her feet, she went into the bathroom, looked at his toothbrush, studied the shaver and mouthwash he must use every day. Opening the cupboards in the kitchen, she inspected the dry pasta, the spices, the half-empty jar of Nutella. Noticing the dirty plates in the sink, for one crazy moment she considered washing up for him.

This was all crazy, though. Her mind seemed to clear and she realized what she was doing. She had to get out of here. Now. But as she went to the bedroom to start clambering back out the window, she heard a noise that made her heart stop beating: a key sliding into the lock.

In that split second, her mind became crystal clear. Surveying the distance, she knew she wouldn't be able to get out of the window in time. Flattening herself against the carpet, she rolled under the bed, pulling her bag and beach towel with her just as the door swung open.

He stood in the doorway in shorts and a T-shirt, a coffee in one hand and the remnants of a croissant in the other. As he turned to close the door behind him, she saw the line of sweat between his shoulder blades. She tried to not breathe, even though she felt like she was about to start hyperventilating. The noise of the door closing seemed too loud in the silence of the room. She heard him chewing on the last of the croissant, scrunching up the paper bag and throwing it into the bin. He crossed the room and the mattress squeaked above her. She could hear him swallowing the coffee and the soft beeps of his phone as he wrote a text message. Then, when it was almost too late, she realized that he could be writing a text to her. Oh, God. She slid her shaking hand inside her bag and slipped her phone out. It lit up. She quickly pressed the button to open the message, almost dropping it in the process, before the alert noise went off. Sorry last night went so badly, it said. Hope you are okay.

She swallowed. That was way too close. Her hands were shaking. The carpet was beginning to itch her neck and it stank of old cigarette smoke and damp. The box spring was just inches above her nose, and if she reached out her fingers, she could have touched the backs of Luke's ankles. She could see each brown hair up close, see each follicle they protruded from.

After a few more anxious minutes of more texting, none of which came through to her phone, the mattress squeaked again. Luke took a step forward, dropped his shorts and then his underwear, and then she saw the T-shirt fall onto the carpet, as well. Before he walked through the bathroom door, she got a look at him from the neck down: pale buttocks, pimples on his back and black curly hair almost completely concealing his flaccid penis. The bathroom door closed, the pipes squeaked and the shower began to run.

She had only a few minutes, tops.

Pulling herself out from under the bed, she got to her feet, ready to jump out of the room while she still could. Then his phone received a text. It lay on his bed and she could see from there who the text was from: Lizzie. Even though her heart was hammering, she couldn't help but pick it up. I'm okay, thanks for thinking of me.

She opened the sent message folder. He had sent Lizzie the exact same text that he'd sent her. Down the list was almost entirely girls' names, mostly hers, Lizzie's and Ellen's. She opened some at random: Always have such an amazing night with you. Been thinking about you today. They were all things he'd written to her but he'd sent them to so many other people, too.

The water stopped. Throwing the phone back onto the bed, she hoisted herself out of the window. In one swift movement she fell into the brightness of the summer morning. She ducked down and crawled back past the window of the sleeping fat man, back under the low-hanging branch and onto the glaring concrete of the front driveway. Then she started to run, without turning back.

15

Last night I had the dream again. But it's different this time. I watch Bec walk down her street and a car pulls up but she isn't scared. She says hello to the driver. She smiles as she gets in. Firstly the driver is Lizzie, and then it's Lizzie's father. Then the driver changes to Bec's mother, her eyes alight like I've never seen them, her teeth slightly pointed as she smiles a huge clownish grin. The car drives away and I hear Bec crying, knowing she's going to die.

I sip my coffee slowly. The caffeine doesn't help, though. There was no way the journalist had sent that text. He hadn't sent the first one either. I'd been so stupid to assume that.

Someone is after me. Someone wants to do to me what they did to Bec. I need to go. I should have left last night. But the street is still cordoned off, the reporters waiting for me to reveal myself. If I walk down there, my face will be on the front of every newspaper in the country. It's not just that—in my gut I know I can't just leave. To let whoever took Bec keep walking around wearing the mask of a normal person. For there to be no consequences for erasing her from this life. I know I should go, save myself. But I don't. I just sit here, drinking coffee. Feeling trapped.

My phone rings and I almost jump out of my skin. It's Lizzie.

"Hey, it's me," she says. "Listen. Jack told me what you said. I want to fix things. Do you feel like going out for a drive? Maybe grab a coffee?"

"Okay," I say. Even though I know I should say no. I know I should just leave and never look back. "There's a roadblock, though. You'll have to get the cop who's guarding it to call the house."

"That's fine. See you soon."

I watch through the front window, feeling suddenly jittery. I desperately want to tell someone. I need to tell someone. Really, the person I should be calling is Andopolis. But if I tell him about the text messages I'd have to also tell him the truth about me. I don't want to go to jail. Impersonation plus credit card fraud would definitely mean jail time. But worse, I'd have to go back. I'd have to face my stepmom. Maybe jail would be better than that.

Lizzie pulls up in a purple Volkswagen. I run out of the house and get in, pulling the jacket over myself again. As she drives slowly through the hordes of journalists, their yells get louder and louder.

"Rebecca? Bec? Is that you?"

"Where have you been, Bec?"

I hear hands banging on the windows, the clicks of shutters, scrapes of feet against cement. My heart starts to race, like they are everywhere. I press my head against my knees.

"Go away!" Liz yells, honking her horn. She revs her motor, and as the crowd quiets for a moment, she speeds away.

"Ha, I wish you hadn't missed that. Their faces... It's like they really thought I'd just run them down!" She laughs.

Pulling the jacket off slowly, I look out the windows. We're on the main road now. A moment of awkward silence.

"So, you and Jack, hey?" she says, breaking it.

"I dunno," I say. I don't want to talk about him. He's already texted me a bunch of times this morning but I hadn't replied. I knew it was cruel but I had no idea what to say.

"Don't play coy with me," she says. "He always had the most massive crush on you, you know."

"I know," I say.

"Slut," she says, smiling at me. I don't smile back.

"Let's go to that café in the Yarralumla Woods. I can grab some takeaways so we can sit in the park and no one will bother you," she says, trying to clear the air, I suppose. "Have you been there since you've been back?"

When I got in the car I was so ready to tell her everything. Now it feels impossible.

"No."

"Cool. You know, that place was really lucky. It hardly got touched by the fires."

"That's good," I say, barely listening. "Did they do a lot of damage?"

"They wiped out a few suburbs, Bec," she says, looking at me. "It was terrifying. People died. Jack and I sat on our roof watching them get closer and closer until we had to evacuate."

"Sounds awful."

"It was."

Silence again.

"How's your mom going?"

"She's okay, I guess."

"She seemed a bit weird when I was over the other day."

I tried to remember what the mother had been doing that day, when Lizzie had been standing in the doorway crying. She'd seemed the same as always.

"Weird how?"

"I haven't been around her in a really long time but I remember her being so strict. She looked like she was sleepwalking the other day, though. I almost didn't recognize her."

Strict was probably the last word I'd use to describe the mother. I couldn't imagine her being anything close to that. Except for that moment in the garage yesterday when she'd basically ordered me to get out.

"I used to be a bit scared of her. I was so sure she thought I was some dumb blonde, that you should have someone better as a best friend."

I pull off my jacket and lean back. Perhaps this coffee won't be bad. At least it will be a distraction from thinking about the text message yesterday and that awful hurt look on Jack's face when I left.

"I guess it's losing a child. It must affect people in different ways," Liz is saying.

She looks over at me, then stares down at my dress, a funny look on her face. It was one of the slightly more adult dresses in Bec's closet, made from a brown gingham material.

"Do you remember when we got that dress? It was from the Bus Depot Markets."

"Yeah," I say, and she still stares at me, as though she's expecting more. "That was a fun day."

Lizzie says nothing and I realize she's pulling over. We're next to a huge lake; there's no café around anywhere.

"Are you okay?" I ask.

She turns the car off, but doesn't say anything. She just looks blankly ahead of her, at the wide blue lake and the black swans floating over it. The clouds above are slightly grey, as though it's going to rain later.

"You know your voice sounds nothing like Bec's," she says suddenly.

My heart stops.

"I guess most people might forget what she sounded like after all this time, but I haven't."

"I don't understand," I say, desperately wishing I'd made more of an effort.

"You look a lot like her—I'll give you that. But you don't act anything like her at all."

"Lizzie," I say, trying to save it, "it's me. I'm Bec."

She turns on me, her eyes flaming.

"Don't fucking lie to me anymore. I don't know who you are but you aren't Bec."

I don't say anything. I can't. I feel so deeply ashamed.

"Do you know what happened to her?"

There is no point now. She knows.

"No. I never met her," I say.

Tears begin running down Lizzie's cheeks.

"Why would you do this? You came back and I thought she was okay. Now it's like she's gone all over again."

"I'm sorry," I whisper.

We sit in silence. Staring out at the lake. My body feels cold.

"Please don't tell anyone, Liz. Please. I couldn't stand to do it to her family."

"As if you give a shit!"

"I do." And I really did.

"Please, Liz. I'll leave. I'll tell them I want to start fresh and I'll call them every few weeks. You won't ever have to see me again."

"Get out of my fucking car." She hates me.

"Someone is threatening me. I'm scared."

"Yeah, sure."

"I need your help." She says nothing, so I continue, my words tumbling on top of each other. "I think the person who took Bec is still out there. I think it was someone she knew—"

"No more bullshit!" she yells.

"It's not bullshit, I promise."

She doesn't believe me, and who would blame her, really? There's no way she's going to help me.

"Please," I say, "just give me until tomorrow. I need to know who it is."

"I don't know. I'll think about it. But get out now. I'm worried I might hit you."

I unclip my seat belt and jump out of her car. I look back at her. Her eyes are vacant but her mouth is twisted with the force of unthinkable pain.

My head feels hot and heavy and I feel a hard pressure against my chest. I lean against a tree, forcing myself to breathe deeply. Behind me I hear Lizzie drive away.

The evil of what I've been doing hits me hard. This was unforgivable; it was the worst thing someone could do to another human being. I really was going to have to leave.

But I didn't want to. If I left and everyone still thought I was Bec, that she was safe living a new life somewhere, then that would be the end of it all. It would be final and whoever was responsible for what had really happened to her would never be punished.

I look over at the lake; its surface is perfectly reflecting the sky. Bec's body might be in there, floating in a garbage bag, weighed down by rocks. She could be anywhere. The only person who knew where she was right now was the killer. The person who'd texted me. But that gave me an advantage, because they were also the only person who would have known straightaway I wasn't who I said I was.

I think back over the time since I arrived. There must be something, some kind of sign that the person was lying.

The map on my phone directs me and I begin walking home. It is getting cold. I feel vulnerable walking out here in this barren landscape, the only figure amongst the sparse white trunks of gum trees, glowing in the fading light.

I've always been good at pretending. At playing roles. I realize that's what I've been doing here. Trying on Bec for size. Being a tourist in someone else's life. A parasite. Just like the person who had taken Bec, I am always wearing a mask, playing a character. Perhaps because I'm afraid of what will be under the mask, something ugly maybe or, worse, nothing at all.

The urge to leave Bec's life is strong now. Someone is after me. I might be killed. But I can't run away. I have to stay. I owe Bec that. Just one more day. Even if it means getting caught.

I get home just before the rain starts. My phone died and I had wandered the streets in the dark until something familiar stood out. As I approached the street I could see the glow from the cordoned-off journalists area. They had set up lights.

They had no plans to move on anytime soon. Keeping to the shadows, I watched them numbly for a few moments. They were smoking cigarettes, rubbing their hands together to keep warm. Laughing in small groups.

I didn't once consider turning around and not going back. I'd made my decision. Instead I walked around the block to the street on the other side of the cul-de-sac. I could see the second story of our house dwarfing the small cottage in front. I sneaked around the side, keeping low under lit-up windows and then jumping the back fence into our yard. I rushed to the front of the house and now, as the first drops of water begin to fall, I brace myself. Liz might have already called them. I unlock the door with frozen fingers.

"Hey, Becky!" says Paul. He's sitting in the lounge room with his iPad on his lap and his feet up. "Andrew and I were starting to get worried that you forgot we were leaving tomorrow."

"Or that you'd prefer to spend the night with your new boyfriend!" calls Andrew from the kitchen.

Lizzie hadn't called. Somehow, she'd found it in her heart to give me my last day.

"Of course I didn't forget," I say, and the relief is overwhelming. I sit down next to Paul on the couch. The warmth of him next to me is soothing. I feel safe again, just for a moment.

"Good," he says, putting an arm around me. I watch as he scrolls through his emails.

It makes me think of Jack's father, the weird way he looked

ANNA SNOEKSTRA

up at me from his iPad. He didn't seem surprised to see me that day, not like everyone else. A shudder runs through me. Paul rubs my arm, as though he thinks I'm still shivering from the cold.

The way he looked at me was all wrong. Was it because he knew? Knew I wasn't Bec because he'd killed her himself. He'd lied to the police; I knew that already. He must have had a reason to do that. The image of him dropping the hat at the vigil comes into my mind. How did I miss it before? He shouldn't have had Bec's McDonald's hat; surely she would have been wearing it on her walk home that night.

Whatever the parents are cooking smells amazing. I get up and go into the kitchen to have a look. The mom is stirring something in the pot and the father is cutting vegetables. Andrew sits at the table, tapping at his phone.

"Do you want to grate the cheese?" asks the dad, pushing the grater toward me.

"Sure," I say.

Tonight is the last night. None of them know that I will be leaving tomorrow, along with the twins. I try to push the feeling of loss away and just enjoy these precious last moments with them.

"So what are you up to tomorrow?" asks Andrew. "Seeing Vince again?"

"Maybe," I lie. "I might go and see Lizzie."

But it wasn't Lizzie I was going to see. It was her father.

16

When you are absolutely exhausted and numb and hating the world, there is nothing quite like having the house to yourself.

The twins weren't speaking to her and had gone out on their bikes to who knows where, and her parents were at work.

Bec was still in her pyjamas and she had no intention of changing out of them until she absolutely had to. For once her house felt like a safe place from the tornado her life had become. Here, she was safe from her fight with Lizzie, safe from having to look Luke in the eye, safe from Ellen's disappointment. Lying on the black leather couch in the living room, she stared at the ceiling and tried to make her mind go blank. Instead of thinking, she focused on the way the leather felt under her bare feet, the squeaking sound it made if she rubbed them against it. She tried to imagine that this cool, quiet house was her world. That the baking, bright outside didn't exist.

She had three hours until she had to go to work. Thank God she was working with neither Lizzie nor Luke. Slowly, she slid herself off from the couch. Picking up her coffee cup, she took it into the kitchen and washed it, watching the soap suds slip from its surface and gurgle down the drain. She dried it softly and then put it back in the cupboard, like she'd never used it at all. She feared turning on the television would break the spell. With nothing else to do, she went back up to her bedroom.

Yesterday she hadn't wanted to come home, afraid of a confrontation with her brothers. So she'd spent the day wandering around the city alone, sweating through her bathers. Eventually she got so sick of carrying around her beach towel she threw it in a rubbish bin.

She'd been so angry that, when Luke's face flashed into her mind, her fists would clench and she had the overwhelming urge to hit something. She had never, ever felt like that before. The steaming combination of anger and shame twisted in her stomach all day; she was sick with it.

Today she felt a bit better, though, if feeling nothing could be counted as feeling better. Sitting on her bed, she waited for the minutes to tick by. Enjoying these last few hours of being alone before she'd have to go to work and try, somehow, to put on a smile. Being alone here felt so right, so easy. But she knew it wouldn't look good, wouldn't look pretty. She saw herself from a distance for a moment: a hunched back, a blank look in her eyes, oily hair dangling limply around her face. Her gut wrenched at the familiarity of the image: when Max first got back from the hospital, he'd looked just like this.

She remembered the hurt look in Lizzie's eyes when she told her to leave, but then she also remembered Lizzie spin-

ning her and laughing and falling over on top of each other
at the party the other night. She remembered going to the
flower festival together every year, having breakfast at Gus's
at three in the afternoon and feeling like an adult, going
paddleboating and Lizzie screaming as she took them right
underneath the big fountain. Without Lizzie, her life would
be darker. When it came down to it, Luke meant nothing.
She didn't even know him. He had made himself into a mirror reflecting her own desires back at her. Lizzie was different. Lizzie was moody and opinionated and annoying and the
other half of Bec's heart. She would take on the worst things
in the world if she had Lizzie to laugh and bitch about them
with. It wasn't Luke who she should be telling everything
to; it was Lizzie. Without even thinking about it, her hand
shot out for her mobile. She called the number and waited.
It went to voice mail. But she had time. If she left now she
could go past Lizzie's house before work. She'd have only
about half an hour to plead her case, to ask for forgiveness,
but it would have to be enough.

She was only just out the door when she got that feeling
again, that awful feeling of being watched. She kept walking, determined not to look over her shoulder.

When she got to Lizzie's house she was already feeling
relieved. Just the monotonous walk up her street from the
bus stop was comforting. The dog that always barked when
you walked past his gate, the fertilizer on the garden at the
corner that always stank. Things were already getting back
to normal. She knocked softly on the door and waited. For
a moment she thought perhaps she had knocked too softly
and was about to try again, when she heard footsteps come

slowly down the stairs. The door swung open. It wasn't Lizzie's face that stared down at Bec, but her father's.

"Hi, Bec."

"Hi. Is Lizzie here?"

"Aren't I enough?" he said, smiling.

She forced a laugh, not really knowing what to say.

"She's out with Jack. Do you want to come in and wait?"

"Okay."

He took a step back and Bec walked through the doorway, brushing past him. She could smell his aftershave. She hesitated for a moment at the foot of the stairs, not sure whether to go and wait in the lounge room or go up to Lizzie's room. It felt weird to hang out with Lizzie's dad by herself, but then again, if she went and sat alone in Lizzie's room when she wasn't there, she would feel like a stalker. She sat down on their couch. Lizzie's dad sat across from her. The sliding doors were open and the sun was reflecting off the wobbling surface of the swimming pool. The chemical smell of the chlorine wafted into the room. Closing her eyes for a second, she remembered the weightless feeling of floating.

"Did you have a fight?"

"What?"

"You and Lizzie. She's been a little quiet these last couple of days."

"Quiet? I can't imagine her shutting up for even a second."

He laughed, but his eyes were serious. They didn't leave her face. Had Lizzie told him what she'd said?

He sighed. "To be young again. Those arguments that feel like the end of the world and then a week later you can't even remember what they were about."

She forced a laugh again, although this annoyed her. She

hated it when adults trivialized her life like this, but she didn't have enough fight in her today to argue.

"How long do you think she'll be?"

"I don't know. What's the hurry?"

"I've got work," she said, pulling her McDonald's cap out from her bag and showing it to him.

"Oh, yes, working for the man. You know, I used to work for Hungry Jack's."

"Really?" She couldn't care less.

"Yes. It was the 1970s and I spent a summer flipping burgers. I had long hair, too, past my shoulders."

"Yuck! You would have looked gross."

"The girls back then didn't think so. I used to have this girlfriend, before Lizzie's mom. She was a real flower child. Beautiful."

She'd never heard anyone mention Lizzie's mom in the house before. Ever.

"She had these long fingernails. That whole summer I always had scratches all over my back. She used to slice me up every time we had sex."

Bec had no idea what to say to that. Why was he telling her this? The image of him having sex made her feel sick.

"Remember last summer, when you came over when Lizzie wasn't here?"

No. She wasn't going there. For a moment she could have puked, right there on his cream carpet. Looking at her watch, she pretended to be shocked.

"Oh, no, I'm going to be late!"

She usually felt so comfortable at Lizzie's house but now she couldn't help but jump out of her seat and half run to the door.

"Do you want me to tell Lizzie you've come by? Or should it be our little secret?" He winked at her.

"Whatever," she said, not really understanding what the hell he was talking about.

He took a step in front of her and for a moment she felt like he was going to stand between her and the door. But he leaned forward and opened it for her. She squeezed past him, hating the feeling of warmth as her arm slid past his stomach. It wasn't until she heard him close the front door behind her that she realized how fast her heart was beating.

17

The sound of the front door clanging shut carries up to my room. The twins must be loading the car. They'll be leaving soon. So will I. I'm sure I can make this work. I'll go to Lizzie and Jack's dad's house. Just to talk, just to make sure. Then I can leave, call Andopolis once I get out of here. Tell him what I've found out. A part of me feels awful; I've already done so much damage to Jack's family. This isn't for me, though. It's for Bec.

It's still raining outside. I can hear the pitter-patter on the roof. This is my last day in this bedroom. I was lucky that Liz hadn't called the house yet, but I was working on borrowed time. There was no doubt in my mind that she would call eventually.

When I go downstairs the parents are bustling around, getting ready to drive the boys to the airport. After I see Jack's father I'll be leaving. I'll never be able to come back. Maybe I'll go to Melbourne this time.

"I thought your flight wasn't until midday?" I ask. It's only 9:00 a.m. I'd thought I'd have just a few more hours.

"It is," Paul says, "and now they've put that new freeway in it's only fifteen minutes' drive."

"Mom pretends she likes being early, but I think she just wants to get rid of us," adds Andrew.

"You want Bec all to yourself now, don't you?" Paul asks the mom playfully as she walks out to the car. She doesn't say anything in response; she looks a little strange, actually. I guess she's sad to say goodbye to her sons.

"You look a bit pale," Andrew says, looking at me carefully. "You don't have to come see us off if you don't want."

I was almost hoping they'd insist on me coming, anything for a bit more time.

"I've got a really bad headache," I say.

"That's okay," says Andrew, pulling me into a bear hug.

"We'll call tonight, okay?" says Paul, ruffling my hair.

"Okay," I say. I won't be here tonight.

"Do you need some ibuprofen?" asks the mom, coming back in. I hug her, breathing in her sweet smell for the last time. For the briefest time, she really was my mother. It's so hard to say goodbye.

"I'm fine," I say, not looking at her.

I stand in the shadow of the doorway as they pull out of the drive, holding my dressing gown tightly around me. I wave and smile until they turn the corner and then go back into the house and lock the door. I have half an hour, if that, to pack.

Going back upstairs, I put my phone on the charger. I'd intentionally left it off when it died, knowing Jack would probably call and having no idea how I was going to explain all this to him. I have a quick shower, trying to decide whether to leave a note. I'd have to, I can't just leave, but I have no idea what I'd write. I try to remind myself that they were never my family to begin with. Still, the sadness is overwhelming.

When I come back to my phone, I expect to see at least one missed call from Jack. But there are none. Just one text, from Lizzie. I open it quickly.

I'm sorry. I had to tell them.

The text is dated yesterday at five fifteen.

18

Bec was fifteen minutes early to work. She'd walked slowly and tried calling Lizzie again. No answer. It was beginning to get frustrating. They hadn't had a screaming argument or anything like that. Lizzie was overreacting.

There was a huge line inside McDonald's, but she sat at the back of the car park, deciding to wait until the very last moment before she went inside. It was stinking hot, and digging into her bag, she realized she must have left her cap at Lizzie's house. Great—a sunburn on top of everything else. But she still didn't go inside. Luke finished his shift as hers started and she didn't want to see him today. She never wanted to see him again.

By the time the fifteen minutes were over and she opened the doors, she was covered in sweat, and the freezing cold of the air conditioning sent a shiver down her spine. Ellen looked harassed as usual, her hair all fuzzed up around her part and the crease between her eyebrows deeper than ever. Normally she had nothing but respect for Ellen but now she seemed so pathetic. She almost rolled her eyes as Ellen acknowledged her with a curt nod. Obviously, she was still mad at Bec, still thought of her as some dramatic little kid. But she realized suddenly that she really couldn't care less what Ellen thought of her. This woman was in her twenties and she was working at McDonald's and hanging out with teenagers. What had always felt like a second, and more real, family now just felt like she was filling some gaping hole with disappointments and lies. With pathetic people who had given up on their lives.

She started serving her first customer straightaway. She could see Luke coming out of the bathroom with his backpack on and she needed an excuse not to talk to him. There was no way she was going to be able to act normal. As she filled up a large cup with lemonade for the customer, she watched Luke say goodbye to Ellen in the kitchen; smiling his easy smile that she thought was just for her and throwing an arm around Ellen so effortlessly. The anger pounded inside her again, but now she wasn't sure if it was at him or at herself for being so stupid, for falling for it so easily. A cold trickle of lemonade snaked down her sleeve as it overflowed from the cup. She banged it off quickly and shook the liquid from her arm, knowing it would be sticky for the rest of the night.

Gradually the glaring sun declined. The moon shifted from a soft thumbprint in the sky to a perfect silver circle. Luckily, the steady flow of customers kept up, so she didn't have to talk to Ellen or Matty except for barked orders.

She knew Ellen's shift would end soon and then it would be just her and Matty cleaning together. That wouldn't be so bad. She could get through that. The customers were turning from sweaty sunburnt families to drunken squealing groups of young people. No one she knew, thank God. She didn't think she could even force a smile right now. But something about the repetition was soothing. It was helping to stop her thinking. It was just words and movement without room for worries and the consuming sadness and anger that had been beginning to scare her. It was just "Can I help you?" again and again and again.

"Can I help you?" she asked, after a group of guys in polo shirts scuffled away, uncovering the girth of the huge, sweaty man behind them.

Looking up at the fat man's face, she waited for the inevitable huge order of fries and burgers. She always tried her best to stop the judgement from showing when obese people came in, but this time she didn't bother. She looked the man up and down slowly.

"Can I help you?" she said again, louder now, like the man was deaf, but he stared at her, still three steps away from the counter. His eyes looked murky and unfocused and she realized something was wrong only a second before he slumped to the floor.

"Ellen!" she yelled.

She looked over and Ellen already had the phone in her hand. Bec listened as she read off the address to the operator, then watched as she went over to the man and knelt down.

"Are you all right? Can you hear me, sir?" she asked. The fat man's face was turning blue. Ellen looked up at her sharply.

"Bec!" she said, like she was angry.

"What? What can I do?"

"Keep serving," she said.

★ ★ ★

It didn't take long for the paramedics to come. Bec had thought the ambulance outside would deter people, but it didn't. People just stepped over the man's bulging body and came up and ordered from her, then took their burger to a table to watch the scene, like it was happening on a television on the wall.

Later on, it was her job to mop up the man's urine. He'd pissed himself at some point and the puddle gleamed in the centre of the store. *This is the worst thing ever,* she thought. Worse than when she had to clean behind the deep fryer, and the oil had solidified into greasy mountains speckled with dead flies. Worse than anything.

When everyone left, she and Matty cleaned up in silence. He didn't even try to talk to her. Normally she would worry whether he was angry with her, but right now she didn't care. She hated it here now. It felt like her real home. A cold place.

19

2014

Who did you talk to? No one has said anything!

Lizzie doesn't answer. While I'm waiting, it clicks into full focus in my brain. The thing that had been niggling at me at Lizzie's house, the half-formed memory that my mind knew was important. Something that hadn't ever quite fitted.

The parents had never asked. In some way or other, everyone else had hinted at the question or asked it outright. But neither of the parents had. Not from when I first spoke to the mother from the police station until now: they'd never asked where I'd been. Coldness takes over my body. I pull the dressing gown back on top of the towel and over my wet skin and put the phone in my pocket.

The door to the garage creaks when it opens. I stand in the position I'd been in the night before last, then look over my shoulder. The mother had been looking at the two large cardboard boxes, carefully closed up with masking tape.

I unpeel the masking tape from the first box. It makes a

dull tearing noise. I hesitate for a second, my hands shaking, then pull the flaps open. The inside is full of books. I pull the books out, waiting, expecting to find human hair or bones. But there's nothing. The dust gets up my nose and I sneeze, scaring myself as the loud noise fills the room.

I unpeel the masking tape from the second box. But I can't look. I know what I might find. I don't want to see her face. But I have to open it. Slowly I pull open the flaps. More books. I pull these out recklessly, but it's obvious they're all that's in here. I put them back, my heartbeat slowing.

I was wrong.

Thank God, I was wrong.

I could almost laugh. My head is swirling. This is all so crazy. Nothing makes any sense. I need to get out of here. The stair squeaks under my bare foot as I step up toward the laundry door. I stop dead, looking down at my dirty toes. There are two stairs left before the laundry.

Pushing the cardboard boxes aside, I stare at the small door that goes under the house. I won't let myself hesitate this time. I lean down and pull it open. Instantly I have to cover my mouth. The smell is horrendous. I start to gag. But I can't stop. I force myself to look into the stinking blackness. There she is. Rebecca Winter. Curled up in a ball like a sleeping child. Brown bones, some remnants of flesh still attached, the back of her skull caved in.

20

Bec, 17 January 2003

Bec slowly walked up the hill after getting off the bus. She wasn't in a hurry; she already knew there wouldn't be any comfort waiting for her. Sweat slipped down her neck. She wiped it away, her skin feeling greasy. The fat and oil from the kitchen would always cling to the crevices of her face after work, the cranny between her nose and cheek, behind her ear, under the cleft of her jawline. She stopped wiping. Instead she let it flow out of her pores and push out the thick grease of the dead cows with her own living oil. The heat felt suffocating. The air itself smelt burnt and it stung her throat.

When Bec finished work she'd looked at her phone, hoping for a moment that there would be missed calls from Liz. But her screen was blank. She didn't want to think forward, to imagine going through the summer without Liz; to go back to school and not be friends anymore. More than anything, she wished she could take back the last week of her life. She wished she'd never said such mean things to Lizzie; she wished they'd never planned to do the stupid exorcism at all. If she had only done what she usually did, and forgot all about the presence in her room, the strange things that happened at her house, everything would be normal now. No one would be annoyed with her and she wouldn't be angry at everyone and everything.

Turning the corner, she could see her house at the top of the hill. For a moment she felt like her throat might close up. Stopping for a moment, she turned away from the house and breathed slowly. In through the nose, out through the mouth, until her throat loosened again. Her phone buzzed and a stream of joy and relief went through her. She pulled it out of her pocket, her hands shaking slightly in their hastiness. But it was Luke.

Hope you are doing okay, been thinking of you still.

Before she could even process it she had thrown her phone away from her, not being able to repress the burning anger this time. She wanted to hit something, to break something. She ran up the hill. She didn't want to have this violence and hatred inside her. She wished she could purge it out somehow. Unlocking her front door as quietly as she could, she ran up the stairs, pulled her clothes off in the dark and got into bed. Closing her eyes tight and hoping, somehow, that the feeling of nothingness she'd felt this morning could come back and replace the hate that was taking over her body.

21

I stand over the bones, knowing I need to turn away, knowing I need to run. But I can't bring myself to close the little door, to lock her back into the stinking dark. My head is spinning and my vision is pulsing. I can smell her, smell the last of her decaying hair and flesh. I bend over, sure I am going to be sick. Nothing comes.

The garage door vibrates slightly, the noise amplified in the silence as the car comes up the street. The squeak of rubber as its wheels turn and it pulls into the driveway. For one sickening second I think the door might open, that they'll see me standing there, half-dressed, over the skeleton of their daughter. But the car stops and the engine cuts and I hear the car doors open. I have a few seconds.

The door to the crawl space fits into place with a click and I slide the cardboard boxes back in front of it. They'll be walking down the path now. The scrape of metal on metal as their key turns in the lock. I run back into the laundry, shutting the garage door the instant before the front door opens. Oh, God. They'll see me coming out of here. They'll know I saw it. I stand motionless in the laundry, trying not to make a sound.

"Bec?"

The tiles are cold under my bare feet. The dryer whirls around quietly. As long as they don't think I saw it I still have some time, if I can just get out of the house.

"Becky?"

I can hear the mother's feet shuffling on the carpet. She's almost at the laundry, about to go up the stairs to my room, but she'll see me as she passes.

"How did it go?" I call back, randomly pressing buttons on the washing machine.

"What are you doing in here, honey?" the mom says. Her face looks different as she stands in the doorway—her eyes look shiny and her skin is strangely waxen—but she's smiling. She looks happy.

"I can't figure out how to make it work. I want to put a load in."

"I'll do that, honey. You should be lying down if your head hurts," she says.

"I know. I just want to help," I say, forcing myself to speak as normally as I can, even though my limbs are quivering, desperate to run. Even hearing the fear in my voice might be enough. They can't know.

"That's nice of you, Bec. Where are your clothes, though?"

"I left them upstairs."

"Well, go and get them."

I force myself to turn slowly, to walk and not run. She turns the machine on, water gushing into the empty barrel.

"Bec?" My shoulders tense.

"Yes."

"Your robe is filthy."

I look down at it. The hem is dark with muck from kneeling in the garage.

"It must be from when I went outside to say goodbye to you," I say weakly. She knows I didn't go outside.

"Well, give it here, then."

"I can bring it down with the rest." My voice sounds strange, higher and forced, but I can't help it.

"Before it stains," she says, her arm outstretched.

She's not asking. I pull it off, feeling horribly exposed in just my towel. She takes it from me. And, as she does, my phone starts ringing. The pocket of the robe lights up. She doesn't stop, though; she doesn't hand it back.

"What are you doing? My mobile!" I yell, but she drops it into the machine. I lunge over, plunging my hands elbow deep into the hot gushing water. The ringing softens as it submerges, warbling as I pull the phone from the robe's sodden pocket. It stops ringing; the screen is black.

The mother pulls detergent and fabric softener out of the cupboards, ignoring me. She did it on purpose. There was no way she didn't hear it ring. Maybe she even saw it in my pocket, and that's why she insisted on taking my robe. I run away from her, up the stairs, wrapping my arms around the small towel that covers me.

I close the door to my room and wedge a chair under it, then pull on some of the new clothes; they itch and smell of plastic, but it's so much better than being naked. I sit down on the bed. This is really happening. My body starts trembling.

They killed her. One of them killed Bec and pushed her

into that dark hole. My breath starts coming in short bursts. They knew. This whole time, one of them knew. At least. They'd just been biding their time, waiting for Andopolis to lose interest, waiting for Paul and Andrew to leave. I wrap myself up in a tight ball, trying to smother the sound of my shallow breathing. I can't panic. I have to get out of here. But all I can think about is her skeleton under the house, balled up like a scared little kid. It has been here this whole time, hidden in the dark.

The window. I push myself up. The reporters are too far away to hear anything, but I can see them there. Miniature men with miniature cameras. If I could see them, maybe they could see me. I press myself against the window, waving wildly. One guy puts out his cigarette. The rest of them don't even move. I could try yelling out to them, but the parents might hear before they do. I could jump out. It's two stories, so I might break something, but I'm sure they would notice me if I was falling through the air. I have no other choice. I try to open the window, but it doesn't budge. Putting everything I've got into it, I pull until my muscles feel like they're ripping, but it won't budge. It's painted shut. I slide my fingernails underneath it and pull, screaming silently as they tear under the strain. It doesn't work; my fingertips are throbbing and bloody. I begin to breathlessly cry. I can't open it. The only way out is through the front door and I don't want to go back down there. I feel like Rapunzel, locked at the top of a tower. No way out. I could try to break the window, but the glass is thick and they would almost definitely hear it before I got a chance to escape. Then they'd know. I would be bundled up next to Bec, twins rotting together.

No. As long as they didn't think that I was on to them maybe I could still just leave. Maybe I can walk out of the front door like I have done so many times. Wiping my wet cheeks, I force myself to breathe. I am a good actor. I can do this.

The house is silent as I slink out of Bec's room. The only sound is the faint whirr of the washing machine. I hold a pile of dirty clothes, just in case. My heart pounds as I walk silently down the stairs. The front door gets closer. Five steps away, three. Then I am there, at the foot of the stairs. The front door just a few paces in front of me.

"Bec?" I turn to see the mother standing in the living room. She's holding a pair of kitchen scissors. The dad is sitting on the couch, watching me.

"Yes?"

"Where are you going?"

"I have to see Andopolis," I lie. "He'll be here any minute."

"You're bringing him your dirty laundry?" says the dad. I don't know what to say.

"Let him come inside for once. If you've got a headache you might be getting sick. You shouldn't have to wait outside in the cold," she says, as though nothing is wrong. As though she is not holding a pair of sharp silver scissors in front of her.

I look from them to the door. I might be able to make it before she plunged those scissors into my back. The dad stands up, taking a step between me and the door. He takes the washing out of my hands.

"Do as your mothers asks," he says.

"I was wondering if you'd let me fix your hair?" she says, eyeing my split ends. I swallow.

"Okay."

She seats me in the kitchen and puts a towel around my shoulders. The dad stands behind us, watching.

"Your hair was always so pretty. I can't believe you've let it get this bad," she says, softly brushing it. The bristles scrape against my scalp.

"This won't take long, don't worry. Vince can come in and have a chat with me and your father. I would like to know how it's all going."

I try to turn to look and see if the father is still in the room with us. She jerks my head back, so I am facing forward.

"We don't want it to be crooked."

The scissors are cold against the back of my neck; I hear the sharpness of them as they snip through my hair. I hold my hands tightly together under the towel.

"This is going to look so much better."

"Thanks." My voice is strange and high again; I can hear my own fear in it. But she doesn't seem to.

"Nice and neat like it used to be." I can feel her breath against my bare skin as she talks.

A strange noise comes from somewhere in the house. A kind of strangled crying.

"What was that?"

"What, honey?"

"That noise."

"I didn't hear anything."

"Where's Dad?"

"He's probably having a nap."

I hear the noise again. A painful sound.

"Chin up," says the mother, wrenching my face up so I'm looking at her. She slides the scissors next to my ear.

"I really should see if Andopolis is here yet," I say, looking straight into her eyes. How had I never noticed how strange her eyes looked, glazed and shiny and never quite focusing on you?

"Almost finished," she says.

A loud echoing bang. I jolt in my seat.

"Careful, honey. I don't want to make a mess of it."

"What was that?"

She doesn't answer. The scissors snip again and again. I can feel the tears starting to fall and I can't stop them. That sounded like a gunshot. I need to get out. But with one slice of those things she could slit my throat.

"Please, Mom!"

"One second, Becky," she says.

I cry silently, listening for the father, but hearing only silence. Then she pulls the towel off.

"Go and have a look in the mirror!" she says. "I think you'll like it."

I turn quickly, half running to the front door. She's letting me out. I can go. I turn the handle, but it doesn't move. The door is unlocked, but it won't open. I throw my body against it, desperately trying to force it open.

"Careful, Bec. You'll break it," says the mom, walking past me with a dustpan and brush.

I notice something wedged underneath the door from either side. I throw myself at it again, my shoulder crunching painfully, but it doesn't budge.

Out of the corner of my eye I see Bec's face. Her mouth

crumpled in pain, her eyes full of fear. I whip around. It's the hallway mirror I'm seeing, my own reflection. My hair has been cut into the same neat bob as Bec's. I'm seeing what she saw just before she died. I finally know what happened to her and now we're sharing the same fate.

Then I smell smoke.

22

[faded mirror-image text from previous page bleed-through]

Bec, 18 January 2003

Bec wanted to start the day off right. She made her muesli slowly, chopping an apple into slices to mix in. Something she meant to do every morning but never bothered with. A proper breakfast was important. That's what her mom always said. She ate slowly. There was no rush, after all. It's not like she had any friends to see. Bec decided to do the dishes, too, perhaps to put off deciding how to spend the day. She cleaned her bowl and coffee cup carefully, drying them and putting them back in the cupboard like her mom always did.

It was amazing how much difference sleep could make. Last night, Bec had felt an overwhelming sense of impending doom. But today, that seemed so silly. So dramatic. She remembered she'd felt that way in the past and nothing bad had ever happened.

She had a feeling deep in her gut this morning that everything was going to be okay. All the dark feelings of the night before were gone and she didn't feel so helpless anymore. Today, she would change things. She would call Ellen and tell her she didn't want to do closes anymore. Then she'd text Lizzie and tell her that she could have as much space as she needed and that she was sorry. It wouldn't fix everything, but having a plan made her feel a lot better. Everything could be put back into place; she was sure of it. As long as she could find her phone, that was. She couldn't believe she had enough anger inside her last night to throw it like that. She almost laughed, imagining what that must have looked like, but she was also a little bit proud of how tough she would have looked.

After her shower she put on a clean cotton dress. She wasn't going to hang around all day moping, she decided. She was going to go out, somewhere. Maybe get in touch with someone from school she hadn't seen in a while. After all, it was getting ridiculous to have only one best friend. There were tons of people at school who she knew wanted to hang out with her more, but she had always been so content with her life the way it was that she would blow them off. Not today. She spent a long time in front of the mirror, making sure her hair was perfectly straightened and trying to get her makeup the best it had ever looked. There was something about looking good that made everything feel so much more in control.

She stood up, turned around, counted to three and then whirled back around and examined herself. In the millisecond before her eyes adjusted to the familiarity of her own face, she saw a pretty, carefree young woman. Good. Now she'd have to go and dig around someone's front yard for her phone.

Something flashed across her doorway, something that wasn't meant to be part of the image. It was Paul, and he was holding a kitchen knife. He didn't look into her room but kept walking; she could hear his feet padding lightly down stairs and the door to the garage open and close.

Bec began to slowly put away her makeup. Mascara, blush, foundation—all back in the box she kept it in. Her hand was steady. Looking at herself in the mirror again, her eyes didn't adjust. She didn't recognize the white circle reflected in the glass. Her fingernails pushed down into the flesh of her hands and somehow she had to stop herself from thinking about it. Tiny crescents were left indented across her palm.

Without deciding, she left her bedroom and stood at the crest of the stairs. One step down and then another.

As she did, the block in her mind that stopped her thinking about the secret slipped away.

She tried to push them out, but it was too late. The block was gone and all the things she didn't want to think about were in front of her.

They'd said they were the only ones who were real. She remembered standing in their bedroom, half turned toward the door. Them smelling of bath time and clean children's skin. The last light of the long summer day blocked out by the closed blinds.

"Does that mean you hate me?"

"Yes."

Her mind flashed through the dead beetle collection she'd found in their closet, the strange emotionless look they sometimes had in their eyes that she'd learned to ignore, the clumps of feathers she'd sometimes find in the garden and every so often a dead, mangled bird. She'd hoped it was the cat getting them. But that was before. She could ignore it then, easily. That was before she knew.

That day. Last summer. She was meant to be babysitting them. She didn't want to think about this, but it started unspooling in her mind without her being able to stop it. Every time she was happy they'd tell her she was ugly, and every time she was angry and broody they would crack jokes and give her soft hugs. If Lizzie was there it would have been different. If she'd had her job at McDonald's it might not have happened. Her mom had given her ten dollars a day to look after them. When she'd agreed, she hadn't known what it would be like. Eventually she'd stormed out of the house. She'd sat for an hour on the steps of the local shops, slowly devouring a killer python jelly and watching the families come and go, the tail of the jelly getting smaller and smaller as she sucked it down to sugar water.

Bec had heard the lawnmower as she walked up the hill, but she hadn't really noticed. It was just like any other summer sound that had no significance: the warble of a magpie, the hum of a cicada. Then she realized the sound was coming from her own yard. She'd broken out into a run, not knowing what to expect but knowing it was going to be something bad. Little kids don't mow the lawn.

She tried to stop the memory there. Tried to force herself to think of something else, to think of what she looked like from the outside, standing on the staircase like that. If her dress looked nice, if it was too short. But she couldn't push her thoughts outward. She couldn't imagine herself here and now. She could only see herself back then, running up the side of the house. Standing panting in the backyard.

It had taken her a second to realize what was going on. The lawnmower was running and the boys were giggling wildly, but they had their backs to her and she couldn't work out why. Then she heard the yowl of the cat over the motor.

Molly was buried in the ground up to her neck and the boys were mowing toward her. Her eyes were gaping wide and her ears were slicked back against her head. She was straining, trying to free herself. But it was too late, it was already too late. Bec had only enough time to look away before the mower went over Molly. The engine stuttered for a moment, then went back to normal. Her brothers turned around when she started to scream. There had been so much blood. She'd run to Lizzie's house, forgetting she wasn't there.

Lizzie's dad and brother had smiled at her like it meant something.

It wasn't a thing her head could process. Bec realized quickly that it was better just not to think about it at all. Paul and Andrew were always sweet to her after that and she found that she couldn't help but love them. This ugliness didn't belong in her life.

She stood at the bottom of the stairs, her body feeling cold and numb. She could just go back up to her room, grab her bag and shoes and leave. Beetles, birds, cats, dogs. As the twins got bigger, so did their prey.

The laundry door swung open silently. The light was on but it was empty. She took a step inside, half thinking they might be hiding somewhere, when the door slammed shut. She whirled around just as Paul jumped off the cupboard behind it, a brick raised above his head. Her arm shot out and connected with the brick, making a sickening thudding sound.

Her vision turned white for a moment and a sharp hot pain ran up her arm.

"You didn't get her!"

Bec hit the floor, falling from the force of the impact.

"Only cos you slammed the door."

"You should have let me. I got her so good last time."

"Yeah, but it was my turn. It's better this way anyway."

Her vision slopped and twisted; she felt like she might be sick.

Something tugged against her wrist. It was Andrew, tying her old skipping rope around her wrist. The rope was blotched with red stains.

The half memory of the Maltese terrier they were torturing in the basement earlier in the week came back to her with such force that it almost pushed the wind from her lungs. The images were hazy, blurring and running together. But she remembered the blood pouring out of its opened-up chest. She remembered Paul dragging the half-dead thing across the ground with the skipping rope. The sound it made was like a human scream.

She pushed herself to her feet, shoving Andrew away from her. Adrenaline was pumping through her now; she couldn't feel pain in her arm anymore.

"You've been following me, haven't you?"

They just stared at her with their identical blue eyes.

"We wanted to see where you go."

"And you were the ones who smashed me in the head that day?"

"You forgot to take us to the pool."

She'd seen their bikes tossed in a pile in the driveway as she walked from the car into the house. She'd even noticed one of the wheels still slowly spinning. Maybe she'd known then.

"Is that why you are doing this to me now? Because I didn't take you to Big Splash?"

The image of the superglue and razor blades she'd seen in Paul's backpack was still fresh. She imagined slippery wet legs going full speed down the water slide toward the blades. That was something she couldn't ignore.

"We're just sick of you. We think you are going to tell on us—"

"And we've never tried it on a person before."

Then she saw the glint. The knife was in Paul's pocket.

"You're fucked! You are both so fucked!"

Their faces broke open at that, and they started giggling in the way she always loved.

"You're naughty, Becky. You're not meant to use that word."

Something inside her broke. She pushed Paul over, using all her strength. He yelped as his side hit the ground. She grabbed the knife out of his pocket and held it above her head. Andrew grabbed at her, clawing at her arms and back, trying to climb up her body. She pushed him off, sending him flying across the room. She didn't realize he would be so light. A moment of shocked silence and then Andrew sniffed, tears welling up in his eyes.

"You hurt me, Becky."

Her mind was all muddled up. Every part of her wanted to go over to him, to make sure he was okay.

Paul looked over at Andrew and Bec saw something pass between them.

"We're sorry, too," said Paul, his eyes filling with tears, as well. "We were only fooling around. We love you."

They pulled themselves up and came up to her, putting their arms around her gently. She still held the knife up high.

"We just want you to spend more time with us, okay?" Paul looked up at her.

"Okay," she said. Her voice was hoarse.

Later, when she goes into the kitchen, the sky has turned red.

23

The house is quiet. There is no sound from the parents' bedroom. I hear the mom pottering around softly in the kitchen.
The acrid smell of smoke still lingers in the air, though I can't
tell where it is coming from. It was faint to begin with, like
a burnt dinner. But now I can feel my eyes begin to sting
from the thin haze.

I am Bec. I am living her final hours.

I sit on the sofa, waiting. Waiting to die like she did. It
makes sense this way, I realize. I was living her life, so I should
die her death. There is no way out. I run my hands over the
cotton dress, soothing myself, waiting for something to happen. I wonder what Bec had thought about before she died.
Had she remembered her brothers or thought about the career
she would never have, the husband she would never meet?
Had she been angry with her parents for this ultimate be-
trayal, or, when the time came, did she still love them? Ac-
cept that this was her fate?

I keep running my hands down the sides of the dress. My mother used to rub my back like this when I cried. I thought I had no memories of her, but this one comes back full force. I rub my knees, too. They jut out of the grey cotton, cold and covered in goose bumps. I hadn't had time to put stockings on. A thin white scar runs the curve of my knee. I touch it with my fingertip and a sudden hysterical giggle escapes me. When I was eight, I'd tried to do a trick on the skate ramp with my bike. My mom had just died and I had felt reckless and desperate to prove myself. I still remember the laughs of the teenagers, the world tipping upside down and realizing I was going to hurt myself the moment before the impact. The smell of hot concrete and steel.

And with that everything comes into sharp focus.

I am not Bec. I had my own life before this, my own identity, and I could have it back.

I have to call for help. It's a risk. If they hear me then it's over, but I've got to try. I have got to at least try to survive this. I take a deep breath and walk quietly into the kitchen. The mom is at the sink. She has taken all the crockery out of the cupboards and is hand washing it again, scrubbing at the squeaky-clean porcelain.

I move slowly and quietly, taking the cordless phone from its stand on the bench. The phone beeps as it's released. I wince.

"Do you like it?" the mom says.

"What?"

"The haircut?"

"Oh. Yes, I do."

"Good. I'm glad. I think your brothers like it better this way."

"They've gone home. Remember?"

"They'll be happy to see I've neatened you up."

"I guess."

She hasn't turned to look at me yet. She keeps doing the dishes, methodically cleaning each one.

"Good idea to call Vince, honey," she said. "Find out what's keeping him."

Was that a threat? Was she trying to tell me she was on to me, trying to call my bluff? I back out of the kitchen. She still doesn't turn her head, doesn't slow down or speed up.

I dial the police and hold the phone to my ear, ready to whisper. But there's no sound of ringing. Instead I hear the thick silence of another room. The other phone, it must be off the hook. The one in the parents' room. I don't let myself hesitate; I don't let myself imagine the father sitting on the bed waiting for me.

Their door is open an inch but I can't see inside. I put out my hand to push it all the way but I can't bring myself to do it. I'm too scared. My heart is hammering and my whole body is shaking. The doorknob is cold under the pads of my fingers. I have to do it.

My mouth opens to scream as the image opens up in front of me. But no sound comes out. The white sheets are red. Sopping with congealing blood. The father lies in the red pool. I know it's the father only from his clothes. He's propped up in the bed, his hands around a sawn-off shotgun. His face and brain are all over the white wall behind him. Next to him is an empty bottle of whisky. On the pillow next to him is a roughly scrawled note.

I'm sorry, I couldn't keep pretending.

Lying on the floor is the phone, knocked off its hook. I

notice a gory piece of skull on the cream carpet near my feet. The mom will hate that; it will definitely leave a stain.

My vision starts to dim. Everything feels cold. I turn away, leaning against the wall. My muscles tingle and I realize I'm sliding down the wall to the floor, but I can't help it. I just let myself fall. I hear the soft thud as my head hits the floorboards but I don't feel it. I see my stepmom in front of me, the way she looked the night I left. Her face creased up with anger, sweat dripping down her temple from the force of it. Spit flew from her mouth as she yelled.

She wanted me to go to jail. She was happy I wouldn't be part of her new family. I hadn't meant to push her. But all of a sudden she was by my feet. The dishwasher had been open and she'd fallen sideways, protruding belly clipping the corner. It made a shockingly loud crashing noise. She rolled over onto her back. Red blossomed at the crotch of her beige maternity pants.

I focus on breathing. In, out. Don't stop. In, out. Just keep breathing and everything will be okay. My vision begins to get brighter. My head begins to feel cold where it touches the floor. I can smell the lemon bleach on the wood and the smoke; the smoke smells stronger now. Thin vapor skirts across the floorboards in front of me.

I force myself to get up, pushing the image of what I've just seen out of my head. I just focus on breathing. In, out. The smoke is coming from the laundry. I press my weight against the wall and stagger toward the doorway. Going toward the sound of the washing machine, spinning my dressing gown around in circles. I can't see anything in there at first. Then thin fingers of smoke creep through the crack underneath the door connecting to the garage.

Through the silence, I hear the mother's voice. She speaks and then pauses, and then continues. Like there is someone else there, but I hear no other voice. I bite down on my lip as hard as I can. The pain cuts through my nausea. I stare at my feet as I walk toward the father. I don't look at his face; I don't let myself hesitate. I pull the gun out of his grip. His blood is hot against my hand. A sob comes out of my mouth before I can stop it, but I force the feelings back down and look at the gun. I've never touched one before. The end of it has been sawn off jaggedly; he must have done it himself. I imagine him for a moment, sawing off a shotgun in his grey work suit.

I walk toward the kitchen, listening. Breathing softly.

"It's okay, honey. Don't worry."

Then a pause.

"Yes, I'll just stay here."

A pause. I almost hear something in it, something so low it is barely audible.

"Yes. Of course."

I get closer. I do hear something else. Another voice. A man's voice, talking in a soft deep whisper.

My footstep creaks. The voices stop. I take another step into the kitchen. The mother is standing there alone, her hands in the sink.

"Mom?"

She turns and smiles. She doesn't even look at the gun under my arm.

"Yes, sweetheart?"

"Who else is here?"

"When?"

"Just then. I heard another voice. There's someone else here."

"Don't be silly, honey. They're always here."

"Who?"

"Your brothers."

Something hard smashes into the back of my head. Blinded by pain, I crumple to the floor.

"Hey, it was my turn!"

"I wanted to make up for last time."

"Yeah, only took you ten years."

The brothers' voices waft around me. I can't tell them apart. They sound the same, like one person speaking to themselves. When I try to open my eyes, they're already open. But I can't see. There're only vague shapes moving in whiteness.

"Shut up!"

"No, you shut up!"

"Don't argue, boys." The mother's voice is quiet.

"Where's Dad?"

"He's sleeping."

"Pissed again, is he?"

More shuffling of feet. My throat is burning, but I can't cough. I feel the gun being kicked out from under my arm.

"Becky, Becky, how did you get this?"

"We're not complaining, Becky. We're impressed. Little Becky leaves a girl and comes back GI Jane."

They both laugh. Then one gets closer, his heat right against me.

"Oh, I've missed Molly so much," says one of the twins—Andrew, I think—in a high-pitched girlie voice. He's close now, right next to me. "Why'd you have to threaten us, Bec?"

"Have you told Vince anything?"

"If you have we'll kill you!"

"Aren't we going to kill her anyway?"

"Shut up! She doesn't need to know that."

I feel a foot under my head, pulling my chin up.

"So what did you tell him?"

I can't speak. I want to, but I can't.

"Tell us!" Another deep, thick pain as a shoe collides with my side.

"Oh, please, boys. Please leave her alone!" says the mother. Silence.

"What did we tell you, Mom?"

Silence.

"What's the rule?"

"No talking back," she says.

"That's right." I can hear him snicker.

"Now, what do you say when someone asks?"

"It had nothing to do with the boys." Her voice is deeper, filled with pain as she recites, "They already checked onto their flights. It must have been my daughter. She's disturbed."

"Good Mommy."

"Let's get out of here." One of them is coughing.

"You stay there," the other says to me, a smirk in his voice. Then I hear the back door unlock and open and the sound of them jumping over the fence. And then silence. Thick, deep silence. The white gets thicker and I can feel myself slipping again.

When the white starts dimming, I don't fight the darkness. I ride it into oblivion.

24

I'm in the snow with my dad. We're sitting on the chairlift, float-ing through white. I'm scared. He puts a soft arm around me and I snuggle into his parka. If I'm with him, I'll be safe. Soon we'll be back in our cabin drinking hot chocolate. My eyes and nose sting, but not from the biting cold. No. They burn. The white moves and shifts around me; billowing clouds of snow. There is a shadow moving in the white. Something cold touches my face. The chairlift pulls me forward and I slide through the white.

My throat and nose are filled with burning smoke. I cough, trying to get the ash out of me. The cough turns to dry retching.

"Don't even think about puking."

I look around. I'm in the back seat of a moving car. I try to lift my head to see who is driving but it pounds violently.

"Feeling okay?" It's Lizzie's voice.

"No. What happened?" I croak, bringing on another pain-ful coughing fit.

She waits for me to stop before answering.

"I figured out something was wrong from your text. I called but then your phone went dead and I wanted to know what the hell was going on. Me and Jack came over but we got stuck at the gates arguing with the cop. He wouldn't let us through. So Jack got out and started screaming his head off, telling the cop he wasn't the boss of him. He was just distracting them, pretending to be some meathead. It would have been funny if I wasn't so scared." She laughs, a dull empty laugh. "Anyway, while they were trying to figure out what he was on about, I drove straight through that damn barrier. There was smoke coming out of the house. Idiot was so focused on keeping people out he didn't even notice."

"The mother?" I whisper.

"I tried." Lizzie pauses. "It was the scariest thing I'd ever seen. She wouldn't move. She just stood there, doing the dishes, with the room full of smoke. But the journalists and Jack came in as I pulled you out. I'm sure they got her."

"Jack?"

"Do you really want to know?"

I don't. I want to ask her where we're going but it hurts too much to speak. So I just lie still, watching the roof of the car as we drive. After a while she pulls into a parking space and turns off the car. She turns around to look at me.

"Okay, here's the deal. We're at Goulburn hospital. It's far enough out of Canberra that they won't recognize you. I want you to give them your real name, and when you get back to wherever you came from, I want you to call the cops and tell them everything that went on today. Okay?"

I nod.

"Good. Now get out of my car. I'm not carrying you again. You're heavier than you look."

I pull myself out slowly, every movement ripping pain through my broken body. I open the car door, wondering for a second if I should tell her that I found Bec's body. We lock eyes and I can see the pain already bubbling behind her steely resolve.

25

Bec, 18 January 2003

The world didn't make sense. The sky was turning red and it was getting dark in the kitchen, even though it was just past noon. Her brothers had tried to kill her.

Bec sat down at the kitchen table and carefully put the knife down in front of her. Really, she should put it back in the drawer, but she didn't want to let it out of her sight. She envisioned it sliding into her side while she slept. Imagined how it would feel to have that cold silver slice through her skin and muscle.

Quietly, she walked back up the stairs to her bedroom. She could hear the whispering in the boys' room stop abruptly as she reached the top stair.

In the back of her closet was a large gym bag she'd stolen from Myer last year. It was back when she still got a thrill from shoplifting. She knew she'd never use the thing, but she just wanted to see if she could walk out of the store with something so conspicuous and get away with it. Turned out she could.

Bec paused for a moment, trying to remember if she'd ever shown it to her mom. She was fairly sure she hadn't. It wouldn't be missed.

She was halfway through packing when her arm started to hurt. Really deeply hurt. There was a graze where the brick hit and she'd been hoping that was it, but the dull pulsing felt like it was getting stronger and stronger. Tentatively she pressed her finger into her flesh. The pain was sharp; it made tears instantly spring to her eyes. Quickly, she blinked them away.

She chose things her mom wouldn't notice were gone. A thick jacket at the back of her closet that she'd never really worn. It always seemed too practical. Last year's jeans. A few old T-shirts. After a moment's hesitation, she picked up her McDonald's clothes from the floor and put them in her bag and then made her bed.

She'd have to leave her makeup behind. It would be too obvious. The photos would have to stay where they were on the walls, too. She took one, though; she had to take one. A picture of her and Lizzie, smiling, cheeks pressed together.

Her reflection frightened her. The makeup smudged around her eyes, both knees scabby. Dirt on her face and scratches up her arms from Andrew's fingernails. She used makeup wipes to clean herself up as best she could, too afraid to have a shower. Then she opened the back of the doll and started pulling out the money and stuffing it into a pocket of the bag. Part of her must have known this was going to happen; she had been preparing for a long time.

Her heart didn't pound as she walked out her front door and down the hill. She didn't even look back. The sky had gone a dark red and the air made her eyes water. The red fog even covered the sun, so it glowed vibrant crimson.

For a moment she thought of Lizzie, and the first real pain hit her. She tried to push it away. She had to do it. She knew she'd always love them no matter what. If she stayed they'd get her eventually. In her sleep perhaps, or maybe they'd wait until they were big enough to overpower her. She could tell her parents, but in her heart she knew there was nothing they could do. In fact, if she really thought about it, they probably already knew. If she removed herself then she removed the problem. They wouldn't have to pick. It was better this way.

As she walked toward the city, the streets became darker and darker. The traffic lights flashed orange. The heat was overwhelming, her body was slick with sweat and her skin burnt. She wondered if she'd even make it to the bus depot, if they'd let her on a bus to Sydney. Perhaps Matty was right about the day of reckoning. Black ash had begun to fall from the sky around her like snow. But she kept going. Kept blindly walking, knowing she would never go back.

26

2015

I've given up cigarettes.

It's been a year, but even now, walking through a cloud of someone else's nicotine is enough to make me gag.

When I arrived at the hospital they had forbidden me from speaking and strapped an oxygen mask to my face. The only thing I'd managed to say was my name. My real name. Then they'd pushed a tube down my throat to suck out the black mess in my lungs.

The doctor said I was lucky. The smoke inhalation could have easily killed me if I'd been in that house just a few minutes longer. I shiver, although it's stinking hot today. As hard as it is to avoid, I try not to think about that house.

Ducking and weaving through the peak-hour crowd, I make my way toward the railway station. It's eight in the morning, the sun is bright and I'm on my way to the interstate platform. It'll take me a long time to get where I need to go. But that doesn't bother me. It'll be well worth the journey. There's someone I need to see.

I hate Perth central station. It seems like it's either packed with suits pushing and shoving, or it's deserted except for a few creeps eyeing you from the shadows. There's never any in-between. Apart from that, it seems to always smell slightly of stale urine. Summer was the worst, because the concrete absorbed the sun and then it smelt like hot stale urine. I pinch my nose as I wait in line to buy my ticket, hoping the smell won't stick to me. I had my best clothes on, and I'd even attempted to do my hair. Even though it wasn't ideal circumstances I was jittery with excitement. I looked around, smiling at people, which was something I never, ever did. Then I noticed the newsstand inside the station. The excitement died in an instant. The headline of today's newspaper read Winter Twins: Not Guilty.

I had seen it coming, but it didn't matter. It still hurt. In that hospital bed, lying for days in complete silence, I had told myself I was going to clean up the mess I had created. I thought of Bec a lot. I grieved for her, and I promised I would fix what I had broken. Swore to her that I wouldn't let her brothers get away with killing her.

When at last the doctors told me I was allowed to speak, I went down to the pay phone in the lobby, my fist full of silver coins. I started with the hardest call: my stepmom. I told her how sorry I was. She had passed the phone to my dad without saying a word. He had begun to get worried about me after all. When I told him I was going to turn myself in for the credit card fraud, he bought me a plane ticket home to Perth. I didn't ask to move back in with him. I knew we could never go back to the way it was. Not after what I had done. He said he'd pay for a good lawyer for me. Looking back, it wasn't love that made him do that. It was his need to avoid the shame of his only daughter going to jail.

I wouldn't have cared. I'd do community service. I'd apologize to everyone I stole from. I would do the jail time if I had to. Just hearing people call me by my own name would make it all worth it.

After hanging up, I took a long deep breath. I couldn't leave it any longer. I clunked the coins one by one into the pay phone. Slowly, I keyed in the number and listened to it ring.

"Andopolis speaking."

"Hi."

"Bec! Where are you?"

"She's under the house."

I told him everything. Every detail of what had happened that horrible day. Then I hung up before he could say a word, my throat aching from talking again. It was time for me to go home, to be myself again. The only trace of Bec left in my life was the deep scar on my forearm.

Even in Perth, the story reached the papers: Kidnap Victim Sets Fire to Her Own Home. I had swallowed down my anger, and hoped like hell that Andopolis was doing his job to fix this. For months, the story was in the news. Luckily for me, they didn't include anything about how the new Bec wasn't really Bec at all. Andopolis must have stayed tight-lipped on that one. I guess it made him look pretty bad. The mother was okay, too, in the end, physically at least. The firefighters had pulled her out of the burning house kicking and screaming to stay.

I'd watched the news with my hand over my mouth as the presenter dryly stated that they had recovered a decomposed body in the blackened garage. A body bag was lifted carefully into the back of an ambulance.

"Lab results have confirmed that the body is that of Maxwell Brennan, forty-one, who lived next door to the Winter family before he disappeared in 2004."

It wasn't Bec. I felt like jumping up and down. After all that, maybe it was possible that she was still alive.

The twins had a great alibi for the fire. The press had photos of the parents leaving the house with them in the back and returning without them. They must have been lying under a blanket or something. The airline had records of them checking in their baggage at the exact moment the terminal opened, and they had made it onto the flight, three hours later. Despite the fact that there was a two-hour gap in there, I guess Andopolis thought he wouldn't have enough evidence for a conviction.

But then, to my surprise, a few days later the twins were arrested. I watched as Andopolis led them into the station, T-shirts over their heads. He was trying to look serious but the corners of his lips tugged with a smirk. Turned out, even after all this time, Max's body was covered in their DNA.

Once the cops started digging, they linked the twins to a series of murders in the aged care home that Andrew had volunteered at in Melbourne. Holden Valley. The murders were grisly, nasty. So much so that at first they had thought some kind of animal had gotten into the facility. The story of the impending hearing was in the paper constantly. I couldn't have avoided it if I'd tried. Newspapers were a large portion of the trash I picked up from the side of the highway for my community service.

During those long hours on the side of the road I thought

of Jack almost constantly. I called him. He didn't answer. I texted him. No response. I followed the Kingsley blog obsessively. Then the blog disappeared from the web and it was Jack's face I saw in the paper. Just a small photo, right at the back. They'd found the camera he was trying to smuggle into the detention centre and arrested him. Unlike Andrew and Paul's case, Jack's was swift. He got six months.

I was trying very hard to be a good person. Still, I couldn't help but see the opportunity his incarceration provided. I knew exactly where he was. Today I was going to see him and he would have to listen. He was literally a captive audience.

"Miss?"

The line has disappeared in front of me and the ticket booth lady is glaring impatiently at me. I attempt a weak smile and go to pay my fare. Part of me doesn't want to read the paper; I know what it will say. Paul and Andrew share identical DNA, so it can't be proved that it was one of them and not the other who had murdered Max. Of course, the media have already convicted them. Maybe that was enough.

I make my way to the newsstand. There is a dark-haired woman looking at the newspaper, too, her back to me. I wouldn't have noticed her, if it wasn't for how still she is standing. The peak-hour suits knock into her, clicking their tongues in annoyance. Slowly, she turns, like she somehow feels my eyes on the back of her neck, and I look straight into the face I know as well as my own. She's dyed her hair and eyebrows brown, but a hint of copper glows at her roots. Her clothes are perfectly tailored and stylish, like she has a job in fashion. Even after twelve years, it is undeniably Bec Winter.

There are tears running down her cheeks as she locks

eyes with me. Quickly, her sadness turns to panic. My face is showing the expression I had gotten so used to, eyes wide in shocked recognition. Like I've seen a ghost. I try to push apart people to get to her.

"Wait!" I scream, but she is already running.

People stare at me as I chase her down toward a platform. But there are trains leaving; there are people everywhere. I keep my eyes locked on the back of her head.

"Excuse me!" A woman smashes her pram into my shins.

"Hey!" I yell at her. What kind of idiot brings a baby to a station at peak hour? I look around, ignoring the woman's snarky comments, trying desperately to spot Bec again. But it's too late.

She has disappeared into the crowd.

Acknowledgements

To my agent, MacKenzie Fraser-Bub, who pulled this work out of the slush pile. She is such an extraordinary woman, and I feel so lucky to have her in my corner. My editor, Kerri Buckley, with whom I developed a great connection through Track Changes before I ever met her in person, and the amazing team at MIRA, who have been outstanding every step of the way. To Nicole Brebner and Jon Cassir, who both believed in this story.

Of course, the story of this novel started long before all that. To my friends at Kino, who always inspired and supported me over popcorn cleaning and choc-top making. To my fantastic writers group, who kept me on track during the sometimes painful writing process. To Ian Pringle, for still teaching me even though I haven't been your student for a long time, Graeme Simsion, for his wonderful advice, and to Jenny Laylor, for her legal expertise. To Sergeant Kylie Whiting of the NSW Missing Persons Unit and Ken Wooden, coordinator of the Policing Practices Unit at UWS, thank you for your patient answers to my nitpicky questions.

I am lucky enough to have so many dear and supportive friends. My girls Phoebe Baker, Lara Gissing and Lou James, for making everything more fun. To the awesome screenwriter Joe Osbourne, who shares my taste in weird. To wordsmiths David Travers, Martina Hoffman and Rebecca Carter Stokes, for reading drafts of this book and not being afraid to tell me when it sucked. To Allegra Mee, who didn't mind me pinching a lot of our teenage memories. To Adam Long, who always listens.

And of course, from the very beginning of it all, to my family. Amy Snoekstra, my sister, who kept insisting I should write a novel until I thought that it was my idea. To my intelligent, amazing parents, Ruurd and Liz, who encouraged me to do what made me happy, and to my hilarious, kind in-laws, David and Tess.

Lastly, to Ryan, the love of my life.